MOUNTAINS
AND OTHER GHOSTS

for Maeve

MOUNTAINS
AND OTHER GHOSTS

SHORT STORIES BY
DERMOT SOMERS

Diadem Books · London

Five of the short stories in the book
were first published in magazines
and newspapers as follows:

Facelift   (High, 1986)
Nightfall   (The Irish Climber, 1983)
The Lug Walk   (The Irish Press, March 1984)
Whom the Gods Love   (Climber and Hillwalker, April 1986)
The Old Story   (The Irish Climber, 1984)

British Library Cataloguing in Publication Data
Somers, Dermot
   Mountains and other ghosts
   I Title
   823.914 [F]

ISBN 0 906371 63 5 (cased edition)
ISBN 0 906371 53 8 (trade pbk edition)

Published in Great Britain in 1990 (in cased and tradepaper editions)
by Diadem Books, London

Trade enquiries to Hodder and Stoughton,
Mill Road, Dunton Green, Sevenoaks, Kent TN13 2YA

Typesetting by J&L Composition Ltd, Filey, North Yorkshire

Printed and bound in Great Britain by
Biddles Ltd, Guildford and King's Lynn

CONTENTS

INTRODUCTION

Dermot Somers was born in 1947 in the Irish midlands. After completing a degree in Irish and English, he taught briefly, then opted for the illusory independence of the building trade and moved to London. It was not until he was in his late twenties and back in Ireland that he took up climbing and mountaineering — this at an age when many consider it more suitable to give it up! Over the past fifteen years he has travelled and climbed widely—in the Alps, Yosemite, the Andes and the Himalayas. In the early eighties he climbed the classic alpine series known as the Six Great North Faces, culminating in ascents of the Matterhorn and the Eiger. He lives now in Wicklow, in a house built entirely by himself and his wife, Maeve.

In his fiction Dermot Somers draws on his climbing experience, not so much as a subject in itself, but as a framework for the close observation of character under tension in one of the most dramatic of human activities. This is deliberately intended to give the stories above all a sharp sense of adventure and to bring about the confrontation with self through action — a possible reaction, as he now realises, against the static existentialist fiction with which he grew up.

On another level, these stories have a persistent political dimension, moving backwards and forwards in time from the Elizabethan *The Old Story* to the *Nightfall* of nuclear nightmare to engage the abuse of power, be it colonial, social, military or patriarchal.

Somers writes in both English and Irish; this is the first retrospective collection of his work.

FACELIFT

kkkrrRRRUUMPPP.
The front of the buttress lifted clean away from the crag.
BOOOOOMM!
It vanished.

Ex-SAS man Willard grinned over his detonator. Knocked up Sheffield that little lot did! Gritstone fragments crashed around him in the violated dawn. He prised the helmet from his cockney skull and rose to his feet. A shocked pall of dust quivered over Stanage. Ducking low, he ran towards it, weaving from force of habit. Size 12 EBs skidded in the dew.

The explosion reverberated through air and earth; down on North Lees campsite stunned climbers struggled into their clothes; an unattended word-processor in the office of *High* magazine hiccupped acknowledgement; and in Chesterfield cemetery, freshly interred, the corpse of Captain Robert Bennett felt the seismic shock and turned in its grave. Twelve days earlier, in a Belfast backstreet, the captain had been shot in the back. Accidentally, by one of his own men. But his tragic conclusion is not the point here.

Dave Willard had picked up some funny habits in Ireland. *kkkrrUUMPP!* — that sort of thing. Of course the Special Services had taught him a few tricks too — *BaBOOOOOOMM!* and all that. Brought up in Brixton, Dave adapted quickly to undercover work in Ulster. His small brain and powerful body were linked by a short fuse and there was plenty of scope for self-expression. And he was learning techniques to take home to London when the crackdown started there. He need never be unemployed. At first the excitement of Northern Ireland compensated for the loss of climbing, but eventually he grew bored with peace-keeping in Belfast and Armagh and craved again the brutal simplicity of rock.

Home on leave it was next-to-top priority. Down to London first for the prostitutes, then he hit Wales, the Lakes, the Peak as hard and fast as he knew how. But he found no satisfaction. Flesh or rock it was all frustration—secondhand, third-rate. All the good stuff was gobbled up in his absence. Everything he touched felt used; classic VS's with their polished holds and initials carved around the belays; when he rang Vanessa from Euston Station she was booked out, but she slotted him in between nine and ten. 'Ta-ta, Dyve, give my love to the regiment. See yer next time.'

Dave wanted to break fresh ground, climb new routes, see his own unique achievement signed in bold lines upon the landscape and the record. But there was no hidden fruit waiting to be plucked, no innocent gems left for the right man. If it hadn't been done already it was impossible — except for punkish ponces in ballet-tights. He suppressed an urge to rape a few of those, and went back to Belfast to settle simpler scores.

Dave knew now he had missed out, given up a great career in climbing to be dumped forever in Paddyland where a soldier couldn't even get sex. The lucky bastards that went to the Falklands got an ocean-cruise out and back and hero mugshots in the *Sun*. Dave imagined his own picture facing Page Three with the paper closed tight on the pair of them and a rasp of stubble on his jaws. Desperation growled in his throat.

He got all the comics through the post — *Penthouse, Mountain, High*, and bulletins from his old club, the National Front Climbing Squad. His narrow-eyed skull throbbed with news. Nancy-boys and pimps making names for themselves every month while the only place Dave Willard's name featured was in the hit-lists of the North. He grew meaner with deprivation, more ruthless in his work. He made it on to the most exclusive hit-lists. One week he may have been Number One on the Wanted charts for an operation blamed on the IRA which dropped their political wing two per cent in the opinion-polls. But it wouldn't have ranked with a first ascent in Derbyshire.

Dave was thirty-three, the panic year. The present was

septic and the past poisoned. He was unmarried. Unmarriageable. No one wanted an ugly soldier with pig-iron bones, a concrete skull and a career in violence. He had no illusions about his charm. Whores sometimes turned him down although they could use the work. He reckoned the army was the right place for him on that score. Where else could he see dozens of blokes even uglier than himself every day? Then suddenly, at thirty-three, he was terrified it mightn't be as simple as that. Maybe he was queer. . . . Those new harnesses in the magazines were doing it to him. And the ballet-tights. No one could ever lust after the contents of an old-fashioned Whillans! Not without a fetish for surgical appliances!

Dave badly needed a change. He'd seen a lot of hard men break down in Ulster. That was why some outfits were called crack units. His hands shook and sweated when he trained his gun on suspects. He made a last-ditch effort to assert priorities. Captain Bennett had been a climber — only a public-school climber, it's true, but he must know which way was up. And there was a couple of geezers in another unit who used to do peg-routes on Malham . . .

Dave proposed a trip to Fair Head in Antrim. Captain Bennett was reluctant. He smelt the black rot of psychosis on the soldier. What Willard didn't know was that the captain was one of a small group of superiors who blocked promotion for trigger-happy soldiers. On the other hand he welcomed the opportunity to assess the man in a neutral situation.

'That's a nationalist strip,' he warned Dave, 'We'll stick out like sore pricks up there, Willard. Play cricket in Crossmaglen if you want a high profile. Anyway I haven't climbed for — oh, years . . .' Dave hinted that it might be the — ah, the crag that — ah, frightened the captain? and soon they were speeding north from Belfast. The captain recalled that it had always been thus in climbing — ego overpowering acumen.

The trip had the atmosphere of an ill-judged mission, Captain Bennett thin, terse and aloof, Nick Grimes and Roger Wilson, grizzled, taciturn veterans sitting warily behind.

Willard bulked in the front beside the officer boasting obses-
sively about his climbing. There was nothing much to boast
about — classic trade-routes on British rock, a couple of alpine
seasons in which the Aiguilles Rouges loomed larger than the
other side. They listened to him with the inscrutability of
interrogators as a suspect hangs himself.

The cluster of cottages at Culanlough and the hidden car-
park smelled like a trap to the captain. In the normal course of
duty this would be a stake-out. Imagine coming here for
pleasure and walking away from the car! He shook his head in
amazement. He glanced at Grimes and Wilson: hard faces, old
ropes, canvas rucksacks — *The Guns of Navarone* — and he was
reassured.

Half a mile of bleak moorland stretched north to the rim of
the crag, a sudden horizon. The sky shone bright with the
reflection of the sea below. The rough land wore the sleepy look
that screams ambush to the eye trained in paranoia.

'For Christ's sake, men,' the captain urged unnecessarily,
'let's keep our mouths shut. And cover that haircut, Willard.
this isn't Bosigran with John Barry!' Dave grunted, his hand
hovering near his cagoule pocket. He was tempted to park his
gun in the hammer-holster of his Whillans but he refrained.

As they approached the rim, and leaned forward to look,
Dave's lip curled in preconceived contempt. A spit squirted like
gull-shit from his mouth. Stringing out it drifted down fifty, a
hundred, two hundred and ten, twenty, thirty, forty, fifty feet
of — *splatt!* — perfect dolerite, dark and clear, cracked and
cornered, hard and huge. A boulder-field as big as a beach with
every grain of sand a boulder shelved half-a-mile down to the sea.

Dave gulped, swallowed space. 'Not like Cloggy! Ain't
much beside ol' Clog is it? Or Gogarth . . .'

'For God's sake man, Fair Head's about three miles long.
Without a break!'

'Stanage is four . . .'

'And Three Hundred Feet High!' The Captain's voice rose
in anger, 'What do you want, Willard? The Verdon?'

'Lose this little lot in the Verdon,' Dave babbled. 'Wouldn't even notice it . . .'

'Don't know much about geology, do you son?' Nick interrupted. He spat too, but carefully behind him. There was something solid stuck in his throat, something to do with the vertical vacancy below, and he was afraid he might remain attached and follow it over the edge. 'Let's have a look at the guidebook then . . .'

'We'll WRITE the flamin' guidebook!'

'Obviously summat's been done . . .'

Dave spat again. 'Nuffin done 'ere, me old cock! Paddy don't climb. Only just stopped crawlin' abaht on all fours.' He cackled raucously. Captain Bennett closed his eyes wearily in repudiation. He reached into his rucksack and pulled out a guidebook.

'This one is years out of date now. Bought it first time I was posted here. Very keen in those days, very keen . . . Always meant to get to Fair Head . . .' He looked around him sadly and flicked through pages packed with routes, 'Paddy's a bit more advanced than you think, Willard.'

Dave shrugged. 'Easy stuff. Gullies an' that! Go up em' after sheep don't they! Plum lines ain't been touched. Been waitin' for this all my life. This is where D. Willard carves 'is name in bleedin' great letters into the 'istory of British rock. Let's go!'

'WILLARD!' The captain was shaking a rat between his teeth, 'I give the orders! This is Antrim. We're not climbers here. We're the British Army! Don't you forget it because no one else will!' He turned to the others, 'If you men have no objection we'll climb within sight of each other. Two recommended routes here in the centre of the crag . . . An Go Ban Sore . . .' He read it out in his clipped bark. '. . . And something beside it, maybe Beal ack Runda . . . or this other one . . .' He pointed to it on the page, 'Sli na Firinne.'

E1(5b), 280ft. Four pitches, only one — the second one — hard. He liked the look of the name, slender, sharp, sensible, like a clean crack leading somewhere definite. Some of the other

routes were unintelligible thickets of diphthongs and consonants. Peacadh Mairfeach he saw overleaf, and Conchubhar
and Aoife . . . Surely they must be clogged with something
horribly viscous to have names like that. For a strange moment
he visualised off-widths choked with catarrh and phlegm.

'It's Gaelic of course,' he explained, peering at the names,
An Goban Saor E1(5b) 280ft. 'I've seen that word before, s-a-o-r,
Sore Eire I think it was, on a gable in Armagh . . .'

'Bleedin' code-names,' Dave burst out. 'Subversive shit-
house talk. Another way of sayin' Brits Out i'nnit? You know
wot them fackin routes are?' He challenged the captain,
'They're fackin graffiti that's wot!'

Again Captain Bennett's thin mouth snapped, but this time
he said nothing. He understood that climbing was a young
man's sport and that Willard was mourning his youth and
independence in his own violent way. He was not the only
mourner. For a variety of reasons no one had seen the captain
smile since he was posted to Northern Ireland. Gradually his
lips had shrivelled up against his teeth and now his cheeks were
folding bitterly in the same direction. Shedding hair and
features his unhappy head was turning into a middle-aged
skull. He was growing old too fast. Flying milk-churns,
hunger-strikes, bombs, bullets, budget-slashes, ambushes,
assassins, mutinies, murders, civilian slaughter, whitewashes
and cover-ups had strained his Sandhurst resources, but now
Willard was stretching his personal reserves beyond the limit.
Rank was no use to the captain here. Rock — the old leveller —
had stripped him of advantage right down to his nervous
system. He had to climb better than Willard to regain his status
— and after that he could kick the bastard out of the unit with a
clean conscience.

They found the Greyman's Path, a narrow break in the crag
guarded by a huge, natural statue, staring blindly out to sea.
Before passing under a slender column jammed across the head
of the gully the captain examined it for trip-wires. The place
hummed with tension, like a stairwell in the Divis Flats. He gave

the signal to proceed with caution, and dark, enormous walls opened before them. Lik a patrol of skin-germs straying into the oral cavity they marched awestruck along the gums, gaping up at the magnificent molars and the great clefts, crannies and crevices between them filled with fabulous pickings.

Dave ran in berserk circles laying claim to every line. His small eyes bulged with passion and veins throbbed in his low forehead. He would climb them all, ALL, ALL . . . First ascents every one. The captain found them in the book, Burn Up, Creeper, Kraken . . .

'Lies!' Dave howled. 'Forgery . . .'

The crag stretched inexhaustibly ahead. The scale was beyond imagination, and the captain was somehow aware that between them — pooling all their Anglo-Saxon resources and discounting Willard's hallucinations — they possessed virtually no imagination at all. Furthermore, as he stumbled through the labyrinthine boulder-field he was conscious of the prime target they presented to enemy trundlers high on the ramparts. With startling clarity he imagined men in black balaclavas lining up overhead with buckets of bubbling pitch. They would be even more exposed while climbing. A man splayed out on a crux-move looked as if he had been shot already. Often felt like that too, the captain remembered ruefully. But nothing happened and every step he took calmed his nerves and enriched his awe. He paused at the foot of a curling ribbon of rock 250ft high, flanked by two impossible chimneys and capped by an overhang big as a tank parked under another overhang the size of an army lorry — and he was suddenly overwhelmed by a sweet sense of insignificance and peace. . . .

There was no one up there watching him, no ambush, nothing but rock and sky and the purely private choice of success or defeat. People were too small to crowd a stage as big as this; a place for ancient giants! The captain realised moreover that the whole of Northern Ireland was inhabited not by tribal warriors but by ordinary people who were smaller than the places and events surrounding them, decent people who worked for prosperity and earned adversity instead. Peace could never be imposed upon them. It was a condition of the heart and the habitat. By right, everyone should have a choice between happiness and hatred and all their choices would add up to the future. But for too many the choice was ordained by history. It was not easy to understand all that inside an imposed uniform and the captain knew he might forget again as soon as he dressed in barracks. He too was misunderstood in the province.

He tried to think the idea through, but he raised his head and his tight thoughts burst like a flock of pigeons towards the enormous corner of An Goban Saor. The two Yorkshiremen wheeled to their allotted route and the pigeons scattered in disarray. Dave Willard attempted to solo, in passing, a 150ft direct start to the route. Only the hard move off the ground defeated him.

Not far to the right they found Sli na Firinne. A set of perfect columns clean and pure as organ-pipes formed the lower half of the crag. Jamming-cracks divided them and the geometric facets presented offset bridging surfaces. But which groove? Several were perfect. Now he understood the cryptic footnote in the guide: 'Do not confuse with An Bealach Runda.' . . . Pitch 2* From the top of the fifth column climb a circular flake (the dot on the i) to gain a deceptive wall, an exposed hand-traverse, a sensational layback and a furtive finger-crack . . .

He saw the flake first. A hundred feet up there was a dark wheel of rock as if something huge had parked on the pillar and all but one wheel had toppled off. Nonsense! He struggled for the scale. Big as a millstone? . . . no, that would be invisible from here like a lost tiddlywink on a shelf. He flipped that childish image from his confused brain. Once, in barracks he had consented to throw a coin in a pitch and toss school played by some soldiers — off-duty of course. His coin had flipped erratically across the concrete, rolled in a silly circle and then — against all the odds — had come to rest on edge against the end-wall, just like the flake (leaving the pillar aside for a second). He had strolled away to a round of applause. Now he had to climb straight up to the damn thing in front of the soldiers. Pitch! And Toss?

He had forgotten how to climb. He flexed his shoulder-blades wanting wings. The angle was impossible. Had he sauntered up such steepness in his youth? Pretend he was lying on his belly and crawl along the concrete to the coin? Look damn silly . . . Call the whole thing off, spot a sniper? He glanced back at An Goban Saor. Nick was already climbing. Like a good soldier on patrol he checked each move for hostile intent, disarmed it briskly and proceeded to the next suspect. It looked so smooth — so . . . disciplined.

Captain Bennett, here at the foot of Fair Head, down among the roots of Ulster with the wild Sea of Moyle at his back and Britain an obscure smudge on the skyline, was discovering a hectic imagination. It wanted him to climb. Somewhere far back in his mind the hand-traverse, the layback and the furtive finger-crack tickled the hairs on his neck — from the inside. Dave Willard peered up the vertical chute of the first pitch and his tongue rasped across dry lips; 'Not . . . not like gritstone, is it?' he whispered.

The captain selected his strategy. Despite its awesome architecture the first pitch was only HVS(5a). He sacrificed that one to Willard. Ideally he would have sent him down a cave, sealed the entrance and gone climbing himself, but while it was acceptable to lose soldiers in combat one couldn't just take them out in the country and bury them in holes.

On close inspection the first pitch was formed by a pair of parallel pillars two feet apart with the front facet of a third inset behind. The enormous columns were fitted together with the precision of Aztec construction — except that volcanic contraction had arranged sufficient space between the blocks to accommodate human hands. And ergonomics had wisely advised that the cracks should open and taper periodically to form handy pods and slots, and furthermore that the edges of these slots should be slightly rounded to minimise discomfort. Footholds were provided also for a short distance, neat grey incuts for an initial boost. Dave had no excuse to dawdle and the captain was left to resume meditation. He watched Nick overpower a bulge on the first pitch of An Goban Saor. Some would call it cheating, but in military terms efficiency was everything. It justified the means. And knotted slings were a damn sight fairer than grappling-hooks! Still, he felt embarrassed . . . not quite the thing. On the other hand, suppose they were invading this coast — he allowed himself a boyish thrill of conjecture — a quartet of commandos scaling Fair Head to take the enemy by surprise . . . No need for melodramatics, he rebuked himself, the invasion was long over. And the army was staying put. Nowhere else to put it anyway. The captain amused himself for a moment wondering what on earth the government would do with the army if it had to withdraw from Ireland. Put it on the dole? He listened to Willard being employed in the pitch overhead. The rope ran out in jerks. Just as he had expected, no talent. Willard climbed like a successful invasion; brute force and inability to retreat. A cracked cry of triumph cut short the political analysis. Willard was up and almost immediately the captain was climbing.

He was struck at once by the unexpected ease, the upward thrust, the sense of muscle-memory as if the revival of adolescent joy had erased his age. He savoured the friction, the clean, dry rock, the monumental shapes that curved around his hands, reviving his gritstone skills in this smooth, stately, adult context. He recognised the cold, unequivocal smell of rock, the thrilling tension in the nerves, the concentration of the senses and the self. There were red smears where Willard had bludgeoned and he avoided them fastidiously. The fellow had already fouled the crag with saliva and blood and the captain hoped fervently there would be no worse secretions. He intended to stay in front — in case.

Twenty, thirty, forty hand-jams — it was as if the ideal sequence of moves had been drawn from his memory, expanded, repeated and extended until it exhausted the desire for continuity, and then at ninty-nine feet the rhythm broke — a knuckled bulge and flared finger-slot punished ecstasy with excess — and then the belay. Willard squatted, rooster-like, skinned elbows flapping. 'Wot a cracker! Wot a facking cracker! Gobsmackin', eh? Wot'll we call it, Cap?'

'I TOLD you! It's done already. It's called . . .'

'I won't say nuffink if you don't. We'll send it to *Mountain* tomorrow. Needs a good strong name, eh. Touch o' class. Wot d'yer reckon to *The British Empire*? Always fancied that for a route.'

A retro-thrust of revulsion took the Captain to the top of the circular flake. He hadn't even noticed it. He was about to leap lightly on to the headwall when something pushed him sharply in the chest in the manner of a school bully. He staggered clockwise down along the wheel and stared up in surprise. The devious wall above swaggered.

The captain snorted, wrenched himself some slack and charged again. The bulge shouldered him off. He stumbled up and down, up and down, as if the circular flake was revolving stiffly under him. Now he knew that shape — it was a bloody treadmill!

Above the bulge the wall slabbed back. There must be something up there? The dark rock was blotched with pale lichen, all colour and no substance, losing the holds in its piebald confusion. Hanging his head for balance he swung one arm in a swimming stroke across the slab. A hopeful edge. The other hand came up and found another. Tiny pasted petals, he was bound to rip them off and take to the air like a detonated butterfly. Opposing sidepulls only, but he was committed now, too late to change, hanging out of balance. Old muscles crushed the gristle in his shoulder-blades, hauled him across the bulge, neck and head vibrating, feet flailing onto friction. He leaned into a shallow scoop to rest and his body was temporarily out of focus, distorted by effort. It didn't fit his clothes, as if his jeans and shirt were back to front, EBs on the wrong feet. He shook himself into shape and swallowed harsh breath. Hand-traverse . . . layback . . . finger-crack . . . God!

Despite the lichen-stains the rock was meticulously clean.

On his left the headwall rose in an enormous pillar, thick and ill-defined with a blunt arête, unlike the sculptured columns down below. A faint groove continued overhead into inconceivable surroundings, grotesque variations on the vertical. His jaw sagged with shock and then he saw the rising fracture running left across the pillar to the arête. The hasty hand-traverse ... He looked for footholds first. Not a single centimetre of support. Instead a long dark stain where rubber skated ...

He reached out into the crack. The edge curved smoothly downwards like the underlip of a massive, pouting statue. Nothing for it but to reach right in and hope she had her bottom teeth. He plunged in to the elbows, spittle-smooth rock, he rummaged fiercely and the toothless gums closed around his wrists chewing the skin in horizontal jams. He prayed, paddled in space and thirteen stone of flesh and bone dragged dangling from the elbows. The jams were solid — almost suction — and he lurched towards the profile. His breath hissed through gritted teeth and he heard grunting in the atavistic air. It seemed to come from a long way off, as if it was someone else, some unrestrained vulgarian pumping towards the same arête from the other side. Someone like Willard about to smash through the back of the mirror ... the Captain was climbing atrociously but he would not be the one to retreat before collision.

Around the arête everything changed, slipped back under control. A massive foothold appeared, as if it had been hacked out with a well-judged axe. And the old witch's mouth had a single tooth after all—a jagged spike ideal for a handhold and a sling. Above it and a little to the side a sharp inverted V showed how the pillar had cracked and sheared. The captain was struck by the notion that Fair Head could choose this very moment to grind back into shape. He almost withdrew his hands. He was reducing the universe to the clockwork of the human time-scale, and the idea amused him suddenly. He heard a sound from his own mouth somewhere between a giggle and a guffaw. This was good climbing, great climbing. Willard was out of sight below and the captain realised he was happy. God, how happy he was to be doing this! And two and a half pitches still to come!

Opposite him, at mid-height on their route, Nick and Ian were beginning a sinuous corner. He promised himself that one next time. Where to now? A thin flake-crack darted directly overhead. He dismissed it, the traverse must continue left. Captain Bennett swung out confidently to look. The stance was undercut. Instantly the whole world fell away from beneath his body as if a stairway had collapsed and he was left hanging by his fingertips from the landing. Down, down, down he looked, down the pit behind the pillar, down the empty stairwell to an alcove in the basement, and for one terrible second he imagined his own skeleton in that shoe-cupboard far, far below.

He shuddered back on to the foothold and raised his eyes to the layback overhead.

'E1, my arse!' he thought profoundly.

He concentrated on placing protection. Suppose — fumbling for psychology now — suppose this was at ground level, a standard layback, say the Right Unconquerable, the ultimate classic. That had been no problem once with a bit of nerve, and this couldn't be half as hard — or long. He hoped! Putting myself on the line for this, he thought resentfully, — the first ascent had it easy, knew what to expect. Wish it could be my route . . . all this effort for nothing . . . He flexed his fingers and his will, grasped the fine-edged flake, thrust one foot high against the wall. A dry sting in his thigh where the varicose knot lurked. He hung out on white hands. Don't look, he ordered Nick and Ian silently, Don't look now. Trust the protection! — that was essential. The solid Moac in a slot, the sling around the tooth. But the rope ran diagonally across the arête and now straight up the crack, rope-drag plucking at the ropes. Fingers trembling with doubt — Run for it! The reality of the Right Unconquerable returned. Someone had shouted a warning as he fumbled for that final hold. He had looked down and his innocent second — face a blank now — had strolled far back to observe the move. The rope ran in at 45 degrees, tight as a guyline, the first nut popped and the rope unzipped the layback neatly from below. As his top nut swung towards the shoulder-belay in the boulders he found the hidden handhold in a hurry and stern words startled Stanage.

He was racing up the layback now hand over hand, hoisting an anchor up a flagpole. He made twenty feet in a single burst, then bridging holds appeared and took the strain out of the final steepness. But the flake was growing thick and blunt, the crack behind it shallow. At the end of tenacity he reached another foothold. The whole crag was quivering. The layback done and still no belay-ledge!

Captain Bennett wobbled weakly, fingers throbbing, his last protection thirty feet below. The only weakness in this blank rock was an offwidth crack—continuation of the layback —leaning to his right. It dragged him out of balance when he tried to lock numb hands between its flaring jaws. No purchase. Futile fists. Where was that damned finger-crack!?!

Punch-drunk he felt his body fade and fold . . . .and then the wiry reassertion of the will. Twist the wrist and fist. Screw into the groove. Dynamic jamming. Keep rooting, something has to hold? Torsion — the very act of twisting. Sweat leaked into his mouth. He spat salt spray.

Torque — the Twisting Force. He needed Torque!

I'll call it *Torquemada*. Sod whether it's done or not! The Spanish torturer. Willard won't like it. Prefer an English name here. Half-Nelson? His foot jigged without mercy on the hold, and his body began to sag . . .

One hundred and twenty feet below Willard stood up on the belay to ease a cramp. Bored with looking at the sea. Bennett should be on easy ground by now. He relaxed his grip on the rope and stretched his fingers. Leaning out he glimpsed a sudden movement on a distant section of the crag. There was a roof midway on a vertical skyline, a square-cut overhang—and Willard saw a . . . a climber swinging out beneath it, reaching over the lip, moving up. It was happening hundreds of yards away but he knew instinctively it was a First Ascent, that sense of breathless hush about the body as of a substance entering a new dimension. There it was — the ecstasy of virgin flight, the pioneering consummation Willard desired and dreamed. He imagined it as triumphant self-projection, a sustained ejaculation of the ego. Seeing others at it, was like glimpsing an orgy from a passing train.

Willard unclipped from the belay and leaned far back for a hungry look. Limned in sunlight the usurper clung to the front of the overhang, graceful as a gecko. With baleful, expert eye Willard measured up. Ten pounds of plastic properly placed would land the bastard in the sea with an armful of overhang to keep him down. . . .

. . . Overhead, Captain Bennett slowly folded backwards. His fists uncurled. Fingers scrabbled in the groove, scraped towards the rim, found a thin, deep slit . . . and held. Incredible!! A finger-crack where he had fought for off-width jams! He tried to see what saved him, peering around into the groove. No matter how he craned it was invisible, tucked away in secret. It nibbled at his fingertips with furtive generosity.

It was early evening when they rejoined Nick and Ian at the car.

'Well?' beamed Captain Bennett. 'What was it like, chaps? Looked jolly good!'

Nick grinned, 'Best bloody route in the world, sir . . .' and he winked; 'what else can I say under the circumstances?' Driving to Ballycastle Nick suggested beer. The captain hesitated. His initial desire was to get as far from Willard as possible. Not knowing how the brute would behave in a pub. He was no longer a cold professional soldier but a victim of climbing-dementia such as the captain had not witnessed since the days of his college-club. Still he was reluctant to pull rank and spoil the occasion for the others. There were traditions to be observed — not only military but a cragging code as well.

And wasn't it strange — he recognised it now — how the peculiar aftertaste of climbing absolutely demanded beer! If they could get that flavour into bags it would make great crisps, the captain thought. He was no longer surprised by his own ideas.

'Just one,' he agreed.

He was trapped by the oldest trick. He should have got in and bought the one and only round, a gesture — to be cut short at that. But crafty Nick got the first one in and the captain was doomed to four.

They sat in a dark corner of the lounge and immediately a cordon of wary space was thrown around them. Captain Bennett felt himself dissolve eerily in the shadows; the elation of strenuous success was giving way to a numb exhaustion. Roger and Ian were affected too. The pints of creamy Guinness drenched them in sentiment. Memories of British climbing . . . finest in the world . . . Cemetery Gates, Cenotaph Corner, Valkyrie, the Unconquerable . . . caressing each beloved bead in the rosary of rock.

'Bleedin' trade-routes,' Willard scoffed, 'played out all that lot is . . .'

Nick flared, "Ow many 'ave you done then? 'Ow many? You won't find them on 'Arrisons bloody Rocks!' He elbowed Roger to get the next round in as the captain was looking edgy. 'If you can show me better routes bein' done today than Joe an' Don was doin' twenty years ago I shall give thee best. . .' His chest puffed and veins swelled in his forehead in that distasteful manner the captain always associated with patriotism.

'Rubbish! Lot of ol' cobblers that is, livin' in the past. There's better right 'ere for starters. An' I'll be back to sort it aht. Ol' Paddy's not keepin' this little lot to 'isself. Right sir? Me an' the cap'n 'ere's comin' back to Fair 'Ead to clean up.'

Captain Bennett shook his head and sighed. Fair Head deserved better than this. He imagined the courteous pace of development to date, isolated from corruption, no hype, no backstabbing, no cheating, no crowds and — he cringed at the sound of Willard's egomania — no noise. He recalled Stanage on a summer Sunday; like the terraces at a football-match. No peace or healing, no escape from conflict there, no respect for the sanctity of place. The climbing today at Fair Head, once he had cleared colonial paranoia from his mind, had been a virtual communion of geology, space and the human spirit. Admittedly human spirit had suffered a stormy passage, but he hoped he had accepted the prolonged pain and the fleeting joy and learned from them.

Not Willard though. Willard — the captain fumbled towards the start of philosophy — Willard was the . . . the imposition of Self on to the natural world, the rage to conquer, the presumption of power. Willard, the captain realised painfully, in all his caricatured awfulness was peculiarly British, a throw-back, the dregs of Empire. For one micro-second the captain thought he had perceived the role of the entire army . . . Mercifully it was a brief exposure then he was back to the singular again. As long as Willard remained in the North he was part of the intransigence, the . . . the fortifications. Something must be done.

Captain Bennett drained his third beer dizzily and as Willard strutted to the bar he left his chair with a confused excuse. He went into the Gents and out the other side through the Public Bar, into the street.

When they returned to the car there was a folded note under the windscreen-wiper. The captain read it out in a toneless voice, then passed it round:

GOOD CLIMBERS DON'T USE THEIR KNEES. YOU WON'T HAVE ANY KNEES IF YOU COME BACK. SEE YOU NEXT TIME.

Willard cursed scornfully, and Captain Bennett understood how much of courage is ignorance.

'It's a bleedin' con this is! The IRA know nuffin' about craggin'. It's local climbers tryin' to scare us off.' He wheeled towards the pub. 'There's a bastard in there looked familiar. Seen 'im on Snell's Field I reckon. Let's take 'im out . . .'

The captain issued a curt order and Willard was dragged hastily into the car.

An hour later as they sped along the motorway through Belfast Ian opened the captain's guidebook to Fair Head and broke the brooding silence.

'I'd like to copy down the route we done, sir. Mind if I borrow your pen?'

He wrote it out in careful capitals, AN GOBAN SAOR, with details, then lips pursed and head back he stared thoughtfully at the result. He nodded in satisfaction.

Willard was transferred. He couldn't believe the irony. Just when he'd got his hooks into Fair Head he was shifted back to bleedin' Blighty. They said he had been marked down for terrorist reprisal after sustained service. He was awarded a non-committal decoration and a posting to a Midlands plain to protect British plutonium against a women's camp. He had plenty of free time for climbing too.

Willard hit the gritstone hard. Every weekend he prowled the edges probing for opportunity. Every new route was rejected, '. . . done before, meathead. Check guidebooks before submitting claims.' *Climber & Rambler* sent him 'Notes for Contributors' and asked hopefully for an article.

One clear and simple day at Stanage, as he threaded his way through the strident queues, the answer dawned on Dave Willard. The virgin rock he sought was there alright — miles and miles of it — it was buried under all this hackneyed stuff that was being pawed and mauled by the multitudes. It was time to dig deep, clear away the rubbish and begin the New Era.

He approached a buttress and crouched breathless before it. This altar of gritstone climbing was only a block about forty feet high, set four-square into the hillside and separated from similar, less sacred blocks by chimneys and gullies. It was not only horizontally stratified in the usual manner of gritstone, it also had a vertically layered effect. There was a great flake —

narrow at the base, wide at the top — pasted to the front. The edges were worn by countless sweaty caresses.

Dave scraped his jaw and pondered. Just behind that brittle flake there was only a blank and unprotected wall. No use to him! Dave sensed rather than knew his own limits. He moved a little to the right and everything fell into place. A deep, narrow chimney split the side of the buttress from top to bottom. X-raying with his mind's eye he felt a classic fault-line weaving right through the rock. Just a touch of surgery, a simple face-lift. . . .

Down at his Bedford van Dave unpacked the toolkit. There was a false bottom where he kept his emergency rations, the special Northern Ireland kit; four half-kilo packs of plastic explosive, a long-life powerpack, coil of electrical wire and two steel screwdrivers.

In the morning Stanage opened to the dawn like an irritated flower. There was a parasite burrowing among its petals. Squirming inside Curving Chimney (Diff.40ft) Dave Willard poked his putty deep into place. He ran out the spool of wire to a natural bunker among the boulders. Working with practised skill he dug the plus and minus poles out of the battery and wound his cable-ends around the screwdrivers. He pushed one deep into the battery, and held the other like a dagger in his hand.

The rampart lay silent in the rising light. The road below ran empty beneath the trees of North Lees farm. Deserted moorland already purple in the distance . . . About to be stabbed in the heart, the Peak lay sleeping peacefully. The screwdriver plunged. *kkkrrRRRUUMPPP ! ! !*

Overbleeding-kill indeed! The Right and Left Unconquerable had disappeared and most of the rock behind them.

Dave scrambled up the smoking stairway of rubble to the top of the crag. Diff. Maybe — not quite the sculptured classic he'd planned, but a start anyway. Gritstone was too soft, rotten really. Better luck tomorrow with Cenotaph Corner. . . .

NIGHTFALL

Even in the hour of the wolf the Eigerwand was blacker than the surrounding night.

Before he stepped across the bergschrund onto the lowest footholds of the North Face R switched off his radio with deliberate finality. The crisp catastrophe in the tiny headset died and the war preparations were silenced for the first time in weeks. The elemental vacancy of the mountain night drained him of everything but fear, and frost. There were no stars above or below; all the lights of Kleine Scheidegg and Grindelwald were shrouded in the emergency blackout, and clouds masked the sky.

All over Europe the lights were out.

Swearing and scrabbling L arrived on the ledge beside him. His radio stammered armies, missiles, conferences, nuclear fronts, within the dreadful dome of his helmet.

'Where are we?' L whispered in panic. He stank of fear and sweat. A trembling muscular reluctance, like a horse in a night-ambush.

'At the start,' R hissed. 'The first pillar starts here.'

He almost shouted, to release the tension, as if the furtive whispers were its only source. But caution clamped his throat even as his mouth threatened to open wide. They could still be stopped.

R knew history and precedent as instinctively as he knew the grammar of speech. The village policeman sweating up the lower slopes towards the still-unknown Diemberger in 1958, not to prohibit his ascent, but to relieve him of his passport so that his body could be identified later. The sweating policeman was a whole platoon of trained fighters now, with a range of technical weaponry that could drop a man off the North Face as easily as the old policeman dropped the passport in his pocket. And there must be guns and sentries at the tunnel windows high in the face to defend the valley.

After a decade of alpine seasons R knew a little about the intricacy of the Swiss defence preparations. If they had the materials they would have built a transparent dome over the country when the nuclear threat became a promise, but failing that there was an infrastructure of underground shelters ready to gulp the entire population into the earth.

As a student in 1984 R had spent his first season above Grindelwald camping within the shadow of the Eigerwand. Nothing cataclysmic happened in world affairs that year. It was all occurring quietly of course, but in the circus of the public imagination there had been a failure to perform, and Orwell was relegated to a sideshow, a suspected charlatan like Nostradamus and the clairvoyant hermaphrodite.

R didn't take much notice of security-effects in Switzerland on that first visit, travel was unrestricted, and anyway he was dazzled by the extravaganza of the Oberland, all those mountains crowding into his nervous ambitions, shouldering each other for space — the Mönch, Jungfrau, Eiger. Released from little prisons of Kodachrome, they flaunted overwhelming dimensions of flamboyance and ferocity.

But he did notice, in passing, some of those great, camouflaged doors set into tree-clad mountainsides, their keys in the care of giants or computers. And he heard how new roads were designed to double as runways in war, and motorway tunnels as hangers for jetfighters already stored away within the rocky core of the country waiting for the inevitable collision of east and west in the air-space around the cockpit of Europe.

But in particular he noted what the American general had said, hawking it up from his chest like phlegm to be spat in the face of an ancient continent, 'We fought the first World War in Europe; we fought the second World War in Europe; and if you dummies let us, we'll fight the third World War in Europe too.'

The ancient continent turned the other cheek, not in peace

but in indifference. That was a long time ago. People didn't want to know. And now the nightmare had hatched out of sleep and apathy; the rape of reality had begun.

R and L were trapped in Switzerland by the crisis. The border-posts were sealed absolutely.

The air-waves of Europe were choked with variants of a trigger-incident. A British ship blown out of the Mediterranean by a nuclear strike, presumed Russian. But it seemed the ship was transporting American missiles into proscribed waters, and the fall-out from the encounter was threatening the Yugoslav and Albanian coastline.

Washington and Moscow issued cryptic statements and an hysterical rumour revived in the European media that Russia and the US would ally to confront China, the third power. Unaccountable detonations in areas sensitive to conflict all over the world were being traced to launches within Chinese territory. But this propaganda had in turn been fired from behind other equally suspect borders.

At the beginning of the crisis R and L had their Irish passports confiscated, and were ordered to report to the military police every day. Fearing internment they ignored the order and hid in their discreet tent up on the high meadows of Alpiglen, listening in shifts to the news bulletins.

It was obvious that censorship and deliberate confusion were rampant. The BBC was the most apparent offender with its jingoistic hero-worship of NATO. Ever since the new king took over in England the BBC had become known for its propaganda as Big Brother Charlie. Ireland was an associate member of NATO, proposing a kind of Florence Nightingale image for itself in the present crisis, but in craven reality the country was being used for base purposes by the Americans and the British.

R tuned in to the Swiss stations every hour for the weather reports. He got them in French, German and Italian, and they were in succinct, multi-lingual agreement. A depression was storming in from the Atlantic, bad weather rolling relentlessly towards the Alps. The Bernese Oberland, the collective north wall of the Alps, was the frontline obstacle to that trough.

For two day R had sat in seclusion, demented by ambition. He was there for the third year in a row to attempt the North Face of the Eiger. Bad weather and shortage of time foiled the previous attempts. Now there was no lack of time — he was a prisoner in the country — but the weather was going to rob him again. He could not focus seriously on the other holocaust preparing outside the bubble of Switzerland. It was unthinkable. A media exaggeration of a media creation. Humanity was gathering speed on the slippery slope, but it would pull off a self-arrest before the brink.

There had been several Irish ascents of the face in recent years, even an ascent by the Japanese route, but always in the company of a foreign climber. No Irish pair had climbed it yet. A fine distinction people scoffed, but R coveted it. Speed was a competitive issue too. He remembered a remark by the ageing climber who had spread the disputed first Irish ascent out over three days;

'I don't know whether it was the first Irish ascent or the second, but I guarantee it was the Slowest Irish ascent.'

R checked his watch in the streaming rattling dark. 3.30 a.m. More than an hour until dawn. The freeze had been insufficient to tighten up conditions on the mountain. The weather was changing already. They had eighteen hours at the very most to reach the summit before the storms broke.

But as long ago as 1950, making the fourth ascent, Waschak and Forstenlechner had climbed the face within that time, and one-day ascents were a normal feature of the seventies and eighties, Messner and Habeler in ten hours, Boivin solo in seven and a half. Ignoring the part conditions played in these figures R felt a gambler's sudden confidence.

Inching up the initial groove, clinging to steep, wet limestone, he was greatly relieved to find the climbing sound and reasonably easy. Reaching high the fingers hooked good handholds, and the probing boot found solid purchase every time. It was traditional to climb this section unroped by the light of a headtorch to get as high a possible before sunlight, snowfall, any disturbance on the summit turned the icefields into lethal ambushes.

His headtorch was tuned to a mere spark to avoid detection. He was climbing blind, and a sudden loss of faith in an awkward move made him pause in fear and almost turn back. But he heard L cursing just below him, and remembered the secret attempts of the thirties, when men who were publicly branded as fascist lunatics launched their destinies on this face without the security of any previous ascent, determined to force the limits of the impossible.

They were ill-equipped then, and carried crippling packs. Eight men died before the first success. These were in the front row (kneeling) in R's mental picture of heroes. There was no excuse for turning back, and nowhere to go.

The wet grooves led to sloping, scree-laden terraces and ledges where the whoosh and detonation of stonefall brought a rush of sweat to every inch of skin. The transition from dark to daylight failed to produce the spectrum of a fair-weather dawn. Grey, watery light strained through the heavy clouds clinging to the dull horizon. R waited on a small, sheltered ledge for L to catch up. They were still on the rough, stepped plinth that forms the lower third of the climb.

He switched on the headset and flicked feverishly from station to station, accumulating horror as he went. An unspecified town in Germany crippled by the bombing of a military base. No mention of casualties or reaction, just the stark obliteration.

In England a power plant and a notorious research station devastated by sabotage. Radioactivity leaking. This information from a French bulletin while the BBC delivered a tight lipped account of summit conferences and diplomatic meetings. When L arrived his radio was off. It was too distracting to climb and listen simultaneously. He was gasping for breath and could not speak, but he looked with desperate interrogation at R.

'It's okay. Things have quietened down. There's a United Nations conference. Nothing's happened,' R lied.

L craned his head to look up at the climbing above, and his head remained tilted in awe. Tier upon tier of blank, impenetrable walls lifted into the confusion of the sky lit by the sullen dawn.

It had taken a masterpiece of persuasion to lure L on to the climb at all, but R had played it with all the expertise of an unattractive man used to bending reluctant women to his will. It was done by subtle association, conjuring up heroic figures and romantic images until the victims felt they were falling for some great mountain explorer instead of a man who had simply observed the originals and borrowed their style.

He had begun to work on L the previous morning as they lay festering in uncertainty within the bubble of fabric camouflaged on the slope below the face.

They had a small electronic dictionary to which they referred for clarification of the news bulletins, but its vocabulary was irritatingly limited, and they were in constant doubt as to the accuracy of their interpretation.

L wanted them to surrender to the police. He had naive dreams of repatriation based on neutrality.

'Are we going down or not?' he demanded. 'We've about two hours left to check in. After that we're outlaws or refugees, or something.'

Hulking, overdeveloped shoulders made his cropped head look small and immature, but he had the trusting eyes and biddable expression of a youth who could be led if his imagination was enlisted.

R was considerably smaller and older. A conservative in many ways he maintained the traditional Irish style of mountaineering beard, sandy and unkempt, the high-altitude look.

'If we go down now,' he said with convincing assurance, 'they'll lock us up for the duration. We won't be left wandering around in case we're spying or something. And if we stay here someone is going to spot us, and report us anyway . . . maybe even take a shot at us.'

He giggled unexpectedly. 'I feel a bit like Heckmair,' he confided. 'You know, in '37.'

'Heck — who?' L looked blank.

'Anderl Heckmair,' R told him encouragingly. 'One of the greatest climbers of all time. Very good on rock,' he added hastily, emphasising L's narrow speciality.

'He led the first ascent of the Eiger North Face in 1938 with Ludwig Vörg. They took Harrer and Kasparek along with them for the ride. Harrer didn't have a ghost of a chance without Heckmair, even if it was him who did all the writing afterwards.'

Secretly it was a colossal shock to R that his partner had never heard of Heckmair. He had never been in the Bernese Oberland before, and he simply didn't have that traditional obsession with the Eiger which seemed to have run its course with R's generation. L had done some impressive rock-climbs in other areas, the kind of thing that was technically way out of R's old-fashioned reach, but he had limited experience of ice and mixed climbing.

'Heckmair was here in '37 too, for a reconnaissance,' R resumed the theme.

'The Swiss made it illegal that year to attempt the face, on the grounds it was suicide. But Heckmair was a sort of Robin Hood character, he couldn't be kept down. He hid in a bathing-hut down in Interlaken for a while, and then moved up here secretly. He had to stay incognito because he was so well known, so the Alpenhorn player who was laid on for the tourists kept him hidden in his hut and used to give a toot on the big bugle if anyone was poking around.'

'Pretty good.' said L admiringly. 'I like the sound of old Heckmair.'

'Doesn't look too hard though,' he added, craning up at the colossal triangle of limestone and ice that loomed above them, and consequently could not be seen in true perspective. The massive tilted icefields appeared meagre and foreshortened from below, while the high, bulging forehead of the face seemed to merge insignificantly with the prominent cheek-bones. The notorious Ramp, a huge groove-system leading to the upper face, looked like a frowning rock-wrinkle offering easy escape to the Mittelegi Ridge.

'Oh, it's not hard nowadays with modern gear,' R hastened to assure him.

He needed to convince himself too, for he knew all the disturbing facts and figures. The 1938 route consisted of 10,000 feet of intricate zig-zag climbing threading its way to the summit 6,000 feet above the buttercups and gentians of Alpiglen. At every crucial stage of the climb a key-passage to the next section had to be located accurately.

He could recite by heart the worn litany of tragedies caused by sudden storms rendering the White Spider and the Exit Cracks impassable.

But on the other hand, to those who hit the right weather and the right route, the climb presented few problems. There had always been Eiger-aspirants who coached themselves exclusively on that gambling prescription.

'They were fantastic characters in the early days,' R yearned. 'They stopped for nothing and nobody.' His voice conveyed the grandeur of participation.

'Well, the bugle player has a bazooka now,' L answered, as a barrage of explosions resounded among the distant hills. 'And he's changed his tune. That doesn't sound like *Edelweiss*.'

'Just target practise. They've been at it all morning.'

Sometimes it was impossible to distinguish between the reverberations in the distant valley, and the rattling volleys of ice and stone on the melting face.

'Listen,' cajoled R, beginning again when the echoes had

died away, 'did you ever read a book called *No Picnic on Mount Kenya*?'

L who had read half a dozen books in his life and hadn't thought much of any of them, shook his head.

'Well, it's a true story, set in Africa in the last war, an absolutely incredible story but true all the same.'

R began with that sense of munching at a story, peculiar to small-mouthed men with beards. But he had a reputation among the younger climbers for a certain kind of anecdotal experience; he was a mythmaker who had been somewhere in the vicinity of many major occurrences in the mountaineering past. But he had never pulled off a coup himself, so he was obliged to trade in other people's legends. That was the principal source of his urge to contrive a first on the Eiger.

'There were thousands of Italian prisoners of war locked up in a British camp in Kenya. One of them was a dedicated mountaineer, and he had this dream of escaping to climb Mount Kenya. He had never seen the mountain, except a diagram of it on a tin of corned-beef, but it was only thirty or forty miles away. There was no question of escaping back to Italy or anything like that; it was impossible to get out of Africa even if a man could survive long enough in the bush to get anywhere.

'So he and a couple of mates secretly made up crampons and pitons in the camp-workshop, the same way prisoners in an ordinary jail cook up tools and weapons to escape. The difference was that the Italians went and tackled one of the finest mountains in the world for the sheer independence of it . . . and then *escaped back* into the camp again. There was nowhere else for them to go, you see.

'They were missing for weeks, maybe months, incredible adventures of every kind, wild animals, giant plants, glaciers, you name it. And then getting back in without being shot was another adventure. But the camp-commandant turned out to be one of those all-round British types, jolly good show, blind eye, and all that, and it appears he was pretty impressed by what they had done.

'It's a fantastic book. You must read it. I'll lend it to you when we get home.'

L turned away moodily. '*If* we get home.'

His lower lip protruded like that of a sulky boy and he rippled his muscles impotently, staring at the hostile mountains all round the horizon.

'Of course we'll get back home,' R laughed, thumping him jovially on the back. 'But we may as well do something useful while we're waiting.'

L doubled over on the small stance with a stomach-cramp, forcing R to lean out over space a thousand feet above the start of the route.

'Relax,' R advised him roughly. 'It's only tension knotting your guts.'

'The weather doesn't look too good.'

L's nervous chatter was getting to him. 'What's wrong with it?' he snapped. Then made an effort to control himself. 'It's only a bit of cloud blowing around in the bowl of the face. You've seen that yourself on a fine day from below. This face has its own private climate, all to itself.'

'Christ, a big rock only just missed me down there!' L continued miserably, 'I don't fancy this at all. How far up are we? It isn't even good climbing.'

'It'll get better soon,' R soothed. 'We're near the Difficult Crack now, so we'll be sheltered from stonefall by that big, red wall above. The crack is a really famous pitch, just your style.

'We're as well off to keep going now. You don't want to have to descend all that crap down there when the sun starts melting the loose stuff off the top.'

From where they stood, below the bulging red rock of the Rote Fluh, the big icefields were invisible, recessed into the rock, and R dismissed them with a wave of foreshortened illusion, persuading L, and himself too for a moment, that all that livid, white scar tissue — streaming with water and rattling with stones — hardly existed at all.

L looked round in panic as the mist broke up into whipping streamers of misery, revealing the appalling scree-laden desolation of the level where they stood, and the dark wings of the face unfolding above to receive them.

The valley reeled below in a sequence of dizzy, sunlit flashes that denied any physical connection between there and here so that L felt he was looking at the earth from the cockpit of a crazily spinning machine, lost in cloud.

R was moving on already. Accustomed to this kind of scrappy climbing he could see little difficulty in reaching the summit that day. The weather should hold, and the face was a lot less steep than he had imagined. It was even going to be quite easy, he cheered himself with a thrill of relief, the attitude of a man who desired climbing not for its own sake, but for achievement; and if it turned out to be a soft-touch so much the better. Lack of quality would not disappoint R, so long as the reputation was there.

He checked his watch.

The BBC news caused a sickening kick of disbelief in his stomach.

Conciliation had broken down irretrievably due to undefined shifts in the alliances comprising the Superpowers. 'Confrontation seems inevitable,' a tight-lipped British observer threatened.

R shook his head frantically at the failure to specify, as if a blockage in the headset might be withholding the vital information.

Then an excited, almost hysterical announcer described Germany as an 'Holocaust of anti-American sabotage', whereupon the station simply gave up and played Elgar.

France was a gabble of incoherence . . .

On Radio Geneva, one strong, uninterrupted, military voice alerted the Swiss nation over and over again to Emergency Action.

The voice, toneless as a tannoy, insisted at ten-second intervals in the stunned silence of R's brain —

Attention! Attention! Crise Internationale! Crise Internationale! Attention! Attention! Aux Abris! Aux Abris!

To the Shelters!

Stupefied by shock R stared out into the blind mist.

For a moment he felt a phantom hunger devour his senses. Then utter isolation. He visualised streams of humanity pouring down from the hillsides, spilling out of the buildings, melting off the streets and draining through the ground into great concrete silos, human reservoirs — or mass graves. The army would stay close to the surface, gun-muzzles bristling from every aperture in the surface of the country. He stood paralysed for so long at the vision of a whole population sucked into holes in the ground that L almost caught up with him. He was shrieking some hideous warning and waving frantically.

R looked up and saw, silhouetted against the brightening sky, a spatter of rocks spewing over the rim of the Rote Fluh, and arching towards him in casual slow motion, so that there was plenty of time to dive under the cover of an overhang and watch the huge chunks smash thunderously onto the terraces hundreds of feet below, then bound outwards with increasing speed as if volleyed on vigorously by the ledges.

No going back down that rubbish-chute. The face was sloughing like an avalanche-slope.

The tiny voice vibrated insistently in his ears *Aux Abris! Aux Abris!*

He shook his head as if he were being stung.

How could he explain to L what had happened, and cope with the boy's panic, despair, his fury even if he guessed deception?

He tried to frame in simple words the idea that life on the planet might have degenerated into chaos while they were climbing a mountain, but the words jammed far back in the mind — like L's electronic dictionary stunned by an untranslatable idea.

He couldn't face a moment of truth of such monumental

magnitude that human history crashed into it at express speed and stopped dead with the impact.

The people in the valleys, running through the streets, down the concrete subways all over Europe weren't facing up to it either. They were taking the first step blindly, and then the next one into the dark.

Better keep going, and keep quiet, and maybe it would go away like the Cuban flashpoint and all the other crises.

For a fraction of a second his mind was suffused by radiant relief while he imagined it all to be an hysterical fraud by the media, like the notorious hoax Orson Welles pulled off in the thirties when millions of Americans panicked out of all control, convinced by radio-bulletins that New York was being invaded by aliens from outer space.

But, as if awakening from a nightmare, past the blissful moment of relief to the realisation that reality is even grimmer than the dream, he remembered the soldiers in the streets, the confiscation of passports, and the barred compounds, and he knew no hoax could be that elaborate.

It was easier to keep stumbling sickly ahead of L, saying nothing. If he spoke he would have to believe what he heard himself say.

There was something doomed about L, he thought dumbly, as if recognising an indicative smell or a sound, something vulnerable about the way the small head sat on the bulky shoulders. He thought of the youth lured to extinction in the old film *Mort d'un Guide*, and shuddered.

R was finally brought to a halt by a steep, unavoidable groove, slick with water. A frayed remnant of old rope dangled down beside the problem, its dubious point of attachment hidden from view. Recklessly he grabbed the rope in both hands like an enraged bell-ringer and began to pull up hand over hand. What did it matter whether it broke or not? But a sudden sense of survival jolted his body, and he shot a hand and foot securely into the crack.

Arriving on a straggle of bleak and tilted terraces at the foot of a huge, overhanging wall of uncracked limestone R was on top of the introductory plinth, and at the foot of the real North Face.

He gazed around. This desolate spot was one of the most intense deposits of mountaineering memory in the world. The Wet Cave Bivouac was here, and the Stollenloch exit from the rail-tunnel. The pulverised ledges, wreathed in tatters of mist, were crowded with ghosts. Buhl, with his shapeless, hillbilly hat; Heckmair, with a homely shin of pork in his sack, staring out of a measured silence at Harrer, so jaunty with one ice-hammer and not a single crampon-point to his name. Bonatti too, going up and then quietly coming down, not just a hero but a survivor; Hinterstoisser and Toni Kurz tiptoeing past the trap in the gallows floor ... Mingling with the myths he had mouthed so many times, R stumbled in the stage-door of history, through the deserted wings, and onto the empty stage.

All he saw was a dribbling backdrop of uncouth, wet rock, and the swirling emptiness in front of his feet into which both audience and the earth had disappeared. Headset switched off he heard only the scree-chips grinding under his boots, water dripping on worn rock, and the meteoric whine of falling stones.

At the foot of the Difficult Crack, below the Hinterstoisser Traverse, the Swallow's Nest, Death Bivouac, the Traverse of the Gods, and the White Spider, the most poetic route in the world, R felt the antiphonic responses of that revered chant sound in the void without an echo.

L scarcely knew them, any more than he knew the Stations of the Cross. He was just at the foot of the fixed rope now. R heard him grunting below, but the rope never twitched or tightened. L was climbing free. He found R sitting on the dripping terrace like some forgotten tragedy unveiled by a thaw, his shoulders slumped under the weight of his pack and the weariness of total desertion.

L was talking at him, but the words didn't register. A break in the swirling mist and he saw distant slate-grey ridges swathed in ugly cloud.

A storm was threatening, his brain measured instinctively, coming to pour destruction into the shattered bowl of the face.

L fiddled impatiently with his headset. He jerked R's arm.

'What does *abree* mean?' he demanded. '*Abree!* What's *abree* mean?'

R shook his head dumbly. The motion was too much for his self-control. Tears broke loose and trickled down into his beard.

L noticed something of his condition and took it for the dejection of fatigue. Competition stirred in his muscles. He had been slighted by the ease with which R stayed ahead on the unfamiliar mixed scrambling below.

'I'll lead for a start,' he volunteered. 'It'll get the weight of the ropes off our backs. Where's that crack you were talking about?'

The mist closed in again, but R knew the way as clearly as if he had been there before. The photographs and descriptions were printed in his mind.

L flexed his sturdy arms, and the pack settled between his shoulders. He scrambled awkwardly up easy, wet rock and ball-bearing scree, but when he reached the foot of the difficulties and began to move up on steep, black rock he entered his own element.

When R's turn came to follow he found the initial moves strenuous and unbalanced. He had climbed much easier grade fives than this famous four. He was wading through a numb grief that clogged his will and dulled his senses like the immediate aftermath of a broken heart. L swarmed on in the lead, the rope running out eagerly behind him, until he came to a confused halt at the foot of a solid wall that impended above him like the hull of a ship.

It was a mark of their different traditions that L was peering inquisitively up the overhanging wall while R never even glanced upwards but faced immediately out to the left. Even without foreknowledge of the Hinterstoisser Traverse that skirted the obstacle he would automatically look for avoidance rather than head-on challenge.

He had command of himself now. There was nothing to do but go on, even if only to avoid descent.

He felt he was getting close to a basic truth of mountaineering, now that it no longer mattered. Draining Mallory's catchphrase to the dregs, he realised that when it came down to the very bitter end of experience, a man continued climbing a mountain, not because it was there, but because he himself was there.

R suffered the cruel contradictions of absurdity and compulsion at the heart of climbing.

Once over the Hinterstoisser there could be no return, psychologically at least, because that was how it was in the early myths of the mountain, and famous men had died terrible deaths trying to undo that step. Of course it was only a myth. Climbers could descend from any part of the lower face, and often did, though the exposure to danger was considerable.

But L wouldn't know the facts, and now it was necessary to ensure that he continued upwards.

'Out there is the Hinterstoisser Traverse,' R spoke slowly. The saliva in his mouth felt as thick and warm as blood. 'Anderl Hinterstoisser and Toni Kurz found a way out there across that slab in 1936. Hinterstoisser spent the rest of his life trying to reverse it in a storm. He abseiled down eventually over there, and fell to his death.

'Toni Kurz survived for a night and day, hanging on a rope, injured, frost-bitten, and slowly dying of exposure. He lived ten times as long as Christ on the cross, and the only thing missing was the crown of thorns. All the time he thought he could be saved.

'He made up a makeshift line from bits and scraps and hauled up a safety-rope from rescuers on the ledges a hundred and thirty feet below. He slid down the rope until he jammed on a knot just a few feet out of reach of rescue.

'He died of exhaustion hanging there, although they could practically touch his feet from below.'

R stopped, overcome. That legendary body had dangled for

a long time over the abyss of his memory on its old frayed rope, a thick crop of icicles growing longer and longer on the crampon-points.

There was nothing to see but the wet and vacant slab, and some disconnected snatches of the mountain breaking through the mist like phrases from a torn description.

In the disturbed pools of L's eyes R watched the shapeless bundle of death ripple and rotate with the deliberately ugly motion of fear, an empty spider on a long, thin thread having spun all its substance into support until there was nothing left to survive.

L hesitated, weighing the hollow image. Then he added it to his load, and moved out on the near-vertical slab.

A rail of old rope looped out into the mist, but L didn't touch it. He clipped his own rope for protection into the pitons and traversed delicately on rounded holds and curved edges until he reached the upward crack. A veil of mist was ripped away and he stood exposed in clear silhouette on the other side of a clean divide. The intervening rock gleamed in the light with the bland polish of perfection.

R reached instinctively for his camera. Then he remembered, and the motion faltered and fell slowly away.

When the rope came tight and it was his turn to move, he entered the pitch as if it were a wave of cold water, screwing up his features, holding his breath. Jumping in, he immediately grabbed the fixed rope and clipped his harness to it. He crossed the compact slab with the precarious aid of the slender, elasticated banister, climbed the steep crack at the end, and at 10 a.m. arrived in a bleak fanfare of sunlight at the Swallow's Nest.

The small bivouac-niche was heaped over with old snow, and a large turd tumbled carelessly to one side, a signpost to humanity.

L was measuring dumbly the enormous expanse of face visible above them now; they had only rounded the lower jaw-line and still the huge, hollow cheeks of ice, and the bulging forehead glowered in repudiation.

R's limbs weakened at the prospect and the brittle heart in his chest crumpled under a fresh onslaught of pain.

'Jesus Christ!' wailed L, as a flurry of stones pumped down the first icefield. 'How're we going to tackle that lot? It's like the Battle of the Somme up there.'

'Just take it step by step,' R muttered savagely. 'We'll get there. And if we don't, it doesn't make much difference anyway.'

The hopeless abandon of the tone struck L with the force of revelation; appalled by some unspeakable understanding he asked no questions.

R snapped on crampons and grasped ice-axe and ice-hammer in either hand.

The ice was angled at about forty-five to fifty degrees, and it was wet and rubbery after a warm night of thaw. The axes and crampon-points gouged lumps and flakes out of the insecure surface. Pebbles drummed an advance warning on their helmets, but nothing bigger came down until they reached the shelter of the next rock-barrier, where the Ice Hose bulged a continuation, and they looked up to see the sky studded with rocks like stampeding hooves.

Bitter bravery rose in R's throat like bile, and he silently took the lead, kicking and axing his way up the steep tongue of ice that led to the massive Second Icefield. When the ice ran out on bare rock he stubbed and trembled up the grit-sliding, nerve-wracking slabs without grace or protection. The Second Icefield was so enormous they felt paradoxically safe emerging on to its murderous, stone-studded slope, as if they were too insignificant in all that vast expanse to be hit by any of the random debris that came down; and yet every screaming, whining missile seemed to home in on their position, and when the first impact missed the ricochet made a second attempt.

Their tools flailed the grit-encrusted ice as if they were trying to burrow rather than climb, but finally, after hours of bombarded exposure they scrabbled out of the target-area into the relative safety of Death Bivouac. . . .

Again dreams and the dead were pervasive, and R merged almost irredeemably with the frozen memories of Sedlmayer and Mehringer. In 1935 they were the first men ever to attempt the face, driving a hard and direct line into a five-day storm and oblivion in this savage spot.

R was not much more real than Sedlmayer, whose ice-statue was seen, by observers circling the face, to guard the bivouac until winter carried him down.

As he stared out into the shallow clearance of the afternoon at the storm-clouds bulging on the horizon R heard - not the mournful prowling of the old spotter-plane droning a farewell among the deserted pillars of the face — but the venom of a jetfighter slashing the final silence of the sky.

During the traverse of the Third Icefield towards the Ramp, hands slotted between the steep, wafery ice and rock, R felt a deep, crumbling detonation filling, suffusing, swallowing the void behind his back. It swelled over thunder, beyond avalanche, to a pulsating explosion so heavy and ponderous that it extended beyond sound into a physical disintegration of distance, a brain-bruising shock that squeezed off perception from the senses so that he could not judge whether the mountain was moving or still, whether it was wind or heat that sucked at his stunned body; and though the entire face was alive and quivering with disruption nothing was more apparent than a great central stillness of ruin within the growing heart of the sound, a core of silent aftermath devouring the explosion from within. The swollen masses of cloud were closer now, not having drifted in, but as if some mighty force had warped and buckled the space in which they hung.

Consciousness began to filter through R's numb brain, and he stumbled forward into the rocky gully of the Ramp. L was there already. He had lost the power of speech and was retching convulsively, deep sobbing gasps torn by the roots from his lungs and stomach.

R anchored himself instantly.

The rope seared across his shoulders whipping him awake. L landed heavily on a sloping ledge a few feet below, and the rope held him. He was chronically dazed, but the effort of scrambling back up controlled his hysteria.

Neither said a word. Sobbing breath and dripping sweat spoke the language of desperation.

R lurched up the easy gully in the lead, realising helplessly that the hard, steep bottleneck at the top of the Ramp would be in waterfall condition now. All the climbing in his life had led insistently to this moment, but now that he needed over-powering skill and endurance he knew with a stark sense of failure that the ability was not there.

If it depended on him to prolong his own life, then he would die here.

The exit of the gully was blocked by a steep, narrow chimney. Water gushed and swirled down the dark, polished rock, submerging the line of the climb. On the right and left overhanging rock bulged ponderously.

R belayed with slow, dull care, attaching himself securely to five different anchor-points. L was heavy and there was not much protection on that grotesque right-hand wall where Lachenal had fought out his desperate rock-variation to the waterfall on the second ascent in 1947.

He threaded L's rope through a friction belay-plate, checked the anchors again and then pointed at the bulging pitch overhead.

'Now,' he said, 'You wanted rock. Climb that, you bastard.' But no sound emerged.

L barely lifted his eyes. He stepped up to a ledge with the heavy, helpless tread of a man on the gallows, and laid listless hands on the rock.

'Get in some protection,' R ordered sharply.

L fumbled a chock into a crack.

'Clip that peg out on the left.'

L attached his rope to the old piton, and resumed his position, breathing heavily.

'Get on with it.'

His arms tightened obediently, fingers closing on the flaky rock as if he was gouging handholds in it. His feet came up and the boots bridged wide apart on small holds.

He began to pull up. A foothold snapped off, his body plunged, and R was dragged against his anchors by the rope. L stood up again, and shook himself.

Failure was good for him.

This time he examined the problem, and braced himself.

He pulled up powerfully again, but didn't rest or hang on the holds. He used them dynamically, following through on each move, and reaching up fast for the next invisible edge.

He was fifteen feet above the last piton, arched out around the bulge.

His legs vibrated and the muscles knotted in his arms. To his left a big crumbling flake jutted.

L's left hand blurred away from a hold, left foot lashed out on the wall for balance. As his body slewed into a fall his hand clamped the edge of the flake.

He swung violently out from the wall, and the second hand smacked around the shuddering shield of rock.

Feet kicked up against the flake, arching his body out, and then he was laybacking fiercely. A hand grappled over the top of the flake, feet and body swung free, and then, with the irresistible savagery of survival, he wrenched himself up onto the ledge above . . .

Climbing the ice overhead to the Brittle Ledges they did not know each other—frail forms weaving through a superhuman world, particles of rock and ice whirling like molecules, the air itself relentless friction.

A disease of darkness setting in.

Freezing cloud flailed them, stinging skin from bone with the leaded whipcord of hail.

L flapped across the brittle, broken ledges like a bundle of empty rags catching and dragging on spikes and projections. R was fumbling again among the sheltered ironies of history . . . that old overcoat cast off high on the White Spider by Albrecht and Derungs, a black chrysalis that panicked the Scheidegg observers into thinking there was a body in it.

L fluttered against the cracked pillar at the end of the ledges as if he were blown involuntarily upwards, a moth in an updraught, ragged and torn against the steep rock.

The wind hammered and howled. There was no more thought of release. No feel of another fate. Born into this, and the conclusion obvious. But not immediate. They staggered around a corner, out of the funnel. A sheltered terrace.

The wind streamed past, faltered, and dropped to a whisper.

Unbearably heavy in the sudden vacancy they slumped together on the little ledge, an irreducible heap.

Here was the Götterquergang, Traverse of the Gods, beginning of the end.

The ledge ran on, sloping and tilting in the gathering gloom. Utterly bleak and forsaken, it was no gangway but a riddle of steep, icy terraces crossing a buttress to a gleaming notch hundreds of feet away.

The notch was bright because, just beyond it, the White Spider was frothing furiously with avalanche. Unapproachable.

R laid his head down in the dark peace of indifference.

The first storm-squall had passed over; there was a lull, the sky cleared briefly overhead baring jagged stars and cold promise.

Time drifted, disarranged.

On the hulking fin of the Eiger R prowled the cataclysms of prehistory, ploughed the tidal glaciers of ice-ages, and towered over a flurry of peopled time, farms and fields creeping like contagion through the foothills, fading into the immunity of the mountains.

Then the great iceberg of the Eiger, adrift in time, sliced into the densest century, tunnels, trains, tourism, and swarming men like lice or lemmings; and R felt the entire mountain shudder under his back.

Waking, the vibration was real, and he understood that the roaring in his ears was a total collapse of some monstrous balance in the world, a balance as singular as the molecular bondage below the skin of things, tumbling surfaces into the void like graves when the bones and the boxes implode and the wild soil falls askew in pits and craters; and it was a collapse of time too, that tumbled cultures down like castles and burned the debris of paint, gold, and poetry to the smoky ash of centuries in a searing micro-second, while the unrepeatable thunder of destruction rolled and reverberated in the empty perpetuity of a history and future all undone.

He looked out into the dark and saw the mushrooming storm-clouds glowing red, as if he were projecting a bloodshot vision on the night.

A jagged flash of lightning slashed the sky, and then again and again, spreading and catching, igniting particles of flaky fire in the abrasive, breathless atmosphere. His skin burned and seared.

R stared at the face inches from his own. The skin was rising in bubbles, hanging in shreds. The lips were black, and deeply cracked. L was dead.

The lightning stopped, and the hot wind gathered.

Slowly, and without any fuss, cloud closed the sky, quenching the nine billion names of God.

R had time to understand, he was making the last ascent.

THE BOY WHO SHOT JOHN WAYNE

My cousin Tom was right about one thing: I was an outright cissy. A thin, pasty child — not so much from normal malnutrition but from some kind of emotional hunger — I was afraid to fight, no use at football. I slouched around, soaked in the misery of a masculine world. I wanted to grow up as different from everything around me on the farm as was humanly possible. A spiritual life seemed the obvious alternative. Not here of course. Kilnamon or anywhere like it in the Midlands would have been impossible. I knew the place too well to rise above it. There was nothing I wouldn't wish to forget; Uncle Joe's wet farm outside the town, the house unpainted and the haysheds rusting, bony cattle in the fields, briar and blackthorn and the rampant yellow buachalan. Tom was a year younger than I but it seemed the other way round. Even at the age of twelve he was doing a man's work.

My father sent me down from Dublin every summer. I was his link with the land. He grew up here in Kilnamon in the spare forties. When Joe inherited the farm my father shifted to Dublin to better himself, but the only improvement existed in his own mind, I'm afraid. He was riddled with notions of status and failure all his life. Pride suffocated his humour and affection. He was a salesman in a hardware shop, a hardworking, honest man. He used to describe himself painfully to strangers as 'in a commercial way of business.'

The holidays on the farm were supposed to toughen me with manly values. My father can't have remembered his own brother very well. The only values Uncle Joe professed were muscle and money. He had no sympathy at all for me, a pale hostage from the city. And Tom too, poor Tom, uncouth and graceless, with strength to compensate for skill, understood what I never realised — that I was a usurper.

His brief boyhood was animated by two passions; fishing and films.

Both had a strain of violence.

When all my pocket-money was spent and he could steal no change from his father for the cinema he went fishing in the river. Without a word from me, condemned to sit by his side, he flogged the sulky water with hook and line. Later he gutted the bony perch and fried them over the kitchen fire. Scraping fish from a burnt pan is the only act of sharing I recall in the house. I don't know what poison was in our fathers but Tom and I were both motherless.

The Royal in Kilnamon was no more than a mile from the farm. A draughty hall with wooden benches at the front below the screen, lines of chairs behind and two rows of cushioned seats at the very back. Tom went to see every new picture. He was a cowboy fanatic, war-films in second place. Love stories were a source of jeering speculation about sex. Life, as Tom projected it, was explicitly basic. Everything led either to battle or to bed.

I couldn't escape him. He trailed me with him to show his power over an older city-boy. And I had been conditioned to accept humiliation, almost to expect it as a right. The only people I ever got to know in Kilnamon were those who could tolerate the company I was forced to keep, Tom and the bullies who hung around with him. I'm sure there were decent people there too who didn't sneer and curse and steal, but they must have had somewhere else to spend their time.

They haven't come out to welcome me back either. I suppose they'll see how the glasshouses get on first. They've lived near cowshit too long to get excited about an organic farm. It's the only one in these parts. Clean fruit and vegetables for an imaginary market. We're surrounded by tired farmers waiting to sell out to land-dealers; meanwhile they breed pharmaceutical beef and sneer at my pretensions. I've one gardener—farmer, I suppose you'd call him — a self-professed itinerant with a bad leg and a genius for growth. He's an unusual traveller — he's never left Kilnamon in his life. If the farm fails his days will be numbered. He will have backed the loser once too often.

II

When Uncle Joe died last winter I got the news by telegram. I almost missed it. It came to the college months after I had left. Father Boyle brought it round to the flat, I didn't realise they had my address since I'd moved a second time. It was embarrassing to find Boyle standing on the doorstep with the opened telegram. He shook my hand gravely, offered help if required, and took himself off. I resolved to move again.

The telegram was signed J.J. Gorman (Solicitor). The name seemed at once ridiculous and right, though I couldn't grasp the contradiction then. The news itself was no surprise. When I arrived in Kilnamon for the funeral a heavy figure stepped from the church-porch to greet me. I looked away. The last thing I wanted was to meet anyone. I had no connections here. This final visit was a cold duty to the past.

'Sorry for your trouble, Pat! Glad you could make it.' With a shock of displacement I saw Tom's former friend — a coarse hulk of a boy — distorted into an adult. John Joe Gorman (Solicitor). His face was folded in rolls of closely shaven fat. Heavy lips and eyes drooped with professional sympathy. A whisper in the flat accent: 'I'm lookin' after your uncle's affairs. We'll have a chat after the funeral.'

Things were beginning to come home to me in a conspiracy of understanding. I must have been blind till now. There were no mourners in the front seats. I knew there wouldn't be, of course, but ... Thought stalled, my eyes veering around the gloomy church. So much smaller than I recalled. The seats dotted with the same old women in scarves and belted raincoats, as patient as the statues. I knew now they were heavier with fatigue than piety, their weariness was a holier condition than prayer.

The stained glass window above the altar was crudely

made. More lead than colour. How had it spangled my boyhood prayers with such dull glory? I used to see blood in red glass and sanctity in stone-cold shadows, a dangerous innocence seduced by sermons and sacrifice.

Uncle Joe's coffin rested on trestles before the altar, so transient it was already sliding through the candlelight into the dark. I knew no comfort to offer. John Joe tiptoed exaggeratedly forward, took a mass-card from his inside pocket and propped it on the lid. He genuflected reverently and returned to kneel beside me in the front seat.

Uncle Joe had never entered the church before to my knowledge. Once, when we were loading hay into the loft I felt his coldness momentarily abate. I knew I had a religious duty to perform. Stuttering, I asked if he would come to mass with us next morning. He spat into the cart very close to my sandals. His speed increased and very soon he was pulling hay from under my feet. I was forced to jump aside to avoid the flying needles of his fork.

And Tom would only come to watch the women and make a nuisance of himself. He used to sit beside me, silently breaking wind, and then slide away leaving me stranded in guilt. John Joe Gorman also had some kind of anal obsession in those days. Loud, tearing eruptions were his style under cover of the gospel shuffle. All the boys were reduced to hysterical mirth and he was an immediate hero. His father was an important man anyway, a leading solicitor. John Joe always had a summer job in a garage on Church Street.

I looked at him now to measure the change. His face had the same sure sense of life as a source of profit. There was aggression in the bluntness of his head. His jacket was hand-tailored to accommodate hulking shoulders. The trousers were ponderously charged where the heavy thighs met the curve of his belly. How could this solid adult ever have been a boy? He was so . . . so absolutely established in his manhood. That confidence had never come to me. No matter how desperately I tried I could not remember growing up.

We drove behind the hearse to the graveyard. There was no other car. John Joe told me he had gone into his father's business years before. He had taken it over now. He was well used to dead farmers and their wills.

'Well, the old place is yours, Pat, and good luck to you. You'll be wanting to sell up I suppose.'

The blood was singing under my skin with excitement and appal. I had no idea what to think.

The hearse speeded up. No one wished to linger over Uncle Joe.

Independence must take years of practise and I had no experience of it at all.

It was drizzling heavily in the cemetery. I had seen all this before, my life whittled down to a cold solitude by this ritual. A figure tended a plot in a far corner. Under a wool cap a straggle of yellow hair. He straightened and turned towards us in respect as the coffin went down. I saw the crooked angle of one leg against the handle of a rake and suffered that shock of displacement again. The thud of soil on hollow timber, and memory jerked in a new direction. Uncle Joe cutting turf in the bog. He stood in the bottom of the boghole hurling the heavy sods up faster then I could catch and carry them. Every sod punched the breath out of my chest. He never let up the pace. Christian training forbade harsh thoughts about the dead but I kept a voice in my head to think them for me: Now you swine — the phrase formed involuntarily — throw this lot up. . . . if you can —

After the burial I shook the hands of a few old men. They knew who I was, of course. A sliding glance into my eyes, murmur of condolence, and the attention shifted to my shabby lay clothes, the collar and tie around my neck.

I was branded with my own mistake. The only reason I had entered the seminary in the first place was to escape from home and Kilnamon. I traded one sense of claustrophobia for another, deeper kind. But my father was happy. University was out of the question, and if I couldn't be a doctor I had better be a priest. He invested a lot of anxiety in my prospects and I began to see that a spiritual life could be subject to the same values as any commercial way of business.

If I had come from an easier background I wouldn't have entered the Church at all. I'd have gone to England and disappeared into the army or the building trade. That was what Tom did when he fell out with Uncle Joe.

III

Tom started to drink in a determined way when he was about seventeen. He ran up debts on his father's credit and sold off lambs for drinking money. Apparently it was a sudden thing, an explosion, total loss of control. Later, he compromised a girl in Kilnamon, a maid in the doctor's house. He offered to marry her but Uncle Joe refused to let them live on the farm.

Tom came home drunk one night and Uncle Joe threw him out. There was a fight and Tom broke his father's arm. He might have killed him only someone interfered.

That fight had been brewing a long time. Tom told me about it on his way to England. He only called on me to borrow a few pounds to see him through till he got a start. The novitiate made him laugh. It reminded him of the County Home. I asked him where his girlfriend was. He sneered at my innocence,

'No shortage of women where I'm going Pat. No need to bring your own.'

My father was in Luke's hospital at the time for the first of many tests. I asked him if he could persuade Uncle Joe to relent towards Tom. He refused to interfere. Apparently he had fallen out finally with Joe himself over some inheritance that was never shared.

I had my own problems to distract me. Study was absolutely joyless and the vocation a fading echo. Dogma and discipline grew increasingly arbitrary but I had neither the courage nor — I suppose — the freedom to leave the seminary. Illness had forced my father to retire from work and he had everything pinned on me then.

My superiors battled for my integrity and submission. In frustration I thwarted their every effort. I turned vegetarian, an unthinkable thing in the Church, choking on the fatty bacon and stewed gristle. Father Boyle argued that the animal world was created for man's sustenance. The least I could do was allow it to fulfil its God-given function. He preached the Body and Blood of Christ almost as a dietary injunction. Curiously some of my class-mates saw my ideas as an insult to themselves and what they stood for. It was like attacking their religion. They were the sons of farmers and they believed in red meat with a passion.

I was summoned to Boyle's office one morning. I expected an ultimatum but was introduced instead to a priest, home on holiday from England. He made me sit down and brace myself for bad news. I had never known there was any other kind.

He informed me that Tom had died in an accident in London. I made a show of grief and began to feel its effects. Attempts had been made to contact Uncle Joe without response, and the priest in Kilnamon had directed them to me. Father Murtagh wasn't sure of any details — he had simply brought the message in passing — but at last he admitted having heard that Tom fell from the balcony of a dancehall during a brawl. Whether he had fallen or been thrown was another matter, but he was a ganger with McAlpine's at the time, and sudden death was not unknown.

Father Murtagh insisted that this report was probably a myth. He had come across the same story before and it had been the same dancehall in Camden Town, the one they called the Buffalo. Apocryphal, he called it.

He promised to send me details on his return.

Almost immediately I received a letter from Uncle Joe. I had never known him to write a word before, but it was strangely articulate. First he informed me coldly of my cousin's death, as if it was no more than his duty to let me know. . . .

And yet in spite of the tone it seemed a personal letter. That 'Dear Pat' must have cost a mighty effort to a man whose voice was shaped by anger. I felt he was reaching towards me in friendship or despair. He explained that having fallen out with my father and lost his own son he was considering the question of his soul now that time was getting short. He doubted that he had such a thing as a soul, though and what did I think of that?

I panicked at the thought of responding to real human need. I knew exactly what he meant for I doubted that he had a soul either. He said he knew my father was dying. It was the first time I had seen it put so bluntly but I agreed with him on that too. Uncle Joe was a man of few words and no illusions. He expressed neither sympathy nor regret, and I interpreted this hardness as a refusal to ask for help. I went down to see him in Kilnamon.

The house looked as if it had been deserted for years. I found him down at the bottom of the farm mending a wall. There was a tractor ploughing behind him where the river used to swamp the land. But it was all drained now, the best of rich, black soil folding over behind the plough. He saw me alright though he didn't show it till I was halfway along the headland. Then he left the stones and came slowly to meet me.

It was one of those rare moments when I realised I was a man to other men. As a boy he never acknowledged me at all. He took my hand briefly now as if I had passed him something casual. The roar of the tractor absolved us from small talk. I felt the curiosity of the driver as he swung into another furrow and moved away. I thought it was an aimless stroll we were taking then, a refusal to sit down and meet each other's eyes. Now I know that we were 'walking the land', measuring me against it.

Uncle Joe was no longer the big man I remembered. I had grown tall myself and he was stooped with rheumatism. He shuffled beside me in a pair of blue overalls and wellingtons, an old tweed jacket, a shirt without a collar. The corded hollows of his throat shocked me with their frail tension. Shaving must be near-suicide, I thought. His face was lined and angular, grey hair combed severely forward onto a bony forehead.

The farm was neglected. Broken walls and rotting bales of hay. But good land and plenty of it. Drainage had doubled the arable acres. Perversely I regretted the loss of the wetlands that had depressed me so much as a fretful boy. The succulent flags were gone from the riverbank where poor Tom used to trail his line in anger and frustration. There was no habitat now for the heron that used to flap away at our approach. Tom had vowed to kill it for stealing fish.

We tramped for an hour almost in silence. Eventually, with desperate delicacy I asked him if there were any ... any problems I could help him with. He snorted — as close to laughter as I ever heard.

'You're not cut out for the confession-box,' he grated. He looked at my cheap black suit and sandals sarcastically, '... whatever else might be in store for you!'

But he talked briefly about his son. He had never forgiven the broken arm. I mentioned the story I had heard. I wanted to know if Tom's death was accidental or deliberate. The old man spat.

'The way I heard it, he took pneumonia sleepin' rough. He was on a drunken batter, and he took pneumonia out of it. That's how I heard it.'

He left me to take my pick of the stories.

All of a sudden he seemed unbearably vulnerable in his hardness. He had missed everything that mattered, and so had I. I saw him pared down to the loneliness of the bone and was moved almost to tears.

My tongue was somehow loosened. I told him he had read me right, I hadn't the makings of a priest and never would have.

'What does your father say to that?' was all he wanted to know. His lack of any interest in me at all made me feel a fool for having confided in him.

'I haven't told him,' I replied. 'The least I can do is stick it out for the few months he has left. There's no point breaking his heart.'

There was no response. His pale eyes were screwed up, staring into the corner of a field.

I visited my father in hospital almost every day. Part of his skull was shaved and the blue marks of radium treatment were spread across his scalp. He was shrivelling into the old striped pyjamas. One day his condition had deteriorated visibly. There was a letter in his hands. The paper was crushed. He plucked at it with gaunt fingers as if he wanted to shred it and didn't have the strength.

'Read that!' He tried to throw it at me.

The letter was from Uncle Joe. I hoped it was reconciliation, but there was an ugly dread in the pit of my stomach. There, at the bottom of the page, was the kick in the belly.

'. . . It must be a hard blow to see Pat leaving the priesthood. He told me about it himself and maybe it's all for the best. My own blackguard let me down worse . . .'

I raised my eyes from the page and tried to catch my father's dull stare. There was nothing I could say, no lie I could tell. He had turned his face to the wall in more ways than one.

Uncle Joe died a year after my father. I had long quit the college and thought they had let me go. In a flat in Harold's Cross I tried to organise a future for myself. I put in for jobs but my past was a problem. I didn't want anything that would take a spoiled priest as a guarantee of humility. Somehow it seemed I must end up in Australia sooner or later. There was something doomed about me that demanded exile. I was thinking of London for a start when Father Boyle brought the telegram around.

IV

After the funeral John Joe brought me to the Imperial Hotel for a drink. There was no legal ritual in the Castle Street office. He produced the will in a corner of the hotel lounge. It came out of his inside pocket. I wondered how many more wills and mass-cards were stored away in there like obituaries in a newspaper file. Without stirring a hand I owned fifty acres, a house, and assorted sheds. The very piece of ground I least wanted to see again on the surface of the earth was entirely mine, The sense of possession was impossible to grasp. They might as well have made me a bishop after I turned my back on the church.

To add to my confusion I got a whiff of John Joe's business style. I understood now why we hadn't gone to his office. We were in it.

This dark corner of the lounge was his by recognition. There were several people at the bar anxious for his attention, but when they saw him with a client they kept their distance. Two brandies arrived unordered. I was used to minerals and the occasional glass of beer. The first sip staggered me.

John Joe was spreading papers on the table.

'I'll have to eat something,' I mumbled. 'I got nothing on the train.'

'Easy now, Pat. Easy. We'll fix you up with lunch as soon as we settle this bit of business.'

'I'll get a sandwich or something . . .' I escaped to the bar. In the long mirror I could have sworn I saw John Joe shaking his head at the barman.

'Any chance of a cheese sandwich?' I was trembling with hunger. He shot a glance over my shoulder. 'Ham!' he grunted reluctantly.

'No. No meat, thanks. Have you nothing else?'

He hesitated and then relaxed. 'I'll see what I can do for you. Pat isn't it? Sorry for your trouble. I'd have been there this morning only I had to open up here.'

I went back to my seat warmed by recognition.

John Joe seemed thoroughly familiar with the farm. He had all the values at the tips of his fingrs. He estimated a potential price. To me it was a lot of money. He could drop a nought and it was still a lot of money to me.

Uncle Joe left no debts. That was why the farm didn't look prosperous. He never borrowed for development.

John Joe was into his second brandy. It had been cold in the graveyard. The flesh of his hands was pudgy, unused.

'I don't want to jump the gun right after a bereavement, Pat,' he said, 'but I think I know the score here . . .' I could imagine him intimidating widows. 'You'll want to sell, Pat, isn't that right? You've had your own troubles by all accounts, but that's no business of mine. There'll be a tidy sum here to invest in something steady for the future . . .'

The implication that my position was common knowledge and even a source of shame infuriated me.

'. . . I have a local client interested in the property already.'

'Who?' I asked, startled.

John Joe's mouth tightened. He couldn't snarl at me to mind my own business like he used to.

'Tim Brophy,' he said after a pause.

Tim Brophy! I was amazed. Uncle Joe had mentioned the name with the usual dismissive spit the day we walked the land. Brophy was the fellow who farmed the scraggy patch to the west. I didn't think he'd have the kind of money Gorman was proposing for Uncle Joe's — for *my* farm.

I was in no doubt about selling. And I wanted the money as quickly as possible. Dreams were reeling through my mind already. But I'd make sure John Joe didn't get a penny more than the minimum commission. I wouldn't give him the satisfaction of instant assent either, although it was hard to imagine anyone buying a farm near Kilnamon.

There was a lot of petty revenge to catch up on. So I said I'd think about it and let him know.

His mouth tightened again, and then formed a professional smile. — Ah sure, he knew well how upset I was after my uncle. Wasn't oul' Joe like a father to me when I was a kid. And all the rest of it! I rose abruptly to leave. The sandwich hadn't come. John Joe circled my shoulders with a heavy arm and drew me towards the bar.

'We'll have a drink out of respect for the dead,' he decided, 'and the other fellah too, God rest him! I always knew he'd come to a bad end.' He chuckled.

'Ah you wouldn't understand, Pat. You were always a nice quiet sort of a fellah. But Tom was a real hard chaw. Jasus, man, he was one tough fucker . . .'

We sat on high stools in front of the bar. This was a new occupation for me and I wasn't too sure how to handle myself. The dizzy feeling could be due to the change of fortune as well as hunger, but it seemed best not to aggravate it with alcohol.

I asked for coffee. Again the barman looked to John Joe for advice and I insisted.

'Maybe you'll take a drop of something in it so.' he wheedled.

'On the house . . .'

'I will,' I said. 'A drop of milk if you have it.'

From where we sat I could see through an open hatch into the public bar. While John Joe reminisced I stared at a startling face beyond.

The man in the bar had his elbows propped on the counter. A glass of Guinness stood in front of him. His chin was cupped in his two hands. The shoulders of his donkey-jacket were still soaked. I had seen him an hour ago standing to attention in the rain.

At first he seemed in a trance, lids hooded over wide-set eyes. Heavy strands of straw-coloured hair hung down both sides of a broad forehead and high cheekbones. His skin was dark, the colour of freckles all run together into a single brown.

With a shock I realised his eyes were not closed at all. He was looking back at me from under the lowered lids. It was the stare of a horse-dealer into a tourist's lens. I felt my face flush from the neck upwards. I knew I would have to wrench my eyes away in defeat. Then, as if a statue moved, he dropped his hands and his dark face dissolved in a confusing grin. He moved abruptly away, long hair swinging just above his shoulders. I heard a sing-song voice address the barman.

John Joe leaned across and followed my eyes.

'Tinker Ned!' he grunted. His face screwed up in contempt. 'You never met that fellow, did you? He'd be after your time . . .'

He called the barman back. 'What did you let him in for?' He indicated with his head, 'I thought I . . .'

The barman protested mildly, 'Ned is it? Sure I can't bar him for nothing. He's no bother.'

There was a growing suspicion in my mind about John Joe, but I was too absorbed to pursue it now.

Of course I knew Ned!

He was only a boy of twelve when I was fifteen, but he was very much of my time in Kilnamon. I couldn't believe John Joe had forgotten. He was leaving for another appointment.

'Ring this number tonight when you know your mind better. Don't leave it any later, Pat. Strike while the iron is hot.' Would he never go? He was whispering close to my ear. I felt the hot brandy-breath on my skin. The huge hand was drawing a chequebook from an inside-pocket.

'If you need an advance now for anything Pat . . .'

I brushed him away with barely concealed disgust. I could still hear Ned's voice in the public bar.

I delved for his surname without success. Had he been refused one?

He lived with his mother in a council cottage outside the town when I was there. Tom had stories of the travelling man she married. He didn't stay around long enough to see his son. On another occasion he told me Ned's father was a black-haired local who got suspicious of his son's colouring and took off for London in protest. I didn't understand the implications, but I'm sure I sniggered anyway. A lot of people took the calamity of his origins out on Ned himself. Those who didn't blame him kept their sympathy very quiet. He was a handy scapegoat for every tool or farmyard fowl that disappeared. I took his guilt for granted because he was so untamed, forever blazing in the fields and streets with crazy energy.

He understood his heritage and flaunted it. His yellow hair grew long and the cheekbones and flattened nose were fiercely tribal.

He refused the drab accent of the Midlands and adopted the tone of the Connaught tinkers who passed our way with covered wagons and hooped tents. But Ned was a lot more colourful than these originals.

Tom had a strange bond of hunter and victim with him. They played out rituals of cruelty and pain from time to time, determined perhaps by the moon or the river floods. I was miserably grateful when these distractions took the pressure off me. But nothing could break Ned's resilience. His scrawny body bristled with belligerence after every beating. He was the kind of mongrel pup that takes on a pack of terriers because it knows nothing but resistance.

Ned and his mother lived off the back and front gardens of the cottage. They hardly ever bought food. That was akin to an admission of crime in Kilnamon. There were stories of stolen food hidden in the house, huge heaps of bones ground into powder to fertilise the garden. And it was true that strange vegetables grew everywhere. Even in winter there was growth. People said there were herbs for poisoning dogs when Ned went stealing chickens at night.

During the dull summer days Ned reminded me of a character in a film I saw; a young Apache kicking around a white settlement without a tribe of his own to go to. He was an outsider. The only one besides myself. But I knew how to keep my Dublin mouth shut while Ned was always in danger of being lynched for open subversion.

He resisted all the rituals that bound the people together in blunt solidarity, the Church, the GAA, the FCA.

In the middle of a football match when Kilnamon Juniors were trouncing the opposition for once, Ned raced across the pitch and stole the ball under the eyes of the population. It was his answer to the constant accusations of theft. The ball came back later in a shower of glass through the window of the pub where the team was drinking.

Ned went on the run for a week after that. He only returned when word went out that his mother would be taken into care in the County Home. A truce was declared to stop her becoming a burden on the ratepayers. That was the reason too why Ned was never committed to Letterfrack or Daingean — even after he joined a Corpus Christi procession with a pair of knickers on his head and an expression of such childlike piety on his face that no one could possibly stomach the insult. Grown men thrashed him out of the parade with sticks torn from the ditch, and his yells of defiance drowned out the hymn-singing children.

I asked Tom once if Tinker Ned was 'mental.' He considered the question seriously. Madness in its various forms was his favourite subject. He admitted that Ned was as smart as anyone else in the school. He could read, write, and do sums. He even liked Irish. But this intelligence was taken as definitive proof of Ned's cunning insanity. I was curious about his knowledge but I could hardly understand a word he said to me. His voice went up and down in wild bursts of fluency, like birdsong or a foreign language.

VI

Ned, too, was obsessed with the cinema. He got in in exchange for cleaning out the hall afterwards. The boys competed with each other in leaving disgusting surprises under the chairs. He carried subversion into the dark hall. Ned cheered whenever a cavalry-officer got an arrow in his throat, or the great white hope was beaten to a pulp in the ring. He was fiercely dedicated to the wrong side, up for every renegade and snake-eyed redskin.

There was a cult of John Wayne in Kilnamon during my second-to-last summer. His films were coming through in batches. The local accent was ideal for adopting his coarse drawl. Tom, John Joe, and all the boys swaggered loosely from the hips as if they had artificial legs. Ned filtered through the shadows like an Apache scout.

He was twelve the year of John Wayne. Tom and John Joe were fourteen. And I was a craven fifteen.

The poster for *Pony Soldiers* went up midweek. Showing Friday and Saturday. Wayne wore US cavalry uniform in the poster. He rode a white horse and brandished a sabre. In case anyone thought he had gone soft there was a Winchester Carbine stuffed down beside the saddle and a six-shooter in a holster on his hip. He was all things to all men.

Tom and John Joe were broke on Friday night. They were in trouble over some vicious misdemeanour and couldn't raise a penny anywhere. I had the price of a single seat but for once I couldn't be bullied into giving it away. Yet with the loyalty of the victim I waited till they could go with me the second night.

The reports of the film were spectacular. The entire Friday audience was sworn to go again. Tom and John Joe got the cash together on Saturday. They had ten Woodbines as well, and made up in thick smoke and loud farts for the humiliation of the night before.

I remember nothing of *Pony Soldiers* until the moment John Wayne stood in his stirrups to lead the assault on the Indians. The sword flashed high above his bare head. His voice spat gravel as he ordered the attack. The camera stayed low and held him centre-screen, his arm raised in a salute to action, body outlined against the sun, the whole world shuddering with the thunder of a white crusade.

In the breathless silence an object whizzed over the audience and shattered against the screen. A violent stain exploded across John Wayne's chest, red blood drenching the Arizona sky.

John Wayne went galloping, galloping into attack, his great heart bursting across the screen. The wild laugh of the assassin rang out at the back of the cinema. The projectionist in his fright grabbed the film and ripped it out of its reel We watched John Wayne and his white horse jerk backwards into oblivion, as if Tinker Ned's shot had blasted them off the screen.

The lights came on for interrogation. The screen was savagely bright and bare, red ink dribbling down the centre. Blood on a blank wall. Evidence of execution.

Tom and John Joe were the first away. Chairs went over backwards as they led the chase. Violence was about to build upon sacrilege, and I followed. The street was quivering with cold light. We caught Ned so easily he must have waited for us. At the end of a closed alley he stood crying in the shadows.

Tom, John Joe, and I closed in silently.

He was dragged to the garage where John Joe worked. The crime called for a secret court and a dark punishment. We knew Ned's act was an attack on everything we believed in.

There were a dozen boys crowded in the store-room, seated on tyres, a row of grim faces under a naked bulb. The windows were covered with flattened sheets of tin. The store was full of cold steel and dirty rubber, the tool-room of an ugly dream. I sweated and shivered. Ned, pinioned in Tom's grip, gaped like a wild bird, a goldfinch or a yellowhammer.

John Joe uncoiled the air-hose from a hook inside the door. He kicked a switch and a shuddering hum filled the room. When he squeezed the trigger a jet of air hissed from the nozzle. A black needle shivered in judgement on a cracked dial. The glass was a star of pain.

'It's the treatment, Ned,' John Joe promised quietly. 'You know the treatment don't you, Ned.'

The boys leaned forward in their seats. My legs trembled beyond control. I was going to be sick.

John Joe smeared the silver nozzle with axle-grease. He squeezed out another jet of air.

I did not understand. The atmosphere was sacramental.

Tom had one arm clamped around the victim's chest. The

other hand was fumbling with Ned's belt. Ned began to laugh. Hopeless and high-pitched it had nothing to do with humour or defiance. The walls were throbbing with the rhythm of the compressor. I heaved myself towards the door. No one looked around. John Joe was closing in with the hose.

When the heavy shutter swung behind me I stumbled forward into the cool night. The sound of Ned's hysteria receded into another world, faraway and skin-deep.

I didn't see him again that summer. The holidays were over. During the winter he had an accident with a tractor. His leg was badly broken and it mended crookedly. The next time I met him he had a severe limp. He was slow and shy, easier to talk to.

Obstinately, despite the facts, I blamed the twisted leg on the punishment.

VII

The barman was clearing his throat to catch my attention. He jerked his head expressionlessly at the hatch.

'He wants to buy you a drink.'

I hesitated, then slid off my stool and went through to the dingy bar.

'No use paying lounge-prices for it, Ned. How are you?' His handshake was hard and dry. Under the abundant hair his creased forehead and old eyes made a disturbing contradiction. My eyes dropped to his awkward leg. It occurred to me suddenly Ned might be thinking of my twisted vocation in the same way.

There was a silence. We needed some foundation in the past, something free of pain.

'I never thought you'd stick this place, Ned!'

'Ah, it's not too bad. Where else would I go?'

Are you still out beyond . . . ?' I tipped my head vaguely. 'Still there, Pat. I'm on me own now this last few year.' I nodded, 'That's hard luck . . .' So hers was the well-kept plot in the corner by the wall.

'Sorry about your uncle, Pat.' It sounded awkward as if he wasn't sure it was the right thing to say. I raised my eyebrows sceptically. Ned grinned. 'Ah, Joe wasn't a bad oul' skin. He kept me goin' the last few year anyway. When work was hard to get.'

'You worked for Uncle Joe?' I said incredulously. 'Well, nothin' much like. We only kept the place tickin' over. He was always fair with the few bob though. I'll give him that.'

I was staggered by this revelation of a secret side to Kilnamon. I would have expected Joe to class Ned as thieving scum.

The ploughed field flashed through my mind. Last year, by the river! I thumped the counter in recognition:

'That was you! On the tractor! Right?' Ned grinned selfconsciously and changed the subject.

'I saw you inside with J.J. Will you take a drink Pat?'

I looked at his own glass. 'I'll have a bottle of stout, so. Thanks Ned.'

Then I said slowly, as it dawned on me that he wouldn't have been gardening in the rain, 'You were there today too, weren't you Ned? At Joe's funeral, I mean. . . .'

Ned shifted on his stool and looked away. He wouldn't be drawn on his allegiances.

I persisted, on a new tack. I needed knowledge badly.

'What do you think of J.J. now?' I asked cautiously. I had to know if my version of the past was real. Ned rolled up admiring eyes. Under the yellow hair the flesh of his face was flat and hard.

'Oh J.J. is top dog now Pat, fair play to him. There's no holdin' him. He has it all stitched up.' He recited this proudly, as if we were all riding the wave of J.J.'s success. Then he winked, and muttered from the corner of his mouth, 'I only come in here to annoy him.'

I was lost again. 'How d'you mean?' He gave a start of comic surprise. The way he used to look years ago when I was ignorant of something he thought was common knowledge.

'Sure, Johnny owns this place!' he said wonderingly. 'Did you not know that?'

The nods and hints. Hushed respect. I knew it alright. I just hadn't realised I knew it.

I took a long pull on the bitter stout, swallowing my innocence.

'He's looking after the . . . the arrangements for me.' Ned was non-committal, pouring his bottle. I knew he was taking it in. My tongue was loosening.

'I believe Tim Brophy wants to enlarge his own farm.' I began. Ned choked over the rim of his glass and began to wheeze with mirth.

'What's the matter?' I demanded angrily. I was feeling foolish again.

'Brophy hasn't an inch of land to his name. He leases them few acres along the river.'

'Who owns it then?' I asked hotly, although I knew the answer now.

Ned looked at me again in wonder and pity.

'Who do you think?'

We moved to another pub where we could talk, and Ned told me of the factories promised to Kilnamon. Development was on the way. John Joe was buying up land to build houses in the expected boom. He reckoned he'd be building suburbs along the river in five years time. He'd be into national politics by then too. Uncle Joe wouldn't sell him an inch although John Joe bought all round him.

'I suppose you'll sell, Pat?' Ned asked gloomily. 'Why wouldn't you. There's nothin' doin' around here.'

I knew then I was going to dig my heels in. Obstruction was the best weapon against power. Perhaps it was the alcohol but I felt a sweet lump of obstinacy where my soul should have been.

I wanted to see my farm again. I stood in a new relation to it now; there was freedom as well as fear. I couldn't stay in the old borstal of a house though. I hadn't the nerve for that yet. But I could take a room here in town and go out tomorrow early. . . .

The thought of booking a room in a hotel, just like that, suffused me with the real, intoxicating taste of possession.

PURE NATURAL HONEY

He fell off her old bike near Legale. No damage done, it was at a standstill anyway. A lady's model — a rusty, black, high-Nelly without gears. Mike was trying to cycle it up the ferociously steep road above the Guinness Estate.

Síle stood leaning on slightly more modern handlebars and watched him with delight. She mopped perspiration and drowning midges from her face, shook back a sunlit mass of curly, brown hair. She looked like an ad for simple, healthy living. Mike was much too vivid to be quite wholesome as he wrestled with the hill, so black-haired, blue-eyed, young and alive that there had to be badness in him somewhere.

His old Volvo had taken these Wicklow hills without strain the day he picked her up hitching to Dublin a month ago. He wore a neat, grey business-suit then, white shirt and tie and serious leather shoes. At first glance he so resembled a solicitor that Síle felt like a throwback to the hippies. There were sinister objects — vague plastic torsos — on the back seat. He produced a smile so unexpectedly bright that she tingled with shock. The farmers and businessmen who gave lifts to Síle — she was tall, tangle-headed with clear skin, full lips and a striking wide-eyed face — were always predictable in their manner. Never objectionable, just shades of ordinary. But this one radiated a magnetic sense of energy and humour, barely suppressed — a lively actor playing an accountant.

Síle had her stylised country clothes on against the weather as she hitched; black broad-brimmed hat, brown handknit scarf, tweed waistcoat, lumberjack shirt, jeans and boots, and a good deal of her own handmade jewellery too. She knew she'd overdone it a bit but she felt pleasantly exotic in an old-fashioned way as his neatly cuffed wrist with a severely digital watch changed gears beside her knee.

He looked fit and slim to her appraising eye, no rugby or gaelic brawn; if he played football he'd score quick, clean soccer-goals. For the first time in months Sile was sharply aware of her own singleness. She searched for space to stretch long legs. He glanced in approval, 'Pull back the seat.' She saw plenty of strong, white teeth, an intelligent mouth — and he hadn't dived across her to find her seat-belt.

'Scenery or speed?' The car hesitated slightly at the junction before choosing the mountain-road to Dublin.

'Do you live around here?' He began to be predictable, 'You don't sound local.'

'Quite close . . .' Careful, against her instinct, not to give too much information. 'You don't sound local either.'

'Just moved down! I love it even though it's a long drive to Dublin, but I don't go every day . . .'

'Neither do I — I work at home mostly. . . .'

'Me too! I've a terrific house. I'm modernising it . . .' Their eager information overlapped, broke off in laughter.

'What do you do? No let me guess. You're . . .' he studied her quizzically and the car wandered, '. . . you're a potter!' He slapped the steering-wheel straight and laughed, not at all unkindly, amused, as if he knew her well already. 'Or a poet! You could easily be a poet, all that hair — and dressed for the imagination, as well as the road.'

'If that's how it works, you must be a computer-programmer,' she put him briskly in his place. 'No, I'm not a poet — though I wouldn't mind. I'm not a weaver either, by the way. It's my turn to guess. You're some kind of engineer . . . or is it pharmaceuticals?'

'Pretty good, you must be a gypsy! I design special projects for the countryside,' he ad-libbed gleefully. 'Jails, abattoirs, schools, morgues . . .'

'Oh God, I'll walk, so —' The car breasted the ugly treeline and she stared entranced as the mountains flooded the morning with banked-up waves of colour. 'This is why I live in Wicklow. . . .'

'Me too!' he agreed brightly. 'I love all that space. The imagination can breathe . . . And I'm not an engineer. I'm a kind of —' He pretended to wince, ' — Well, a sculptor actually. You'd hate my work though; it's all plastic and steel, and viciously modern.'

He was full of self-mocking relish, 'Anyone who weaves or knits or hurls pots *hates* me!'

'Sculpture? Is that it in the back?'

'God no! Display-models for fashion-shops! That's just business. They're always looking for something different, so I sell them squares and cubes and it seems to suit them. Clothes aren't made for human beings anymore.'

'Neither is your sculpture by the sound of it. I work in fashion-design by the way. For people, not robots. No, don't apologise, I know the sector you mean — though I don't think I'd care to cater for something I didn't approve of!' She looked at him sternly, amazed to be so intimate, and then smiled at the consternation on his face. 'All my work is traditional,' she explained. 'At least, the materials are. Though I try to do something original with them — if I think it's an improvement that is. I'm still a student, so I'm working at various things — fabric, fashion, jewellery — at the moment I'm designing furniture for a diploma-project; I'm bringing the chair designs up to town today, and I'll be finished then, free . . .'

'Furniture?! I'm doing my house and studio. Can I see?' He brought the car to an impulsive halt on the verge and turned towards her.

Funny, she didn't feel a bit nervous in a lonely layby with him, just defensive about her work. 'I told you it's very traditional,' she warned. 'Nothing sophisticated, but they're solid and they work, and anyone could have them in a house beside the TV or the dishwasher. That was my brief, and I believe in it too. Okay?' she challenged.

'Okay,' he agreed absently. 'Let's see. Mm, nice drawing for a start anyway — I could never draw.' He studied her artist's impressions with lively appreciation, and then turned busily to detail.

Síle turned away, suddenly embarrassed that he had her so easily in the palm of his hand. Was he laughing at her? Unsettling too to see her work appraised with such detachment as if it were a business proposition. Until now she had traded among friends and fellow-students. This guy was intriguingly different, but she was annoyed that she had delivered herself to him for judgement. He was definitely younger than her, probably no experience of design at all.

She peered at her drawing again; not much at first to distinguish it from a traditional wooden chair of the more elaborate kind with a round, inlaid seat and a semi-circular back-support projecting forward in two sturdy arm-rests. She'd emphasised all those characteristics, and then altered the proportions for a more — well, rakish appearance. These chairs looked as if they were ready to dance and only waiting to be asked.

The motifs to be carved on the wood were semi-original ideas; they meant to imply motion, a difficult thing with something as stable as a chair. Síle felt confused. He was still studying them, as if memorising the design — or was he composing something plausible to say?

She turned to look up at Tonelagee, the sun now kindling the heather to golden warmth, and she seized on the memory of the heart-shaped lake up there, hidden except to those who made the effort to walk up the mountain.

'Ever been up to Lough Ouler?' He interrupted her solitude.

'Yes, often, I was just thinking of it — Well, do you like the chairs?'

'Definitely! Respectable without being genteel. I hate smugness, don't you? I can imagine elderly aunts being tempted to too much sherry in those. There's a sense of discreet sin about the shape.'

'Is there?' Síle was amused. 'That doesn't sound like me. When I sin I'm not a bit discreet — I get carried away . . .'

She stopped, embarrassed again; she didn't usually get carried away quite so soon. 'Sounds interesting!' he encouraged innocently with wide-open eyes. She noticed again their compulsive colour.

Probably no bluer than ordinary eyes really — it must be the vivid way they caught the mountain-light that brightened them. She found herself laughing with him, as if they knew something between them that no one else knew.

The other thing about his eyes was the way they distracted attention from the rest of his face, as if they were compensating for a plainness which of course he didn't suffer from at all. He was too dangerous to be left driving around picking up romantic young women and setting them down again as if they were shapes in clear plastic for displaying garments. Síle was veering towards indiscretion and steadied herself for whatever he might do next.

What he actually did was fold the drawings carefully, hand them to her, gaze up Tonelagee with narrowed eyes and murmur, 'Terrific site for a hotel up there!' Then he started the car and drove away. She was relieved, not only that he hadn't made a pass at her and put her in the difficult position of refusing the desirable — but also because she'd have been bitterly disappointed by such predictability. Particularly after he'd liked her chairs.

She was used to being pursued, but how to pursue? Did he live on his own, that was crucial.

'Do you live on —' lost her nerve '— on the main road?'

'No, up the back behind Annamoe. I can be on the hills in minutes from my door!'

'Lovely! Do you get out much?'

'Not until the studio is finished. I know the hills pretty well though — I used to belong to a mountaineering club in college.

'Hey! . . .' an idea struck him. 'Maybe we could do some walking together!' He turned towards her, beaming with pleasure, and the car almost left the road. 'Look out!' she cried, and threw her hands up in fright.

He fell off the bike again trying to force it straight uphill. Then
he got smart and began to zig-zag, a wobble at each verge and
a horizontal lurch across the road and back. He might make it
that way, but it would take at least a week. A sheep popped its
head over the wall agog with critical alarm. He wobbled the
wrong way in response and plunged back towards her.

'Let's leave the bikes here at Pier Gates,' Síle pleaded, 'you'll
never get to the Sally Gap. We can walk down by the lakes here
and up Knocknacloghoge instead — save Lough Ouler for
another day.'

'Okay, you'd need the muscles of a postman to pedal this.'

'It belonged to a District Nurse,' Síle scoffed. 'She used to
overtake motor-cars! You haven't got the legs for it.'

He stretched long, fine limbs for her inspection, 'Are they
up to walking do you think?'

Plunging downhill at the half-walk, half-trot the slope
requires he caught her swinging hand and closed his own
around it.

'In case I get lost,' he confided.

'Get lost!' she parodied, but she held on tight and gazed
with absurd contentment at the quiet lake below, a fringe of
forest along the near shore, then a sandy beach and the big
house behind it guarded by steep slopes, a boulder-field along
the far side, and above it a huge, hanging mass of rock. Out of all
that tranquil enclosure the lake drained south along a green
valley-floor between tawny slopes of heather and fern. A
second lake, Lough Dan, was partly visible a mile away
surrounded by low hills that rolled lazily away on every side
without any of the crowding steepness of a mountain-range.

'Isn't it beautiful?' she sighed, feeling sentimental and apt.
'It's got everything — trees, water, rock, heather, sand . . .'

'Midges,' he slapped busily at himself. Síle was above minor
irritations, only something volcanic or nuclear would disturb
her now. She pointed across the valley with her free hand. A
small area of hillside lay softly lined with ridges and furrows,
blurred by heather, almost re-absorbed into the earth.

'Lazy-beds, the remains of old potato-drills. Look at the colour and texture! If you could knit it or weave it just as it is!' she teased longingly. 'Plastic will never mean anything rich like that.'

'Of course it will, when we've lived in a plastic world long enough — then it'll be quite normal . . .

'Look,' he continued briskly, getting it straight, 'you see things in a different way to me, Síle —' And for a terrible moment she thought he meant something more important than the view, '—I mean, we both love the oaks and all that, and we hate the creepy dullness of the conifers, but in a way I walk to get *above* the — claustrophobia of the earth and the bog. Sorry if it sounds pretentious, it's not meant to. I don't look at my feet. Sometimes the ground hems me in with its gravity, it's full of memories and promises of — of decay . . .'

She was staring with profound anxiety and interest, and he laughed nervously at himself. 'Don't get me wrong! I agree the mountains are lovely, that's why I'm out — well, part of the reason —.' He grinned and blushed but didn't stop. 'You like the density and the texture of the mountains Síle, you'd like to wrap them around you like tweed or a plaid rug, but when I look at the hills I like to see space, not substance. I don't think it's the way most people look. To me the landscape sort of gets in its own way sometimes. You know those photographs with huge hunks of geology and vegetation stuffing the frame? — I find that boring, even if the colours and textures are . . . interesting. D'you think I'm a philistine . . .?'

He watched her worriedly and at the vigorous shaking of her head he plunged on: 'What I like is lots of shifting sky shaped by the profile of the landscape. Wicklow is very friendly that way; it's so rounded and open it lets the sky through in great curves and arcs. A tent of light. And I love the way the lakes reflect it, and make a full circle —'

He seized another strand, '—I'm the same with houses and buildings, I sort of look past them and in between. There's plenty of people concerned with the density of things. I think it's really important to appreciate the spaces — the way light is allowed to make its own designs . . . It doesn't happen at all in Dublin because it's flat and sort of *tight*; if I had to live in a city I'd definitely go for New York . . .'

'I see . . .' Síle broke the flow. 'Town-planning as sculpture —'

'Well, that *is* what I try to do in my work. I know you haven't seen it yet, but that's *it*! It's always groups of objects arranged so that I can emphasise the spaces between them. The trouble is, it results in draining the objects of any meaning in themselves, otherwise they'd take over; you know, as if letters and numbers were just the limits to the space between the ink and meant nothing more than that. See what I mean? —' and he bounded in front of her waving his arms vigorously, '— think of a number, take your own age, twenty-three; I bet you've never examined the shape of that space between the two figures before! Or your name; you make extraordinary patterns between the letters every time you write it. Why shouldn't that be important? I'm trying to liberate that space.'

Síle's hand had cooled by now, and her heart was steady with caution. Was he garrulous — or actually inspired in some hectic way? It was very important that he should not be a sham! She still hadn't seen any of his real work. His house was empty while he rebuilt the big attic as a working space. She was impressed by the enthusiasm of the project, but she needed hard evidence as to what he was. She needed to see his work.

'Maybe you can see my problem now, with the sculpture I mean? People say it's all very well, but they want to buy Objects — they don't want to spend money on Space which they feel they own already! Now if I could make objects that were both valid in themselves And definitions of space I'd be on a winner. . . .'

'Make a chair!'

'A chair? A Chair! Why a *chair*?'

'It'll give you discipline in structure.' Síle was very firm.

'Good furniture is unobtrusive — it's sort of invisible in a way, and yet it defines a room. You can concentrate all you want on the spaces and shapes within a chair — but if it doesn't work as a seat than it's worse than useless. Burn it! There's nothing worse than a chair that doesn't work . . . except maybe a jug that dribbles. Oh, and that's another idea; I don't want to set you up as a craft-centre, but you could design all sorts of pots and jugs that make fantastic statements with the space between them — everybody knows the urn/faces trick — but if they don't pour properly, I'll take a hammer to them . . .'

'A chair!' He sneezed it quietly again, 'Could I make yours, Sile?'

'Mine? Of course! I'd love to see it made. Can you do all that stuff, wood-turning, carpentry . . .? That's real craftsmanship. Much harder than sculpture.' She grinned.

'Just leave it to me!' He grabbed her hand again, his bright face full of restored confidence.

Mike threw the door open and she walked into his studio screwing up her eyes. She was ambushed again by the vigorous light inside the attic. There was no sign of rafters, roofing-felt, or the underside of slate. The white room was full of long windows angled across the hilltops at the sky. Bright surfaces and mirrors intensified the daylight; like passing through a door into foreign weather.

The room was empty still, he'd been working on her chairs. She looked around for the dark, rich wood. Mike was silent for once, and then she realised — they were there . . . She was looking right through them.

A gasp of disbelief and she turned a withering glare on him. He quailed but managed a weak grin. She strode across the room, heels hammering the bare floor. Her chairs alright — but pale, transparent ghosts of her intention, not timber at all, but a thick see-through substance moulded smoothly onto a thin steel frame; a parody of texture — what had he done there? For she saw that the chairs were indeed the colour of some strange kind of wood; a subtle stain had been added to the plastic, and there were traces of texture too, at random; one seat had the undeniably natural grain of wood — though when she felt the surface there was nothing there. Then she saw the mandala from a child's marble embedded within the ghost of a knothole, and she understood the trick — the textures and the marble were all inside, pressed onto internal layers. . . .

The seat of the second chair had hints of fine, old lace in it, and a blurred corduroy imprint too as if someone had thought of sitting in it while it was still soft. She ran a fingernail across the furrows and ridges — 'Lazy-beds,' he reminded nervously — but there was nothing there on the surface except that infuriatingly funny blandness. And there was a sense of — well, of Exposure about the glassy chair. She had a disconcerting flash of someone — herself? — sitting naked except for a see-through plastic mac, seen from behind drinking gin?

Mike was still grinning at her — his eyes held the only deep colour in the room — his expression a blend of enquiry, apology, affection and sheer cheek. She knew she was being - not ridiculed or parodied, but . . . laughed at? No, it wasn't that either, and whatever it was she was beginning to mind less as he smiled at her. He simply couldn't resist statement — like the day at Luggala. There it was, embedded in the thick arm-rests of the chairs, that day again — strands of moss, heather, blades of grass, leaf-imprints, and somehow as well a stitch-motif from the Aran jumpers he detested . . .

. . . But the joke was on him — for the whole thing was beginning to work, in detail if not quite in total. It gave character to the vacant plastic. She followed the exquisite footprints of a bird small as a wren around the rim of a seat until it took flight. It was so meticulously done that it revealed his respect for the materials he satirised as clearly as if she had found a scrapbook of pressed flowers under his bed.

And the colour too, a kind of tawny, golden transparance owed more than a nod of submission to wood. She returned again to a tiny tuft of moss, a few blades of grass, a quartz pebble and a twig or two, arranged so that between them they conjured up a whole landscape; and something warm and permanent — the rhapsody of the scene — settled into her heart.

Mike nudged her attention impatiently downwards. He tilted the chair to show how the legs had been moulded to her design — but as she bent closer she saw that he had infiltrated a joke in the form of tiny labels into the mixture, so that the carved sections of the legs now resembled slender bottles and jars stacked on top of each other. The labels were transparent of course — strings of oldfashioned print just beneath the surface.

A plumply tubular section near the seat read Pure Natural Honey, and she giggled helplessly because the smooth plastic with its delicate, mellow stain did indeed look fit to spread on bread — homemade brown of course. There was even an uncanny trace of something like honey-comb stirred in. Just below it, the next section was labelled Vintage Cider Vinegar, the same colour was equally apt and the taste of honey turned apple-sharp and sour in her mouth. He'd caught her lifestyle exactly, for another label announced Twelve Year Old Whiskey and without effort the rich substance glowed amber.

There was Lemon Tea as well, complete with rind, and a plain section of leg at the floor that contained either wine or urine — but the two words, and samples, were so remarkably similar that she didn't dwell on that, in case he was taking the p . . .

'Okay,' she surrendered, stifling laughter. 'Okay, you win; though I wouldn't sit in one! I don't see why you changed the shape —' She pointed at the D-shaped seat and a missing arm, '— was the symmetry too much for you?'

He danced in front of her, beaming with relief and pride, grabbed a chair and swung it between them. He sat down solidly, braced his left arm on the single arm-rest, grabbed a sketch-pad to his knee, and with elaborate motions showed how he could sketch freely without any obstruction to his right elbow. It made devastating sense.

'That's all very well for you!' Síle fought to the end, 'but it's selective design. One-offmanship! What about me — I'm left-handed?'

'I know! And this is the Ciotog-model; this is *your* chair!' He pressed her into the other one, taking a delicate liberty while he did so, and she found her left arm unrestricted while her right was supported. The opposite to his.

He thrust the sketch-pad at her, drew his chair across and placed it down beside her. The cutaway sides of the seats butted perfectly together, while the two interrupted back-rests now made a continuous arc. It was an intimate double-seat. Síle slapped her forehead; she had just spotted the purpose and the punch-line. As they sat pressed warmly together, he slid his arm along the joint backrest and tightened it round her shoulders, 'We're arm-chair mountaineers!'

'Wait a second, hold on —' she was still a designer, 'what about a normal couple, right-handers, how will they get on . . .?'

'Who cares?' He shrugged her firmly against him. 'Let them make their own chairs.'

CLIMBER AND WALKER

Always a revelation, every season, that first view of the Alps, impossibly elegant, the evening spires gilded with alpenglow; or black, triangular teeth in the morning slicing a high, icy dawn. Once she saw them in moonlight, the moon itself a galleon of light sunk behind the reef of the Aiguilles, so that an inverted, misty shadow, notched and crested, haunted the night-sky above Chamonix.

And though she had climbed the cleanly equilateral face of the Blaitière and found it wanting in quality, the mountain still projected an image of tapered perfection. And the blank, comb-crested facets of the Peigne, just to the right, looked as solid and pure as if the scree-chutes of the hidden descent were a spillage from some limestone memory.

She looked up with perplexity at the Frendo Spur, an easy climb, but a great one, her first in the Aiguilles, its ethereal snow-ridge supported on a springing pillar of rock and soaring above into a high horizon of light. She remembered tottering there once, below the final rocks, hammering her trembling legs down into the deep post-holes kicked in the snow by a hundred other feet, feeling the rush of falling space sucking her down, so that she leaned forward in the footsteps and thought she saw her own wild-eyed face reflected in the blind mirror of the snow. The first cable-car to the summit swung through the air a few hundred yards away, and she wept for the barred security of that cage.

Now she could approach that single memory from many points of view: perched on the exalted rib of ice, an escaped cage-bird terrified by freedom; looking back from the swinging box of the cable-car at a minute crumb of life on the knife-edge of eternity; and standing here on the edge of town, transported through five years and five thousand feet of space by the dizzy flight of the first escape.

Climbing had not become any easier after that, but she got used to the pain. It was a matter of perspective, realising that even the harshest moment would have an aftermath of relief.

Cathy was tall and lightly built, with a sense of concentrated strength about the shoulders, a kind of muscular grace. Unruly black hair was drawn back with severe practicality in a Doris Lessing bun, but now stray wisps and curls framed an expression that was radiant with arrival. She heaved her rucksack off the pavement and trudged on, after her companion, towards the familiar campsite.

Her elation was rebuffed by Peter's silence and a profile that seemed more than usually tightened by lines of age and fatigue. He had said very little while contemplating the Aiguilles. It was his first time back since a serious accident put him out of alpinism for four years. His partner died in a fall on the Eckpfeiler, and Peter was slow to recover from his own injuries. But he had been climbing steadily at a good standard for more than a year now, and his ambition — with a chill undertone of vindication — was to return to the Alps and make up for lost time.

'Weather must be good; there's not much snow about,' he remarked flatly. His voice carried none of the enthusiasm good conditions should induce. It might be simply travel-weariness, but to Cathy's disappointment it sounded more like depression. On the occasions when they climbed together she recognised that Peter's attitudes to mountains and to climbing were completely different from her own. She was a romantic, and felt as if all the imagination and fantasy of the long, wet winter was about to be realised now among the mountains that crowned the whole horizon, while Peter glumly tried to see them as three-dimensional topos to be climbed via cracks, corners and slabs with clearcut techniques and grades. But there was a dark side to his vision, which, if it predated the accident might even have caused it: sometimes mountains terrified him though he would not define the fear. Cathy visualised it as something like the brooding menace in Victorian mountain pictures.

'Remember that day on the Midi-Plan? I think it was the best day I've ever had here,' she said cheerfully, trying to revive an occasion that scintillated with laughter and light, a rebel crystal in the past. It was the last day of her first season and they raced along the snow-ridge that divides the human habitat of Chamonix, its forested slopes, alpine meadows, and granite walls from the great, glacial smother of the Vallée Blanche. A single day that might be the only reason she was here with Peter again.

'Will I ever forget?' he said ruefully. 'I thought the Envers glacier was going to avalanche any minute and sweep us down to Montenvers like surfers. All that fresh snow. The Grandes Jorasses was wiped out.'

He lapsed into a contemplative silence and she caught a chill reflection of what that polished day had meant to him: the Walker Spur on the Grandes Jorasses, buttressing a remote corner of the sky, clad in the white rags of its own bad weather, — *that* was where Peter wanted to be, straddling that vast rock-rib, the greatest climb in the world. Not plodding along a snow-saunter with a novice.

She was barely aware of its existence then, and the pleasure of a perfect day had remained intact until she looked inwards now and discovered with a shock of recognition the same Walker Spur standing out in sharp relief against the background of her own ambition. She tasted briefly the sour flavour of Peter's point of view, and felt diminished as the Midi-Plan, Frendo, the Dru, the Gervasutti Pillar, Route Major, shrank in status from unique experiences to mere reconnaissance trips for one great climb. The Walker Spur was the secret they were both harbouring silently — he like a grievance or a wound, and Cathy like a hidden talent.

They trudged out along the forest-road towards the squalor of Snell's Field, heavy boots dragging through the gravel, slouching under the weight of rope-hooded sacks, and buffeted by the constant blast of passing cars. Under the grime and sweat Cathy's face flickered with suppressed excitement.

'Fancy a crack at the Walker?' she remarked breathlessly to the downcast profile.

The expression cleared slowly, a cloud drifting aside to let sunlight filter in.

'Well ... there's not much snow about,' he responded, nodding thoughtfully.

Two days later they were on the North face of the Dru. It was early August, the weather had been stable for several weeks and conditions were good — very little ice in the cracks and the snow-ledges clear. Peter went into overdrive, the confidence of a man who had forgotten how brutal a mountain can be. He wanted to travel light, hammer the route in one day. Cathy refused. She was not a fast climber, she argued, honourably disdaining to imply that he would hardly be a speed-merchant himself after four years' absence. And anyway, it was no harm to get used to carrying a bit of weight.

So they bivouacked on big ledges a few hundred feet above the start. Climbing solidly from dawn the following day they struggled out onto the Quartz Ledges below the summit well after dark. They were both exhausted, but Peter had suffered a psychological deflation as well. They swapped the lead after every pitch, except once low down, when Cathy opted out of a foul, wet chimney with a twenty-foot icicle jammed in the back of it. She acknowledged immediately that blunt male arrogance was the most effective weapon to force that kind of problem, and was rewarded for her good sense by the next pitch, an exposed ramp and a fine, steep crack. Having climbed with a wide variety of partners over the years — including continentals — Cathy had no neuroses about ethics. She clipped gratefully into pegs whenever they presented themselves, and climbed free when that seemed logical. Peter was impressed by her steadiness, and embarrassed by his own lack of it. He was way out of touch with alpinism. Her experience was particularly obvious in route-finding; she seemed to know instinctively where to go, while he felt totally lost in a vertical wilderness of ribbed and seamed rock. The route was twice as long as he expected, and a good deal harder.

On the summit bivouac he devoured the extra food Cathy had insisted on carrying, and that irony was not lost on him either. She was wrapped in the light sleeping-bag she always brought, while he tried to hide his shivers in an anorak and overtrousers.

Seeing him stare silently into the darkness in the direction of the Brenva face of Mont Blanc and the Eckpfeiler buttress where the accident had stamped its epitaph on his past, Cathy realised they didn't know each other at all. Hers was a silent alpine career; she certainly didn't publicise it herself, and not being attached to any particular scene or climbing group, no-one else knew the full scope of her achievements. She climbed mostly with men to whom she was introduced casually; occasionally they didn't even speak a common language. People who did hear of her ascents usually assumed she was a second anyway, not a leader in her own right.

Cathy enjoyed climbing with Peter at home because it was unusual to find a man who didn't want to use her for some purpose or other. Some were looking for romance or sex with their climbing, many wanted a perpetual second, some felt their own climbing contrasted impressively with a woman's. Peter seemed to want someone who didn't talk a lot, and was free, like himself, midweek. They both worked weekends and this kept them at a distance from the normal climbing scene which conducted its initiations, graduations, assassinations, and post mortems on Saturdays and Sundays.

She couldn't resist a curious question. 'What's it like to be back, Peter?'

'Not great' he admitted honestly, after a long silence. 'Not worth freezing for anyway.'

'Still,' he shivered and pulled himself together, 'we have to pretend, haven't we? I mean you have to admit the futility of it all, it's obvious — and still believe in the value of it at the same

time. It's a kind of juggling, keeping two contradictions in the
air at the same time. I feel if I told the truth about mountains I'd
never bother to climb another one, but then the illusion of value
is worth believing in for the sheer beauty of the defiance. It's a
myth, but it's a mighty one.'

'Defiance?' She recoiled in bewilderment thinking of the
serene aesthetics of the faces ranged around them in the night.
'I thought the great thing about climbing is that it gets you away
from all that kind of thing.'

A week, two more routes, and two minor storms later, they
tramped up the Leschaux glacier towards the little hut perched
like a tin drum on the moraine. The north face of the Grandes
Jorasses rose above them. More tiny pilgrims picked their way
over the devastation of the glacier converging on the hut. Peter
was fretting over details, the forecast, the amount of snow,
bivouacs, food.

To Cathy it all seemed simply impossible. You couldn't
climb that blank, overpowering pillar that thrust into the sky as
if it was about to blast off into a bigger, purer universe. But she
was going to climb it. She knew. Two days later she intended to
stand, invisible from here, an angel on the head of that four-
thousand foot pin.

Heart and head filled and reeled with awe at her own
power. Peter was trying to forecast the best way up the glacier
to the foot of the route. He fussed.

'There'll be footprints,' Cathy said absently. 'And
headtorches.'

'If we leave the hut at two,' Peter calculated 'we should be on
the route in a couple of hours. Before dawn anyway. And if we
go like hell and we're lucky, we should be on top in a day.'

The hut was full; every new candidate for the Walker was
greeted with a sardonic shrug by those already there. Such
good conditions, and a good forecast, were rare — nobody
would back down, even if their numbers cheapened the

experience. The guardian, a young Frenchwoman, took Cathy aside and advised the Croz Spur instead. There was only one party going for the Croz while eleven parties were bound for the Walker, she said, rolling her eyes and r's dramatically. Cathy discussed it with Peter but he wouldn't hear of it. It was the Walker or nothing.

She felt the same. She gazed sadly up at the unearthly pillar glowing in the evening light and felt she would be just another acrobat in a circus troupe. And still she wanted it. Her instincts had been compromised.

They bivouacked below the hut but Cathy could not sleep. The air grew heavy and turgid, and the golden nails in the night-sky blurred and disappeared. The forecast was wrong. You could never forecast for the Walker; it made its own weather.

At about midnight it began to rain, fat heavy drops that penetrated the sleeping bags like little water-bombs. Draping their raingear over the bags they heard each other cursing and laughing in a kind of idiotic relief as rain soaked the tension into an anti-climax. They slept until dawn, when the sun shot up without the slightest trace of guilt. No one had ventured out of the hut. It was usual to start the climb either before dawn or else in the late afternoon in order to reach a bivouac on the face by nightfall.

As they ate a silent breakfast before descending to the valley a pair emerged hurriedly from the tin shack and headed up the glacier in the direction of the Spur. With surprise and interest Cathy recognised the weather-beaten rucksacks and old-fashioned gear of a central European couple who had sat solidly among the flashy crowd on the terrace the previous evening. Czechs or Yugoslavs, she thought. The square-faced, sensible-looking woman spoke French and German readily to people near her.

Cathy got to her feet and began to pack, her back turned against the valley. A surge of nerves in her stomach constricted her breathing, but her face and voice were relaxed.

'We might as well go up,' she said.

They reached the frozen waves of crevassed ice at the foot of the face in two hours. Briefly the pillar appeared to Cathy like some great war-sculpture, a broad, bronze horse upreared with hooves thundering against the sky. But that was Peter's style of paranoia she realised, and hoped that he could visualise himself as the masked rider standing up victoriously in the stirrups for the duration of the climb. Looked at coolly, she saw that the Walker Spur was like any other big rock-climb, a broken, foreshortened buttress lying back against the sky. Of course she could only see about a third of it, but that was a reassuring illusion in itself, and it certainly looked climbable — a short ice-slope, a rock-step, and a long stretch of easy ground below the first barrier of slabs.

Peter was striding ahead on the glacier, setting a punishing pace, obviously winding himself up to take a run at an obstacle. He was still sweating from his exertions when she caught him up at the foot of the ice.

'We'll have to move fast,' he grated. 'It's dangerous here at this time of day. There might be stonefall.'

'Not half as dangerous as burning ourselves out. Relax, Peter, there's only one party ahead of us.'

He looked at her resentfully, feeling the criticism.

'We'll solo up until we hit something technical,' he ordered, producing his ice-axe. He had opted stubbornly to carry the little Terrordactyl with its outrageously drooped pick, which had been unjustifiably popular during his last season.

Cathy would have preferred to rope up, but she did not want to aggravate the tension, and there was a reassuring chain of steps cut up through the little icefield. Peter moved up without gloves — so that he could use the steps as handholds too. He struck at the ice above his head with the Terrordactyl, and uttered a sharp howl of pain. A little knob of ice had trapped his thumb against the handle, and the force of the impact ripped away the nail at one side. A jagged edge of nail like a broken shell stuck out at the side of the thumb, and little globes of blood dripped and dissolved on the ice, It was the kind of injury to take to a doctor if it happened at home, but here there was nothing to do but swear and continue climbing.

There were flat ledges above the ice, and a rock-bulge with a short jamming-crack running through it. It was grade IV, but as Cathy dropped her sack on the ledge to take out the rope she saw Peter, to her great annoyance, attempt to solo it. She was about to express her exasperation forcefully when he stepped back down cursing his injured hand. He tied onto the rope and clipped into a peg for protection with the expression of a man going to the gallows rather than a mountaineer embarking on the route of a lifetime. She had seen that expression before on the faces of strangers who found themselves committed to something above their ability, but with Peter it was different, he simply didn't believe in what he was doing. He was here out of bravado or defiance, not desire.

Above, there was a long stretch of mixed ground, awkward scrambling on broken rock embedded in ice. They moved together, the rope between them, Peter still leading. Gradually Cathy's awe at the overwhelming situation relaxed into confidence and she began to catch up on Peter, taking in coils of rope as she went. The guttural Europeans were only a short distance ahead. They were climbing in pitches, the man leading and belaying every hundred feet until his partner reached his position, when he surged forward again.

Cathy saw that Peter's headlong momentum derived from his determination to pass the other pair. She wondered what he was going to do for route-finding when he found himself in the lead — he was certainly no Cassin — but she stifled the sour thought.

Soon Peter passed the woman as she stood on a ledge belaying her partner, and a minute later Cathy drew level with her. She was about forty with a cheerful weather-beaten face, wide-set grey eyes, and big, white teeth. She grinned amiably as Cathy saluted her in French. The woman answered in English and chuckled at Cathy's surprise.

'Where are you from?' Cathy called curiously.

'We are Romanian,' came the proud answer. 'You are English, yes? American?'

Cathy cleared her throat. There was something emotionally charged about the encounter, two remote countries meeting in this spectacular place.

'I'm Irish,' she shouted back a little more loudly than was necessary. The other woman beamed a delighted understanding. She pointed at Peter churning ahead.

'He is good, yes?' she asked. 'You will be okay with him, yes?'

Cathy understood. The Romanian woman automatically assumed she was simply a passenger being guided up the mountain by the man in the lead. She felt a great surge of affection for the cheerful woman, below her now. She wanted to shout, 'He's not bad, but I'm a lot better than he is.' Instead she only smiled, said 'Good Luck' with a kind of despairing warmth, and swarmed on after Peter.

They arrived together at the toe of an immense buttress of bulging slabs. The scale was vaster than anything Cathy had faced before. Her courage shrank. The parallel pillar of the Croz Spur rose on the right, another column of the proscenium arch, while the snow-hushed theatre of the Vallée Blanche, waited for the tiny climbers to give the performance of their lives.

Cassin had arrived here in 1938 from Italy, never having seen the area before, and had marched straight up this mighty pillar without a pause.

1938 she thought in an agony of amazement, contemplating the apparently impenetrable barrier above; this was 1983, they had every conceivable climbing tool and technique at their command now, and it still seemed impossible.

Peter was consulting the description nervously. Then he was off again, a rising traverse leftwards, searching for the key to the barrier above. Wait till we get to the real climbing, Cathy thought grimly. She was reasonably content to let Peter dash about now on this easyish terrain if it kept his mind and his nerves occupied.

An uncertain shout ahead — 'I think this is it' — started her moving again along a lip of ice that lay against the rock. Peter was belayed at the foot of a steep groove.

He had spotted a piton higher up.

'I *think* this must be it,' he muttered doubtfully. 'I'll go up and have a look.'

'That's okay, it's my turn,' Cathy said reassuringly.

'Are you sure?' He wore a troubled expression.

'No problem. If it doesn't work out I can always lower off that peg.'

She began stepping delicately up the steep shallow groove, bridging deftly between small holds and tiny ribs. It was a technique she developed to a high degree when she didn't trust the strength in her arms, and learned to let her feet do most of the work.

'Bridget' someone had called her mockingly when she was seen bridging a strenuous layback corner.

Peter scrambled up, wincing silently when his thumb touched the rock. They wandered erratically up ledgy slabs until the walls closed in ominously above them penetrated by the unmistakeable Rebuffat Crack, where the hardest technical moves on the whole climb are located. Cathy took off her rucksack and sat down.

'I brought EB's for this pitch,' she announced happily. Peter looked down at his great clumsy footwear, then up at the delicate, overhanging dièdre with its small, sloping holds. He sat down glumly and prepared to belay her. His blinkered outlook had scorned EB's on an alpine route.

Using the pegs in place it was not particularly difficult to swarm up the first crack, and then came the move of VI, a long step across on friction, off-balance, to a sloping hold. Peter found it desperate to follow. He blamed his thumb and his boots, justifiably enough, Cathy felt, and gave him a tight rope. With a flash of egotism that shook her Cathy wished the Romanian lady could have been on the ledge below.

They traversed on ice for several ropelengths, and then up

another section of broken rock towards the 75m dièdre. Cathy simply strapped her rigid crampons on tightly over her EB's for the ice to save putting on her boots again.

Peter looked on in appal, and when Cathy told him patiently it was a customary practise now for short sections of ice, he took on the righteous expression of one for whom alpinism would never be the same again. When they reached the foot of the great corner Cathy whipped off her crampons and began to lead again. The crisp, golden granite gave beautiful climbing with the boot-heels constantly silhouetted against the chaotic glacier.

There was a moment of uncertainty on every belay as she silently offered Peter the option of leading through. He dragged with him a grizzled air of misery up onto the belays, which mingled with the smell of their sweat to generate a sense of depression, and Cathy couldn't wait to be off again, springing elatedly up the superb rock.

Over and over again the resounding name of the climb rang in her head and once she seized a handhold, a solid flake of golden granite, and tried to shake it like a door-knocker as if she were attempting to stir the whole mountain, whispering fiercely to herself, 'This is the Walker Spur. The Walker Spur.'

She was afraid this might be a sign of delirium but suspected it was really a symptom of enormous happiness. There was the beautiful thrill of arrogance in doing all the hard work too.

At the top of the dièdre Peter decided to lead the slabs and traverse to the short abseil at the foot of the Black Slabs. He was slow but looked happier to be out in front and Cathy was content with the arrangement. The early evening sun was shining obliquely on the tilted towers above. They were looking for a suitable bivouac-ledge. A traverse led abruptly to a notch with a weathered hank of ropes hanging down diagonally towards a blocky pedestal.

With the querulous gaze of a blinkered rock-climber Peter was sizing up a traverse that avoided the well-known abseil.

'That looks okay across there, and it avoids all that messing with the ropes, and climbing back up again. I'll have a go at it.'

Cathy regarded him with surprise and dislike. 'Don't you think if it was a better way it would be in the guidebook,' she said pointedly. 'You're hardly the first to spot it. There must be some problem out there.'

'I'm going to give it a try,' Peter said obstinately. 'Looks okay to me, and it'll be quicker.'

He was obviously salving his ego in some private way, and Cathy belayed herself with extra precaution. Peter edged out onto the slab and it was clear immediately that it was harder than it appeared. He fiddled some protection into a crack standing on his tiptoes on the bald rock, and lurched across onto a sloping hold. He was committed now and could not return. His expression made it clear that he regretted his position, but he would not admit it.

Cathy's impatience gradually froze into anger as he tried ineffectually to step farther out on the slab. She concentrated on the mountains across the glacier, the rock reddening in the setting sun, and picked out the climbs she had done, the East face of the Réquin, Mer de Glace face of the Grépon, the Ryan-Lochmatter on the Plan; she had stitched her way up and down the seams of the Aiguilles without ever visualising the unity the complete ridge possessed. The real route over there, she grasped from this magnificent viewpoint, must be the complete traverse of the Aiguilles.

Her reverie was stamped out by the scrabbling of Peter's feet and a harsh cry as he skidded off the foothold and slid down the slab. The rope came tight around Cathy's waist with a jerk. There was no danger. Cursing hoarsely Peter swung back, she tossed him a loop of rope, and he dragged himself back to the ledge.

'Sorry about that,' he gasped. 'It's a lot harder than it looks.'

Cathy laughed. 'Depends on who's looking,' she told him cheerfully. There was no use getting upset, and suddenly she felt sorry for Peter, out on a limb in his climbing, and out of depth in his feelings.

Above the abseil there was a small shelf carved out of an ice-ledge, large enough to seat two bodies with their feet hanging down in space. Cathy was determined to raise Peter's spirits to the level of the occasion — her own satisfaction depended on it too. She had great difficulty with her toilet arrangements in the confined space, whereas Peter could simply stand casually on the edge of the ledge.

Eventually she forced herself to abandon years of reticence and do something similar while he melted snow for the evening meal.

She remembered the absurd contortions she went through on previous mixed bivouacs, and managed to reduce Peter to a semblance of mirth describing some of the more embarrassing scenes.

Late light accented every needle-point in a sunset world. Two tiny climbers stood up like millimetre marks on a ledge on the Croz Spur; the sharp ridge of the Periades supported a row of barracuda teeth and the spire of the Aiguille du Midi pointed into the sky like an arrow poised for flight.

The second day unreeled a slow spool of tension and pain. Cathy postponed satisfaction, and simply endured. This climb was too big to enjoy. It had to be fought for, and pleasure would come with success.

From midday onwards she was constantly in the lead. The weather held steady, a clear sky and dry rock. She felt her dazed thoughts emerge occasionally as staccato prayers, let the weather hold, let my strength hold out, let us get off today . . ., please let it get easier . . . But it never got easier, and sometimes it felt so hard she thought she must be off-route.

Peter staggered up the relentless rock towards every belay, his face white and strained, teeth gritted, cursing every hard move and shouting for a tight rope. Stripped of superiority, his illusions had caved in. Feeling him drag behind her like a brake, Cathy realised how easy it would be to hate someone. But when she saw the jagged pain of resentment in his eyes she realised with a shock it would be much easier for him to hate her. He was the one who had to swallow the bitterness of failure.

All through the morning and afternoon she hoisted her exhausted body upwards from hold to hold, up thin cracks, wet grooves, exposed ribs, and awkward chimneys, watching the distinctive sprawl of the pillar below her as it tumbled lazily into the blind labyrinth of the glacier, the distances so great that motion was meaningless. One particular pitch she had heard described as an icy overhang, 'Sometimes the hardest pitch on the route'. It loomed askew in her imagination. Over-reacting to the ominous prose of the guidebook she dimissed all the technical problems she encountered as nothing to the doom-invoking overhang she expected above.

Of course that took some of the sting out of the lower difficulties, made the climbing more automatic, and when they finally reached the little overhang she laughed aloud in near-hysterical relief. It was easy in comparison to some of the pitches she had dismissed below. A couple of stretchy aid-moves and she reached over the bulge and thwacked the ice-axe with deep satisfaction into a pocket of frozen snow. She was about to pull up strenuously on the axe-handle when she realised with dizzying elation that this was the last of the major difficulties and felt an irresistible urge to celebrate. She clipped an étrier to the axe-handle and, instead of the muscular lunge demanded by speed, she moved up luxuriously loop by loop enjoying the frivolity of the situation as she stepped regally over the bulge. As soon as she gained a ledge she whooped with uncontrollable delight. Nothing could stop them now.

'What was that in aid of?' Peter growled irritably. His hair was plastered to his forehead with sweat, his eyes were sunken and bloodshot over a grizzle of beard, and he looked like a stranger who had been hooked by the end of her rope as it fished in the depths.

'We're going to make it,' she yelled exuberantly, her voice cracking with strain. 'We'll be up in an hour or two.'

'Not we . . . *you're* going to make it,' he told her miserably. 'I haven't done anything.'

'Don't be ridiculous. You made all the moves too.' But the reassuring words sounded hollow in her own ears. She didn't believe them either. Climbing was about motivation, and if you didn't really want to be there then you didn't have it. But there was a thoughtful look in the stranger's eyes now, and his mouth was firm.

'He's telling himself he's done it,' Cathy told herself with a stab of amazement. On any other climb she would have dismissed the matter, believing a partner's reactions were his own business. But the Walker Spur was different. Maybe her instincts had been compromised, but she would not let this achievement be denied. Peter wouldn't need to tell actual lies to distort the truth in his favour.

'The Walker Spur ... with Cathy,' she imagined him announcing quietly with his customary lack of detail which people took for honourable reticence, and they would all visualise Cathy being piloted up the mountain.

Well, not this time, she thought fiercely, as she began climbing again with renewed vigour. On the next ledge, as she waited for Peter, she began idly framing an article about the climb. And while she was at it she might set the record straight about a few other routes too. Why not begin at the beginning, as you stepped off the train, and caught the various visions of the Aiguilles; gilded with alpenglow in the evenings, raking the frozen sky in the morning, and there was that moonlit night . . .

THE PRIEST'S BREAKFAST

From below I'd seen him seated on top of Slievenadubber, hard and hunched as the statue of Ó Conaire in Galway's Eyre Square.

I ran steadily towards the summit, threading a path between the Holy Wells that name the mountain. Close up he bore no resemblance to that benign old storyteller — he had instead the hawkish look of a hill-farmer.

Had I scattered his ewes? Was it lambing-time? I was hill-running in Connemara, anxious not to antagonise. Gnarled hands clamping the knob of a stick he sat astride a rock surveying time and the earth. Old eyes narrowed to focus on my arrival in running-shoes and shorts. Beneath us the sea, inland the Twelve Bens.

'Día dhuit,' I offered nervously. He answered in the local gaelic, drawling consonants and vowels, jaws slack so the words came from further back. 'Dia's Muire dhuit. So you ran the mountain. You're not the first, a mhac. Slíabh na dTobair, the Hill of the Wells, has been raced before —'

'I suppose so. Hill-running is popular now.'

'Long before your time. Sagart is gréasaí . . .'

'Who won?' Sweat chilling, I was anxious to be off. Sagart is gréasaí had the slow echo of folklore, the priest and the shoemaker . . .

I'd run for hours already, wild rocky ridges close to the coast, not a soul in sight — all day swooping under a dizzy sky while the smooth Atlantic shone and islands drifted on the skyline. Then Slievenadubber had drawn me on to the spiral of its well-marked path. I ran past the village where I'd meant to stop, and began to climb. Only the parish calls it by name — to the rest of the world it's a spur on a Galway ridge. The path zig-zagged the slope and crossed fourteen streams, or one stream fourteen times, the Stations of the Cross. The junctions were dug out and ringed with stones to serve as Holy Wells. Rough crosses stood askew beside them. On one June Sunday every year a procession prays at all the wells. I said no prayers, but the mystery of mountain pilgrims — some still barefoot on the screes of Croaghpatrick in neighbouring Mayo — stifled the running-pain.

The path was twice the length it looked, full of cunning detours to collect the wells, and the added length gave the feel of a high mountain. The people's summit was this hollow on the ridge where the old man sat and counted the rocky parish, its strip of shore, and the treacherous fishing-grounds beyond.

'Who won? There's no winning that kind of a race —'

'Dead-heat,' I offered in English. He made a literal joke of that harsh language, 'The two of them are dead anyway, and you may say they're feeling the heat too —' He pointed downhill, the stick sharp and steady as a rifle, 'It happened in the time of Father Clarke . . .' Ignoring my wretched shivering, he faced into his story.

Father Clarke it seemed had been a bull of a man in his middle years, a former athlete, a hero in his youth — he'd jumped a twenty-two foot river with two bullets in his body and the Black and Tans on his heels. And in every sermon after that he jumped the same river again. The priesthood didn't suit the misfortunate man, and there was no choice to quit then. He hardened into age with a habit of solitary drinking and so much frustration in him that he'd as soon club you with his fist as shake your hand. His health turned bad and his limbs seized up with rheumatism. He couldn't escape the parish for they wouldn't have him anywhere else.

Father Clarke turned against his own people and bullied them body and soul. 'Foréigean anama,' the old man called it, violence of the soul. He renewed the ancient march up the mountain—not from devotion, but as another form of spiritual aggression. The head of every household had to trudge behind the muscle-bound priest — men that spent all their days on the sea and the bog and the mountains, and could do with a Sunday's rest. Carrying the Blessed Sacrament Father Clarke headed his grim procession up Slíabh na dTobair and when he reached the top he would look down on his parish holding the Sacred Host on high in a show of power. No man dared cross him — until the shoemaker, that is — and indeed the priest had his own henchmen, the publican, the grocer, the teacher, the civic guard, to carry his power into the temporal sphere.

The shoemaker was a different class of man altogether, but he had his own devils too. He was reared beyond in the hills where there was no living to be had at all, but he was a great man to build anything or make a thing out of nothing and he got himself a name for work. He remained high up on the outskirts of the parish, out of the way of the village; until one night he tumbled off the mountain going after a clifted sheep and lay out for days before he crawled down, so that his injuries never mended and he was left with a twisted leg.

There was nothing for him but to move into the village and set up as a shoemaker, a trade he was known for, where he needn't stir abroad again. But he missed his free and active ways, and as he sat in his little shop chained to the boot-last he turned sour with the frustration of a spoiled life. He fell out with Father Clarke straight away on the matter of the Easter dues, but he was a great hand at the bootmaking while the heavy priest was hard on footwear, so they needed one another to survive.

That's how it was until the priest got a housekeeper. She was a big, shamefaced lump of a girl with a soft look to her, and she was Father Clarke's own niece. She had been in trouble, and of course everyone knew what that meant. But it was nothing to the trouble she was in now, landed below to look after her uncle in all his ignorance and frustration. Of course there was no money for the job, no time off nor any benefits; it was a cross between a vocation and a penance. No one would talk to her either after her shame; it was a relief to the village to find someone lower than themselves. That was how bad he had them driven.

The only one who had a civil word for the woman was the shoemaker when she was in with her uncle's battered boots or passed the door where he huddled in the shadows. He'd call out to her kindly and shake his head at the bitter mystery of their predicament. The shoemaker had an eye for suffering, and he saw the wear and tear the silent girl was taking. Nor was he the only one who thought she was getting worse from her uncle than the fist.

Word went to the priest that his niece was friendly with the cripple. On the eve of the pilgrimage he brutally corrected that error in her ways, then sent her out to fetch his boots for the climb on the morrow. The shoemaker saw the bruises around her dull, tearless eyes — he smelled blood too, and he couldn't get a word or even a look out of the poor girl. He held the boots back for an hour to finish them. In the morning after Mass the congregation followed Father Clarke out of the chapel and up the hill — all but his housekeeper who was sent an hour before to reach the summit by the back side of the hill and have sustenance prepared on top. She had a little pot, a bottle of water, and a few sticks to boil a cup of tea for him after his exertion.

Father Clarke wore his vestments for the climb, and he carried the blessed Sacrament raised before him, gloved in its golden cloth, like the fist of God. No one was ever allowed to pass him on the hill. He must lead his people to the summit as a sign of authority and power. The procession jostled along behind his rheumatic tread and with the terrible hysteria of oppression they jabbered rosaries at his bulging back. At the third Holy Well there was a change in the mumble, an excited buzz, and when the priest dipped the well and turned to spatter a blessing, he saw an unholy apparition lunging up the track behind. The shoemaker!

The man was leaning on a crutch and vaulting forward with the power of his arms and shoulders while one leg swung uselessly and the other barely supported him on the ground. Veins stood out on his forehead and already his face was lathered in sweat. He caught the tail of the procession and the people fell back from him in mortal fear, but he passed them without a glance. Father Clarke held up the Host against the challenge as if it would fling him to the ground or strike him dead. The shoemaker came stumbling on. At the last moment he veered aside to pass the priest but the teacher took a cruel swing at his legs with a blackthorn stick. The cripple fell, tumbling over and over like a tripped hare. He lay still at last, face down at the side of the well, his thin ribs heaving.

The procession moved on in a hurry. As they passed the ruined creature some blessed themselves in terror, some aimed kicks, and one old widow at the very tail, with no hope at all of reaching the summit, scooped a little water from the well and shook it on his forehead. Then she dipped again and made him drink a drop from her hand.

The shoemaker heaved himself upright on the hillside. She spoke to him in soft Irish, urging him downhill to the empty village. He seized her stick, brushed her roughly aside, and lunged upwards again. A terrible grinding noise came from his teeth now, as if there was a broken engine in there driving him on. His eyes burned with a yellow rage and again the people cowered back. The shoemaker left the winding path and lurched straight up the rough hillside where he could not be stopped. At the sight of further challenge, the priest cursed, lengthened his stride and leaned into the hill.

His hobnails rang with effort on the rocky path, and straightway he bellowed in pain. He stumbled a few paces on his left boot, and then roared again. The shoemaker looked full across the hillside and his wild laugh rang out in triumph.

Nailing the new leather onto the boots he had planted two nails full in the centre of the soles, and with all the cunning of his trade had gauged their length and depth to penetrate under heavy pressure. That pressure was on.

To Father Clarke they were the bullets in his body, the

spikes in the foot of the crucifix. They spurred him on to martyrdom. He must beat the godless shoemaker to the top and assert the force of the Church. He strode forward on the nails, and began the race uphill against the devil.

They weren't running: neither man could run. The shoemaker hadn't the limbs, and the priest was bound up in vestments and pain. His feet were wrecked with varicose veins, and bad as the nails were he couldn't remove the boots and go on barefoot.

There was something so unholy in the spectacle of two mad men racing slowly that the people stood spellbound. All except the teacher. He lumbered after the shoemaker and made to fell him with a mighty blow to the head when the priest saw he was outstripped now by his own henchman and gave a strangled roar, 'Back! Get back!'

Curiosity for human spectacle overcoming their fear, the people pressed along the track behind the priest, keeping a distance in case he turned on them. In a croaking voice the publican offered twenty to one on the cripple to anyone who'd take a long shot, but no one would bet against the strength of the priest who was sticking to the track and the Holy Wells, while the other man was taking all the rough ground, swinging uphill between his crutch and the widow's stick. You might have expected the people to be on his side—an unfortunate like themselves—but no. They were for the priest, and every time the shoemaker toppled, or hit himself against a rock and opened up a new wound, they lifted a jeer against him.

They knew nothing of the boot-nails — they were only found later when the priest was stripped for the laying-out, and the boots had to be dragged off his feet by a strong man, full as they were of blood-suction and nailed almost to the bone. Had they known in time they could have seized the publican's odds and cleaned him out.

For the shoemaker it was who won the race.

The girl jumped to her feet as he breasted the ridge and lurched towards her in the summit hollow. She screamed once then ran to him. With one strong arm she stopped him in his final fall.

Pity turned to terror as the beaten priest, his vestments hemmed with blood, bore down upon her. At bay, here in this hollow, she sheltered the dying shoemaker, turning her blank, black eyes against her uncle. He raised the sacrament in his hands, aimed it at the pair, and began to curse them from the depths of his power.

She screamed again, a different scream, dragged the crutch from the shoemaker's body, and swung it at the priest to stop the curse. It caught him full across the swollen throat, but she struck too late and the words gushed forth in blood. The curse was fully spoken.

I . . . yes, yes, I — I was shivering with cold and loathing as the story stopped. Sweat lay icy on my skin, and mist swirled across the ridge to fill the hollow. The figure sat in silence looking down on the lost village.

'What happened . . . ?' Ragged hysteria in my voice, 'What happened to her?'

He made no sound but sat on, like a statue or a stone. I turned in terror, blind in the mist, and glimpsed the girl there, on her knees and burning eternally at the rock. With a bottle of water and the priest's kettle she was trying to quench her hell.

THE LUG WALK

John Paul asked Maria to marry him on the last stage of the thirty-three mile Lug Walk across the Wicklow mountains. He had just located Lough Firrib, in thick mist and rain, with some acute map and compass work.

But the navigation wasn't quite as inspired as it might have appeared to Maria, since John Paul was covertly following the trough of footprints, some ten feet to the side, left by the ninety-two other participants in the walk, all of whom had already completed the course. Furthermore, the footprints were following the pipeline from Turlough Hill to Lough Firrib. Navigation wasn't really necessary at all.

John Paul was thirty-three years old, so he hadn't actually been called after the travelling Pope-show. They were simply the plain names his plain parents had conferred upon a son whose brother had already used up Patrick.

As a boy, with thin hair around a furtive face, he was known simply as John, but he thought of himself secretly as J.P., and sometimes as Justice of the Peace, an image that accorded vaguely with Marshall Wyatt Earp.

But when the Pope toured Ireland with such romantic success — 'Young people of Ireland, I loff you!' — John, like many of the less personable young people of Ireland who had never before been loved by anyone, and would never be again, felt identity stir in his compulsive soul. He launched his double-name first on his very small circle of friends who were jealous of its fortuitous aptness since most of them were of a similar bent, and then on a cynical public, who combined it with the thinning hair and ascetic beard and recognised a failed vocation.

John Paul still lived at home with his resentful mother, a wiry wisp of womanhood, in a redbrick house in Ranelagh. He referred to the box-room he had occupied since childhood as his 'study'. His mother called it his hutch. He worked ineffectually in the Civil Service, where serving ambition is the only real work to be done, and he had very little of that.

The Climbers & Walkers Club was his passion. Actually it had changed its name since the unfortunate initials led to its being known universally as the Country & Western club. It was now presented as the Walkers Club, the W.C., the earnest committee having not yet perceived the irony in the new title.

In the hall at home John Paul kept his rucksack and walking boots. Once, his mother added a forked stick and spotted kerchief, but he missed the point. The boots were the first items to strike his eye as he entered or left the house, and he cultivated an indulgent notion that he might step into them some day at a moment's notice, and abscond into the romantic wilderness.

He kept a long-handled ice-axe in the umbrella-rack for a while to broaden the geographical range of the illusion, but his mother relegated it to the wood-shed, where she found it moderately effective for chopping kindling.

The boots were standard walking-wear, bendy and bulbous like a pair of cut-down leather wellingtons. They actually seemed to suck the bog-water in rather than keep it out.

The rucksack was an up-to-date model in flashy fabric with adjustable waist-belt and a plethora of straps totally incomprehensible to John Paul's mother who tried it out as a shopping-bag on her little trolley, and found the straps kept catching under the wheels.

When Maria joined the W.C. John Paul sized her up as a large woman of little ambition, who would not be seeking relations with men of rock and ice pretension, a companion whose plodding abilities would never outstrip his own. She seemed to be composed, not altogether unpleasantly, of circles; a round head with tight black hair that formed thousands of little key-ring curls; a rotund, round-eyed face that was further divided into circles by the superimposition of round-rimmed spectacles. Shortsighted, navigation not too hot, J.P. judged. The circle motif continued to develop below the neck in all sorts of obvious ways in which John Paul wasn't interested; what he wanted was companionship and solicitude.

Maria was a domestic-science teacher after all, though what science had to do with housekeeping was as much a mystery to the man as to his forthright mother.

He courted Maria assiduously through the introductory Sunday walks; saw her through the difficult period when her new boots cut her feet like steak-knives; and taught her to 'set' a map, with limited success, since very often her view of a landscape was a confused blur. He failed utterly to teach her to refold a map with the same alarmingly practised ease she used on the restaurant menu the Sunday evening he finally asked her out after an intimate 'F.H.S'. (W.C. code for a Foot-Hill Stroll).

But the poker-players's flick of the *Carte* was a false alarm. Maria was not a Good-Time Girl. She ordered a modest salad and a pot of tea, and chattered excitedly about the walk and the fine views the group had enjoyed under her patron's tutelage.

John Paul ordered a grandiose hamburger, with 'Seven Seas' sauce thrown in as a dash of romantic afterthought. The kindly waitress knew he meant 'Thousand Island' dressing, although John Paul always looked like a man who could do with a good laxative.

He spoke with a faraway look in his pale, pink-rimmed eyes of bigger and higher things, of mountains and mountaineering, of rock and ropes and . . . but when he caught the frightened look in Maria's rolling orbs he shifted down a gear or two and confided that he was In Training — as if this were a mystic condition — In Training for a Big Walk, perhaps the Biggest Walk, far bigger than the Reeks Walk, demanding stamina and endurance unknown in the Maum Turks, a thirty-three-mile struggle with nature and the landscape that cut right to the heart of the Wicklow Mountains . . . er, Hills, he amended immediately, when her eyes distended again.

The Lug Walk next year, he announced, was the object of all

his desire and ambition, a snot of 'Thousand Island' slipping furtively down his beard.

Maria giggled nervously. It wasn't just the eloquent sauce, but the sound of the Lug Walk reminded her ridiculously of a bold child being taken firmly by the ear between thumb and forefinger and marched out in front of the class to be chastised. But she thought hurriedly of Lugnaquilla towering immensely above a wilderness of remote geography, and swallowed her giggles, and her questions.

John Paul conducted Maria to her bus-stop with some reservations in his mind, which he had quite forgotten by the following Sunday when, as a qualified member of the W.C. he led his charges on a 'Preamble' (Preliminary Mountain Ramble), which was really just a detour cunningly devised to eliminate several stages of the Glendalough bus-route.

He spent much of the walk deep in monotonous conversation with a breathless Maria, while the rest of the group were left to trample flowers and be terrorised by browsing cattle without advice or instruction.

This pattern continued weekly, with Maria asking questions ('What makes it point to the North?'), and developing a ring of confidence. But as her assurance grew she became bossy too, and like a teacher who breaks down a class by boring it to death, she took over the control of the trudges, rambles, tramps, and scrambles, until the group dwindled to a tiny circle of eccentrics (she was good at circles), and eventually even these fell away, thrown off by the centrifugal force of John Paul and Maria's partnership.

John Paul did not allow the semblance of romance to disrupt his dedication to the Lug Walk. Instead he planned it like a campaign, introducing Maria whenever possible to short sections of the great monotonous marathon that seeks out the most boring sections of high bog in Wicklow and then links them by a devious route that concludes on top of the most complex lump of turf and rock in the county.

Maria walked wherever directed; up or down, wet or dry,

seemed to have no effect on her incessant questions, a tendency that allowed full rein to John Paul's taste for the expression of his opinions, attitudes, and confusions on every subject under the rainclouds or the sun; and since Maria paid scant attention to answers — already chewing over her next question — there was no need for John Paul to be over-concerned with accuracy or truth.

On the slopes of Mullachcleevaun he misrepresented exhaustively the workings of combustion-engines and gas-fridges. He abused his unfortunate mother as a shackling tyrant on the track to Seefin. Once, on the bus to Enniskerry, he expounded an original technique for the use of oxygen at Himalayan altitudes. John Paul proposed that mountaineers should uncoil a long roll of thin tubing as they mounted towards the limits of the atmosphere. Oxygen, being a gas, should automatically rise within the tube from bottles kept at Base Camp, and if it didn't . . . well, the climber could always suck hard.

He got carried away by the theory and, in a flash of inspiration, perceived the possibility of merging the climbing rope and the air-tube into a revolutionary hollow rope. . . .

He was quite unaware that he was the subject of a bus-full of suppressed mirth, and that he was rapidly becoming one of the many comic myths of the walking-scene. Their arguments in the hostels were being greedily collected and embellished by observers (the ultimate accolade), beginning with the evening in Glencree, over a meal of burnt toast and sausages, when John Paul himself asked a burning question; namely, what 'Science' had to do with domestic housekeeping?

Maria responded haughtily that any body of information or knowledge might constitute a Science, to which John Paul replied, banging his empty cup on the table, that it was certainly Science that had determined the temperature at which water boiled but he could not see why she needed a degree in chemistry to drop a tea-bag in it when it began to bubble.

Maria pouted, her mouth the round O of Outrage, and John Paul enquired provocatively whether she had required much Science to burn the bloody toast.

And yet, every Sunday throughout the long, wet winter and the long, wintry spring, they walked and talked, and sometimes it was John Paul himself in his comic-opera tweed breeches, thick plaid shirt, and the absurd balaclava cradling his monkish little head, who grew breathless and had to resort to questions as a ruse to gain breathing-space.

Maria was refining her geometry, tightening some of her rotundities to mere curves and arcs; even the famous fullness of the breeches was slowly waning to a parabolic crescent, assisted in its decline by the friction of innumerable mud-slides taken in descent. A John Paul encyclical would be punctuated suddenly by a high-pitched squeal and the oily slither of overtrousers on wet grass as Maria tobogganed bluntly down a slope upon her back.

They discovered 'Sessions' in January, and took to visiting the Glendalough and Glenmalure hostels on Saturday evenings for a while. As a self-considered expert on the 'traditional' field John Paul insinuated himself into the rabble of guitar and banjo-men frequenting the local public-houses. He was content at first to clap spasmodically out of tempo, like a plain-clothes Christian Brother, to the pedestrian inanities of 'Fiddlers Green' and the 'Streets of London' but his reticence couldn't last, and on the third visit he brazenly produced the harmonica he had been torturing at home for weeks to his mother's distress.

It was in the crowded, festive lounge of the Royal at about ten o'clock on Saturday night.

There was a brief lull in the ribaldry and jollity. The singers were preparing for the fourth assault on 'The Bunch of Thyme', when John Paul rose to his feet with all the gargling solemnity of a white turkey making a speech from the dock, and called for order. He fluttered his bony elbows, waggled his shoulders, placed his cupped hands to his mouth,

and, as a hush of smothered glee fell over the congregation, announced in the reverent, rural mumble befitting the
tradition:

'I don't know the name o' this tune, but I got it from the
playin' o' the Gallowglass Ceili Band.'

He closed his eyes humbly, and blew a long, piercing note
on the miserable wedge of saliva-soaked tin and timber
clenched between his lips.

The crowd released a shuddering sigh as if punctured, as if it
had sat collectively on a long, sharp splinter while the note rose
slowly in pitch gathering and rejecting cracked discordances,
and John Paul's rigid frame was seen to bend forward, one leg
lifting like a dervish about to kick off a rain-dance; then the
note swooped, broke, and slobbered into an unrecognisable
semblance of a tune. It was obvious from the man's frenzied
hopping and jogging that it was a dance-tune, but it seemed to
centre around a very limited number of notes despite the
embellishments and accidentals the crazed musician was
spitting into it.

The crowd gazed at each other with that sublime and wild-
eyed elation that comes upon people only in the presence of
great art—or of supreme idiocy—when an individual displays
absolute mastery of one or the other extreme. Someone noticed
that Maria was humming stridently along with the music, her
eyes closed and hands clasped, a Botticelli balloon. All ears bent
upon the tune she was shaping, since John Paul's version was
unidentifiable.

Dum-dum, da-daddle, da-dum-de-dumdum, Maria sang
obliviously, and continued dum-dum, da-daddle-di-dum . . .
Understanding dawned.

As the second part of the tune broke on the audience like the
opening of an abattoir door the happy voices crashed in as one;
'Ant-y Ma-ry hadda ca-nary, Up the leg gof her drawers . . . . . .

On and on they went, pounding fists and glasses on the
table, stamping boots on the hollow floor, pummelling each

other weakly in the hysterical enjoyment of another soul's insanity, only stopping when hilarity had exhausted them into whimpering submission, and John Paul collapsed into his seat with the beatified radiance of one who has controlled the pulse of his audience.

Elation galvanised the mirth-stupefied crowd and a rib-cracking nudge passed around the circle as John Paul jumped to his feet again, one hand raised authoritatively in the air like a station-master about to send off a train.

'A slow one!' he barked fiercely. The unspeakable instrument went to his lips again, and to the lugubrious chugging and steaming of spittle-choked notes, *Danny Boy* churned out of the station.

Immediately a powerful female voice tore into the silence of non-participation: '. . . the poipes, the poipes are caw-aw-ling,' it asserted belligerently across the room, cutting like a siren into a brawl. An axe-faced local lady with an acidic reputation was not going to let any brat of a Dublin jackeen desecrate the real spiritual anthem of a great and proud people, and she had the voice to back up her intention, a fine nasal abrasion like hard chalk whining over slate!

'. . . from glennnnn to glennnnn annnnd downnnn the Mounnnntainnn side,' she continued aggressively, keeping pace and pitch effortlessly with John Paul while transfixing him with an eye like an engraving tool.

The local team knew they had a winner in their corner.

'Good man, Mary!' they roared in jubilation.

'Give him shtick!'

John Paul was attempting to bow courteously in mid-squawk, thinking he had the cultural pleasure of a duet on his hands, but he forgot to lower the harmonica in time with the bowing of his head and his teeth gnashed against he sharp edges of the metal. Mary stepped up the pressure, contemptuously scenting weakness, and it was only when she abolished the summer and executed all the flowers that he realised it was actually a duel he was in.

He swelled his chest with the wind of challenge and puffed his cheeks like pig-bladder footballs so that the world-famous sighing sequence of notes concluding the first half of the tune ripped out between his fingers like the phantom of the opera wrestling with a Wurlitzer.

In the small bar, just the other side of a baize-clad mahogany door, Tony Maloney, local pool-shark, leaned over the antiseptic green of the table and lined up the shot that was going to pot one ball with a clinical left-hand spin and set up the remainder to win him the fifteenth game of the night, bringing his winnings to the level of a modest weekly wage. He shook his head in irritation as the confused cacophony penetrated the two intervening inches of hardwood.

'Bloody hell!' he thought. 'Sounds like an Orange March in there.' He had absolutely no sense of tradition.

He sized up the crucial shot, and began to concentrate again.

Mary went into the high second half of the verse like a champion coming out for the final round, full of nonchalant, practised venom, showing plenty of power but keeping the best in reserve for the big punch she knew was coming up. John Paul was at full throttle alongside on ' . . . sunshine and in so-ho-row, or whennnn the va-halley's hushed and white with snooooow / Tis I'll be. . . .

'HEEEEEEEERE' screeched Mary violently launching the notorious high note in an uppercut that soared from G to high E with a vicious tone full of bare knuckles. It was no canary — more like an ambulance siren — she had up the leg of her colloquials.

John Paul reeled under the onslaught, and lost his grip.
He hit, and held, high F instead of E.

Critics argued the issue later as to whether the upper end of the trashy implement was simply a half tone out of pitch, or whether, as several observers attested, John Paul panicked at the crucial moment and sucked instead of blew.

Either way, the consequences were disastrous.

Mary held and amplified her 'HEEEEERE' not merely in the service of the song, but asserting her own continuity despite any combination of war, death, revolution, famine, or hikers. John Paul, hopeful that perhaps no one had noticed his slip of the tongue, decided to brazen it out.

Several things happened as the raucous duet chain-sawed through the lounge. Big Jim O'Rourke, a splinter of agony in his ear, gripped his pint-glass so hard that it burst, and deluged his new pale-grey suit in Guinness. For years after it was sworn locally that Mary's voice had shattered the glass, and Big Jim never begrudged her the glory, but for the moment he had business to attend to — he was lumbering towards John Paul, shedding beer-drips like a lawn-sprayer, with the jagged butt of the glass clenched vengefully in his fist.

Simultaneously, the manager hurtled out of that mysterious back-space hidden like a sacristy in the architecture of every pub. He skidded through the bar just as the precision-driven tip of Tony Mahony's cue approached the bottom left-hand side of the cue-ball. The manager burst through the mahogany door and dived into the scrum around John Paul.

The swinging door batted a jagged wedge of sound into the pool-room, driving Tony's cue like a huge darning-needle through the plush green cloth, nudging the cue-ball conspiratorially as it ripped. The white sidled guiltily across the table with a Judas-kiss for the black, which dropped apologetically into the pocket.

Foul shot, and game forfeited.

Before the embarrassed *Oops!* of the balls had died away Maloney was on his way to the lounge, his cue gripped overhand like a Zulu assegai.

John Paul felt himself lifted bodily out of his standing, past a gamut of barbed weapons, by the manager who didn't want blood on the new carpet. The door crashed open as in a Western, except that this was solid oak and not a splintering replica — normally it opened inwards. John Paul hit the road outside with great relief considering it was his turn to buy the next round for the rabble of spoon-players and tin-whistle men within.

As he lay gratefully in the gutter a hard, choking sensation in his throat roused him to panic again, and his fingers flew to his prominent adam's apple. He remembered that prior to his ejection, Tony Maloney had been attempting to push the blunt end of the cue down his throat without first taking the precaution of removing the mouth organ.

John Paul drew an experimental breath. The wheeze in his chest sounded alarmingly like a B-chord. If he expelled the air and produced a C then he was in real trouble. Just as he ventured on the crucial test the door swung open again and the harmonica skittered viciously off the tarmac, striking John Paul in a highly sensitive area. He produced the high-C with no mechanical assistance whatsoever.

Lying in the ditch at Glendalough, like his namesake stricken down on the Road to Damascus, John Paul pondered, and abandoned the fleshpots of culture for the hardship of the outdoors again.

There was a lot of suffering to be indulged in before the great marathon flog with which Irish walkers re-enact Napoleon's retreat from Moscow.

It was late spring now, and all the Heavy Walks must take place before the sensitive growing season ended, so that the armies of booted feet could have the maximum impact on the ecology in order to underline their domination of the mountains.

At the last moment John Paul made a major sacrifice. He bought a new pair of boots — guaranteeing himself even greater pain than the most rigorous Catholic upbringing and Christian Brother education could have required.

The morning of the Lug Walk didn't dawn at all.

It was raining so hard at the Stone Cross in Bohernabreena that light couldn't possibly filter in between the dense clouds and the flying mud. Right from the start John Paul and Maria had great difficulty clinging to the sturdy quartet of walkers he had marked down as his guides through the muck and murk.

They were known popularly as Male Members of the Gents section of the W.C.

Unable to secure a lift to the Stone Cross for himself and Maria, John Paul had eavesdropped on the other group's arrangements, and then simply turned up at their rendezvous. It was proof, not of schoolboy humour, but of a great earnest innocence that the group met opposite the public toilets on O'Connell Bridge.

An elderly Volkswagen, grossly overloaded with five bearded gents and the mammoth Maria, lurched and squelched into the Dublin foothills, belching chagrin through its exhaust. Maria was squashed in the middle of the back seat — having refused the front on grounds of safety — between John Paul and a morose individual who would not speak but was audibly digesting his breakfast porridge.

In the thick of Tallaght Maria made an urgent request for a toilet-stop.

When the driver finally found a suitable spot she was purple with enforced continence, and the entire contents of the car, including the frothing driver whose seat wouldn't tilt forward sufficiently, had to be unloaded into the rain.

At the start they registered their presence and time of departure with a snug man in a tent and were instructed to register again at every checkpoint along the thirty-three-mile route.

Their reluctant 'keepers' attempted to slip away from them on the rainswept track across Seahan when John Paul paused to relieve a blister in an achingly new boot. But Maria foiled the escape bid by scuttling along in their wake, leaving John Paul to hop along behind as best he could.

Reluctantly daylight seeped through the dense rainclouds and illuminated the swirling wraiths of mists that clogged the bog-slopes of Kippure. The silent, bearded men were growing desperate at the slowness of the pace, and Maria's incessant questions — 'Why are they called peat-hags?' — when a suitable accident occurred.

At the reedy edge of a deep rift in the bog each man in turn launched a flying leap to land on the quivering rim of a peat-hag, one of the tall mushrooms of turf protruding from the sticky ooze.

Maria jumped in mid-question and failed to reach the rim. She landed six feet lower on one leg and promptly sank to the knee, driven into the sludge by the pile-driver of gravity. She waved the other leg fastidiously in the rain, but all efforts at equilibrium failed, and eventually she was forced to plunge the dry foot too into the slime. It was immediately sucked into the morass in a welter of bubbles. She stumbled forward, finding no support.

The bog released its grip on the first foot, retaining, however, the boot and sock as consolation.

Now Maria was balanced again on one boot, and waving a plump, pink foot in the air while a row of hairy faces goggled down at her.

Again she toppled forward, and the naked leg dived to the knee, transferring the strain to the anchored boot which yielded its contents with the same squidgy ease as its partner had done.

Maria fell forward, flat on her face in the mud, a pair of fat, bare feet waving in the air.

As John Paul slid reluctantly down towards her the four silent men looked at one another, shook their dewy beards, and melted into the mist.

John Paul and Maria arrived at the Sally Gap checkpoint just as a hurried search-party was being assembled. John Paul offered advice with such officious authority that the group had almost departed on his instructions before realising that the grotesque pair bossing it around was actually the object of the search.

Supplies of official tea and soup had long been exhausted, so they guzzled the marshals' private supply and complained about the shortage. They ignored with haughty disdain the most strongly worded suggestions that they drop out of the running at that point, since at their present pace the walk must take at least twenty hours to finish.

John Paul removed the more excruciating boot, and studied the impatient legs round him. Under his stern scrutiny the ring of feet became increasingly nervous, and an embarrassed pair of wellingtons made a cringing attempt to curl over, one on top of the other, like a child controlling an urge to pee. So hypnotised was the wearer by John Paul's persuasive obduracy that he yielded up his rubber boot with little more than a whimpered demand for later restitution. So John Paul and Maria strode and waddled into the mist again, to the bemused shaking of heads, the single wellington adding a dry, satisfying thud to the triple-squelch of the sodden boots.

Many hours and mishaps later, John Paul — shod now in a second, mismatched, wellington, acquired at the Wicklow Gap — stumbled into Lough Firrib, which he only recognised when the water-level wavered an inch below the mouths of the rubber boots. It was only a few miles to the conclusion now, and he felt he knew this section intimately.

He was wrong, of course, and they would be found the following day on the wrong side of the mountain, but for the time being — in a burst of thoughtless elation — John Paul proposed marriage.

There was a brief and breathless pause while the proposal quivered in the air and a ripple of icy water slopped over the rim of his boots. John Paul resonated to the appalling echoes of his suggestion.

His heart cringed with regret, a sponge wrung by ruthless fingers. And then Maria, with the wild look in her headlong orbs of a compulsive questioner who could not resist what she was going to ask, although it was as ill-timed as a period on a honeymoon, demanded querulously, 'What does Lough Firrib mean? . . . What did you say?'

John Paul considered briefly, not the questions nor the answer, but his own merciful deliverance.

'It's probably a derivation of Firbolg, one of the original Celtic tribes in these parts,' he offered happily, brushing aside his error of judgement like one bum note in a rhapsody.

THE ISLAND

It seems extraordinary now that all three could end up on a rope together. Yes, I let it happen. I suppose it was in part stupidity, and in part my hope that a sharing would resolve their problem — mostly, though, it came about because beyond a certain tension relationships dictate their own events. If Tommo needed to destroy Brian then they'd end up on a ledge together somehow. And if both had an obsession with a third, then, sure as hell he'd be there too. When that level of passion is reached the cogs of the inevitable grind into gear.

Even so — given that *some*thing had to happen — did it have to be on my time? Not that that's the important question. There are bigger issues involved here. A shocking laugh echoes in my ears — confuses me more than the scream that preceded it.

An ideal decision is impossible. If I do not report what happened on the island, if I conceal an attempt on one boy's life by another, then I am an accessory of sorts. In itself that wouldn't bother me too much — if it ended there. How can I conceal the fact that Tommo is capable — still capable — of that sort of desperation? Next time it might really come to a fatal conclusion. And yet, even more insistent than the screech of pain and the laugh that followed it, is the terrible memory of Tommo's tears.

'He — was — *my* — friend!'

I'd never have known it was possible to cry like that — to have held so much pain, rage, grief as he released in that adolescent damburst. The intensity increased and he was shaken by convulsions, weeping solid memories, fragments of friendship, debris of broken homes — harsh shapes dissolving in a flood of acid tears — prams and shattered chairs, torn bedding, a naked doll big as a baby, life-size wads of skirts and coats, linen grey as drowned skin, all the wreckage of a young life spilling out.

He crouched beside me on a ledge above the calm, clean sea, consolation useless. The convulsions quietened. Close as he was his voice when it came was a long way off, muffled in some internal distance where his heart crouched by the flood before it slipped in forever. Grown up now, he could never cry again. Unbearable to renew that pain. I kept a hand on his shoulder . . . the denim might have covered a thin flake of rock.

Below us the sea swayed between the boulders, its grey indifference full of restless burial. It was just as if Tommo's rope was cut and he slipped with his new manhood into the water a hundred feet below.

What good will it do to report his act? I have no faith at all in detention. And they won't find Tommo anyway to put him away: he is drowned deep in his own life.

Instead they'll use the incident to shut down my programme and deprive all the others of the brief freedom we can teach them. For that reason — because this is a pilot scheme, an experiment — my instinct is for concealment. You may think I'm protecting my job, but that isn't it. There are easier jobs than taking screwed-up kids out into the wilds on rehab-programmes. I don't expect to transform anyone, and there's no moral involved in mountain navigation or in paddling a straight line; it's enough for me to get them out — water, wind, rock, challenge, courage, achievement — out from under cover of deprivation to meet themselves not as we, but as nature, sees them.

I can't get away from it though — he could have killed someone.

And Brian's laugh! What goes on in a mind like that? Laughing on the edge of the void. Is Brian so far removed from the ordinary, so subtly displaced he makes a virtue of his alienation? Could that be what Tommo and the group saw in him, an otherness that had them fascinated but quivering on edge? It wasn't just sex — that was only an expression of something more extreme, something that came through in that cruel laughter, a private strength, immune to loneliness, that Tommo understood . . . and envied?

I had them on a sea-crag. They'd paddled out to the island and camped there, the culmination of a three-week course in 'adventure skills'. There were six of them and, to help me, one officer from their detention-centre — a skilled canoeist, I'll give him that, but not strong on the human side. And that was a pity with this first group. I could have done with support, because . . . they — were — *bastards*!

That was the basic problem; as a group — a gang — they were totally unsuited to an experience meant for individuals. It was as if they'd been hand-picked to destroy the programme right from the start.

Mr. Tuohy, the staff-man, muscular, impatient, kept rubbing them the wrong way. He couldn't relate on common terms — his accent, interests, humour were all wrong, and he didn't know how to lie low and get on with his job; he had to keep imposing his well-meaning but superior manner, either pointedly ignoring their behaviour as if it was beneath contempt, or else over-reacting to vulgarity. He'd have suited well-brought up boy-scouts, and I couldn't understand how the mistake had happened. As a result the unruly group couldn't relax and be free of authority for a while, they were forever reacting against the kind of irksome order he represented. In his frustration he tried to draw me in on his side over their heads, incriminating me in the exercise of authority. He couldn't see that the more superior he felt the more absolute was their scorn. Like all boys they would at least have admired him for his skills, but he used canoeing as a means of assertion — they called it showing off — and that finished him altogether.

I suspect Dr. Farrell, director of the detention centre, chose Tuohy for me specially. Farrell (Doctor of what? I still don't know) didn't care much for innovation. He splashed liberal rhetoric about and the centre was full of pool-tables and colour-televisions, but there was nothing personal, nothing from the heart. Behind the chrome and plastic the place was as homely as a fun-palace. Radical measures were being forced on him from above by some political initiative (of even briefer duration if I submit this report). But behind it all, detention to Farrell meant what it said. Tuohy told me his boss believed he was training young misfits for a life in prison and the best he could do was get them used to it early. That kind of belief is self-fulfilling.

That's the other reason why I want to save this programme at all costs — to confound his expectations.

'I can guarantee you one thing with these fellows . . .' Farrell promised as we left his centre, the blue minibus heaped up with ropes, helmets, rucksacks, paddles, boys. I awaited the wise word of experience —

'They'll always let you down. Always.'

Such a failure of inspiration seemed funny at first; I almost laughed. Did he think I understood him, shared his cynicism, this paunchy warder with his pseudo-doctorate, the collar of his wrinkled business suit faintly sprinkled with dandruff, grey hair smeared to his scalp and the shine of a leather chair all over his sedentary life?

What did he think of my beard and jeans, adventure-jargon, liberation of the spirit, diplomas in Mountain-this and Outdoor-that. . . .? I know what he thought. Another fool with no experience of the ineducable — a few weeks with Tuohy and the incorrigibles would sort me out!

And yet — I still come back to it — there was almost a deliberate death.

When I call them a gang, it wasn't just leadership, the kind of thing you can isolate; they were going through all kinds of collective responses too. They had gestures, chants, private slang — but by far the most obvious feature was the pseudo-homosexual phase they were in. No girls in their lives and they were making a ritual of it. It was mostly harmless talk and exhibition — planned as a protest against sexual segregation in the hope, while radical gestures were in, that someone would throw them a few girls. Smart thinking in itself, and it might have worked — a different kind of hunger strike — except they got hauled out on crags and rivers instead. Cold-water treatment. No wonder they resented me. Mainly though, they were just acting out provocative ideas, teenagers with a primary mission in life — to defy!

But Brian was different. He wasn't the leader. Tommo was — more or less — at first. Tommo wasn't tough at all, but he looked savage which goes a long way. He made a convincing act of his instability too. He had to be doing something crazy all the time to feel important — and to make you see he was important.

I saw his file: separated parents, alcoholic mother, juvenile crime, institutions — textbook bad start — but unluckiest of all in need to make an impression. He would always be rebuffed because he was short, thin and vicious-looking. His sharp, blue eyes were much too close together, he had spikes of aggressive ginger hair and a mouthful of rotten teeth. I saw how he tried to make an impact on adults, the way he ran his gang — with fast, funny, dirty talk — but with the best will in the world, all that came over was his head-butting, frontal style and those scaly teeth leering at you. For a day or two I kept him at bay, until I found there was no harm in him. His unfortunate appearance seemed made up of ill-fitting bits and pieces from different faces, not all of the same age or temperament. At first I saw it as a symptom of a fragmented personality until I realised that his experience hadn't disintegrated Tommo at all — it had compacted him with need. He was wholly and inconsolably himself, cemented together by the kind of craving for attention that is inevitably the first phase of pain.

He lived on sugar as far as I could see — sweets, minerals,

tomato-sauce, chocolate. Tuohy was disgusted by the boy's teeth, forever trying to bully him off sugar and onto toothpaste, but Tommo didn't believe it was the sugar did the damage; it was the craving for sweetness, the addiction itself that caused the rot, it was like a solitary blight inside him that made him different from normal people and would poison him eventually. While he waited, he issued conflicting orders, set things on fire, stole anything mobile, and sucked cheap sweets, baring his gums with an appallingly ruminative thoroughness at Mr. Tuohy all the while. He was highly entertaining company when you learned to look slightly to one side of him, the way you treat headlights in the dark.

He was only a puppet when it came to leadership. I was surprised the centre hadn't briefed me on group-dynamics; either they didn't notice — which is quite possible — or else it was part of the conspiracy to sink the outdoor scheme.

Joe Curran was the brains, not Tommo at all. It took me a while to spot because he was discreet. Unlike Tommo, Joe wanted control, not attention. He orchestrated the whole obstinate atmosphere and subverted any success we had, carrying out his will through Tommo while their partnership lasted. And that was the reason for the partnership too, not the fact that they were both from Dublin — bloodbrothers, as Tommo thought, among rednecks.

Joe was cautious, intelligent, never capsized his canoe. He was the boy who spends his time on the dodgems avoiding collision while the others are hellbent on it — but his manner concealed a blade-sharp edge that was exposed sometimes between a bitter word and a soft smile. That edge would never soften because it was the rim of his true self. He was the Director on the other side of the fence, the other half of Tuohy's 'them and us', the one who would always let you down, because that was his mission; you were the enemy and he was going to make you pay. The kind too who always uses a front-man to take the friction.

Tommo didn't know he was being used. At first Joe

conversed pleasantly, sensibly about discomfort, and the value of risk so that I had innocent, high hopes for him, while Tommo foulmouthed me openly, grinning all the time — not meaning the abuse but proud of his ability to provoke. It occurred to me later that it was poor Tommo, trying to communicate the only way he knew how, who gave the abuse — but it was Joe, polite and cold, who meant it.

They weren't bad at the sports — they'd done a bit before and thought they knew everything: climbing was about abseiling, you canoed on flat water, and hillwalking happened when you got lost. They lacked self-confidence though and bravado was no substitute. The principle of the whole thing eluded them. They had a totally different concept of Adventure: theirs was urban, illicit, subversive. I had to make a real effort to realise that mine was just as odd to them.

They ruled out the sea at first with an absolute sense of their own rights that you never get among ordinary schoolboys of the same age — a stubborn sense of the self, concerned only with resistance and demand. Swimming was out because it was too close to washing — hygiene was under protest back at the detention centre. But when the masks, snorkels, and huge, black fins were unpacked the 'dirty protest' collapsed. They wanted spear-guns — it had to be about hunting. They assigned Tommo his own snorkel and warned him to stick to it.

Every shadow under water was 'Jaws!' and they leapt for the beach. When they conquered that terror Tommo would swim up from below and bite them through the wetsuit. When it wasn't 'Jaws!' it was 'Aids!' Their world was full of four-letter sensation.

Orienteering made no sense to them at all; they dealt with it by throwing away maps and compasses as fast as they were handed out. Privately that was alright by me, I'd rather stick to the hills and crags, and the programme was all about 'choice' anyway — educated choice. i.e. you have to do it first before you decide you don't want to.

As I say, they made sense of things according to their own priorities, so hillwalking was learning to survive on the run, or after a bomb. I had to recall a lot of primitive stuff about snares, and edible weeds, although in the long run we had to agree the only realistic thing was to raid the homesteads. Rock-climbing, up and over . . . well, obviously a handy skill.

Maybe they forgot these theories in the boredom or excitement of the action, but I despaired at first, because they would never let me think for a moment they were enjoying something for its own sake. As soon as there was any danger of that concession they began to complain or criticise — because if they got satisfaction from the experience then they owed me something, and they couldn't have that, yet. It irritated the bristly thorns of independence that detention had given them.

One day I brought them underwater to a submerged car off the end of a Connemara pier, an old Mercedes stripped of its emblem and grille. In its murky interior a big lobster flexed his claws behind the windscreen. While Brian distracted him by hanging motionless near the glass I reached in through the passenger window, grabbed the lobster behind the pincers and brought him to the surface, a steel spring coiled in my hands. When I lifted him above the water to show how easily disarmed he was they scattered in — disgust? Puzzled and foolish I swam back down with the outraged creature and replaced him in his car.

Back on the pier they got hysterical satisfaction from a crumpled cigarette Tommo found in his pocket. The lobster was consigned to an oblivion deepened by the fear they'd shown and the excessive effort I was making to win them over. And yet, later on he would surface in their drifting night-talk, a new shape in the imagination, that outlandish crustacean, his claws like Tommo's teeth, piloting his stolen Mercedes out to sea. Sometimes too, as if I'd closed in downwind of a deer or a hare I saw a boy completely lost in profound, unguarded freedom. The slightest move, even a glance or a smile from me and the moment vanished. It might have lasted longer and longer with sunshine and practise but for the constant interruption by that other powerful experience of the self — or the mimicry of it. No one could emerge from a wet-suit or bend to tie a lace without one of the others leaping into a lascivious posture behind him, eyes rolling, tongue lolling.

It was a joke of course, and you had to laugh, it was so absurd; despite sloppy wetsuits, flapping cagoules, scrawny pimpled flesh and faces blotched with cold they never missed a cue. It became a reflex action — stacked together on nervous belays, eyes wide with apprehension they would begin to thrust at one another with idiot-automatism while calculating the drop below and the knots involved in their safety.

Yes, it was impossible not to laugh, though sometimes - tired and replete, mock-dancing to music on the radio — the thing contained a languid affection, and I wondered if they found the pathos in each other poignant . . . if that was it?

In the group of six there were two who didn't play-act. They made the gestures but in a deeper sense Brian and Joe were serious. And the others didn't tackle them so much either — except for Tommo: he even tried it on me once — and regretted it when he was picked up and hurled fully-dressed into the sea. . . .

Brian, quiet, self-absorbed, was older than the others — not in age — so old in outrage that they could never catch up. Tuohy told me about Brian, my star pupil, with the self-importance of one who knows the bad news, the inside-story. Subject to violent abuse from infancy, Brian had stabbed his common-law step-father at the age of twelve. Tuohy said 'stabbed to death!' but that wasn't quite true. When taken into care there was said to be something sinister in his docility at first, as if the truth was incubating and must explode some day. Outbreaks of silent delinquency had begun to occur recently, more enigmatic than serious. Tuohy thought that was why Brian was assigned to me, to see if the dynamics of adventure would release some spring — for good or bad. I began to feel very much alone, trying to hem them in with action and exhaustion.

After a week it was obvious that Brian was the focus of the group-sexuality that undermined all we did. During every bout of exhibitionism — trouser-dropping, mooning through the minibus window (as if the public could tell the difference between their faces and arses anyway!) they referred to him with sidelong glances at his soft features, dark eyes unmoved behind cream-skinned, half-shut lids. He had some dubious power, an effect I never saw, something that came out in the night perhaps — if it came out at all. If it was present during the day it was only a pale reflection of itself and manifested to the ones who knew what to look for.

Tommo didn't get on with him. He was actively resentful of Brian. I noticed it quickly, but didn't know what to make of it . . . Then, in the second week, a crucial change of allegiance occurred. Joe Curran began to drop Tommo — his friend and fellow Dubliner — and Tommo fell very awkwardly indeed. Things were difficult now in a different way. Just when I thought I understood the group and could get the most out of them, everything had changed.

Brian and Joe moved obliquely towards each other on the edge of chaos, not quite looking at anyone, their gazes sometimes tangling, sliding apart like surreptitious torch-beams. And the other three, who would have been fine on their own, grew giddy with tension and regressed into a hectic childhood from which they sometimes emerged for a single frame to show a startling flash of skill, an instinctive hand-jam or a perfect paddle-stroke, only to flounder off balance immediately and disappear under.

Tuohy got into a terrible state of excitement one night — claimed he caught them 'at it' in the hostel showers, Tommo and two of the others. And maybe he did, but it wouldn't have been what he thought, an orgy of perversion. They were always setting him up — in the same way that Tommo stripped his gums at him. It's possible they picked up a few thrills in the process, but that wasn't the point . . .

The same when they mimed drugs, peeling back a sleeve on a tattooed arm, thumb braced against an imaginary syringe, initial grimace of desire and pain, then the face suffused with idiotic ecstasy subtly different from the sex-expression—while all the time a sharply-amused eye was peering out behind the act to see how you were taking it. From the start I refused to react; you don't lecture a boy on pacifism when he squeezes a toy trigger at you. It was interesting that Joe and Brian weren't in the showers that time. Tuohy thought they were the innocent ones. But whatever Brian and Joe got up to, was done for themselves, not for show — it would be a celebration of otherness, a private pact between them.

I discovered that first on the night of the whiskey. We were on a two-day hillwalk with an overnight camp near Mam Eidhneach high in the Twelve Bens. Strenuous walking on steep, rocky ground, stunning views. Three tents: Tuohy (he snored) and I in one, the group divided between the other two. At midnight a row erupted. I awoke through a nightmare — Apaches attacking the wagons. The nearest tent, torchlit from within, throbbed with raucous fury — a bedlam of rage, nausea, tears, and a maudlin slur 'One Day at a Time, Sweet Jesus . . .'

Sweet Jesus, indeed. Whiskey! Tommo was incoherent with drink, fury and betrayal. No sign of Joe though he'd started off in that tent. There were four in it now, fighting bitterly. As far as I could interpret, Joe had left with the bottle and gone to the other tent — Brian's — to give them a drink. Instead of coming back he'd ordered the other two boys over to Tommo. The shift was complete. Joe and Brian were too drunk to stand up, they lay silent and inward as stones, unblinking in Tuohy's relentless torchlight. He dragged them all out in the night wind, shivering and puking. Torches strafed the dark — rubber limbs, toppling bodies, ghastly faces askew like masks. Tears; you could see how much closer one or two were to childhood than manhood and would remain so all their lives.

I couldn't interfere on their behalf. This time Tuohy's anger was official, institutional. We knew who'd brought the whiskey — all he wanted to know was who had bought it. He was prepared to keep them stumbling on the wet mountainside till dawn if necessary. They wouldn't tell him anything at all, even the babies, and yet it was obvious from the disclosures minutes earlier — when I'd asked no questions at all and they were only too keen to betray — that Joe was the culprit.

Tuohy wouldn't believe it — he was determined that Tommo was responsible, and of course it suited Tommo to take the rap, seeing himself with drunken pride as leader of the pack still. Basic to Tuohy's fury and my own sense of foolishness was the fact that they'd insisted the previous day that he and I should carry the provisions since they were the most important loads. We'd been set up — made clowns of. Even I couldn't let it pass.

I asked Tuohy to call off the bizarre inquisition (though it had its funny side) and promised we'd punish them in kind next day. I got out the map and headtorch and, over a half mug of whiskey, devised a forced march.

In the morning, an hour after dawn, we stripped the polluted tents around them and tumbled them from their sleeping bags. Packing was done in silence, and if they ate it was only in queasy defiance. Joe, I noted with satisfaction, was particularly rough, but now that his role was out in the open he carried himself with the hardened aloofness of a convict. The rift between himself and Tommo was final from his side, though Tommo — who looked as though he'd been robbed from his grave — was still trying to patch things up. He fried Joe a slimy egg along with his own, and when the offering was ignored he slithered it soft and flabby as a wound into a plastic bag for lunch.

Brian was the only one in control of himself, eating thoroughly as if he knew what was in store with his usual self-absorbed air through which he seemed to look out on the landscape — quiet stream, grey rock, mountains, drifting clouds as if the world contained his own secret reflection and he

would not care to disturb the surface. It was a superb
punishment — saved from sadism by the amount we suffered
ourselves. Gradually, horribly, it dawned on them that we
were not returning to the bus the quick way as Tuohy had
led them to believe. I said nothing, hoping to load the
consequences onto him, and this silence gave me an unexpected
air of menace so that although they had to follow me for
protection from the wilderness they had no idea whether I was
leading them out, or further in. On the grim slopes of Binn Bhan
(the first time — we would cross it later in the day from the
north) they had threatened to mutiny, but the Connemara sky
closed down on cue and I took a gamble, stalking upwards into
the mist. They followed like frightened sheep.

Secretly I was astounded by their performance, hungover
and shattered, heavy-loaded over eighteen miles of steep,
rocky mountain in bad weather. Maybe they could only
respond to coercion but three weeks ago it seemed they could
hardly walk a sea-level mile.

They endured it in their own — by now — distinctive ways;
Joe was stoic but you could tell he would never forgive; Brian,
dreamy absent, as if he'd set his body in motion and vacated it;
Tommo was stunned at first, withdrawn and grieving — but
every now and than a flash of himself broke through: 'Sir! Sir! —
(he deliberately called me Sir because I was trendy enough to
prefer first names and he reckoned I hadn't earned that yet.) He
stood at the side of a high, desolate pass, rain running down his
baggy anorak, as I prepared to contour down Binn Chorr and
sneak back around the other side. He gestured urgently up the
ridge rising steep and fierce above, 'Sir, sir, can we go up that
one sir? Can we sir?' And the friendly, evil grin to let me know
he understood just what was going on and could always go one
step further than he was pushed. I liked him.

He began to look after the three weaker lads as well, not
from compassion at all but with a great show of protecting them
from my viciousness. He played this card so well — brave,
young refugees victimised by cruel oppressor — that I was

forced at last to swing guiltily back towards the road. At one stage in the afternoon we were skirting slopes within a mile of the minibus but they couldn't see it in the rain, and they were going so well that we spent a further two hours treading rocky humps and hollows in the immediate area. Even Tuohy didn't fully realise what was going on, and finally he more than anyone was pleading for release. To a great extent I was punishing them for my own mistake, for trusting them. And further, it shocked me to realise how little they understood me after a week of sustained effort, how readily they accepted ruthlessness from me as if that was all they had expected. A simple equation presented itself: in their relations with the world they expected to bully or to be bullied, exploit or be exploited. No middle ground of shared respect. If I wanted that I would have to level it out myself on a very steep slope indeed, and one getting steeper by the hour — without any assistance from them.

I gave in at last, sat them down, passed round my flask — and learned an incidental truth; no matter how famished they were their own personal tastes — tea or coffee, sugar or not — took precedence. I chatted for the first time all day, commiserating on blisters, resolving broken ankles, lamenting the sorry decline of our 'adventure holiday' and the great distance still to walk — we were nearly half-way. . . . There might be a way out. . . .

Joe smelled compromise, came straight out in the open, negotiating. I could see him in the future trading territory with the law in some city of blackmailed ghettoes. With the instinct of a dealer he seized my delicate drift. No further incidents in exchange for a short-cut. . . .

The deal concluded he sat back; I think he expected a taxi to arrive. Tommo hadn't sat down at all. There were no cigarettes left and he was smoking a biro or something, chewing imaginary gum. He'd eaten the cold, fried egg and guzzled most of the flask — I couldn't bring myself to drink from it after him.

I marched them tactfully away from the bus for twenty minutes, contoured around in driving rain, and in three quarters of an hour they saw it — fortunately, because I had begun to spot our previous tracks with embarrassing frequency. Even Brian joined the stampede, and I had to restrain Tuohy.

No further incidents; but an error had been committed. I should never have made a deal, however tacit. It brought me out of detachment and into their style. I was one of Them now — along with Tuohy and the Director.

For the final week the weather improved. Connemara steamed and shimmered, lakes evaporating in a heatwave. We paddled out to an uninhabited island for the last few days; the real thing, self-sufficiency, Survival! We brought an astounding amount of food. They preferred to leave nothing to their own resources, just in case. I won't say which island — I'd prefer to reserve that crag in case the programme survives.

It's a big, rambling cliff on the seaward side, sheltered from Atlantic swells by a high reef that juts out into the ocean, half-encircling the cliff to take the brunt of the weather. Even on wild days there is a pool of calm water, wide and deep, below the crag. When the sun shines the pool is a glossy, green lagoon full of cool, weedy mystery, its inward eye rimmed by the shadow of the reef. Smooth caverns burrow into the rock floored with shells and sliding shingle. An underwater archway tunnels under the reef out to the open sea, requiring a cool head and a very deep breath to traverse.

On our first day we abseiled down the cliff on two hundred feet of rope (you could walk down a few hundred yards along but never mind), swam out across the lagoon to the reef, the water so warm the wetsuits were irksome. We scrambled up and over the reef, down to a ledge on the seaward side. The unbridled ocean swelled and sucked a long way below.

One by one they took deep breaths, faces tight with excited apprehension, screamed Death to a chosen enemy, and leapt

onto a rising wave. A long way down, the yell strung out
behind, water lifting solid as glass shattered in a cold crash,
down through foaming light, breath clenched, mask clamped
to the face, streaming through the water, wild emerald — then
lunge for the surface, blinding light, cheering faces. . . .

One by one I led them back underwater through the tunnel.
To get enough depth we climbed up high on the reef and
plunged again. Far away down wet light shone through a green
door in the rock. Kick hard with the fins, dive towards it. Enter
the arch. Cool cavern, open at both ends. A roof of rock above,
dark and sinister, the rubber body rises bubbling towards it.
Blow out air to sink, keep kicking — pinned underwater against
the underbelly of the earth . . . Surging up through the inner
pool of warm, calm water, the world bursting with light and
silence, fish flicking, plankton thick as midges, the cold ocean
far behind. Lungs full of rich, golden air. . . .

I ducked back through the arch for the next initiate. All but
Brian recoiled at the entry where the dark rock pressed down
like a tomb. I had each one by the wrist as if to steer, and at that
point a subtle jerk overcame the hesitation and we were down,
through, out before they knew it.

Yes, I thought about rebirth —

Only Tommo and Brian would follow me back through the
tunnel and then return on their own. But when they broke the
surface and threw up their masks in triumph, recognition
clamped down like a visor and they swam apart. . . .

And yet, more than anything before, the tunnel seemed to
unite us in a real sense of adventure. Even Tuohy didn't try to be
superior but yelled and screeched along with them — told how
terrified he'd been until the thrill took over, and they laughed
and made no attempt to cash in on his admission. I thought we
had it made; peace and harmony.

They got their wetsuits off without molesting anybody, and
then grabbed harnesses and ropes. We were going to climb two
hundred feet to the top along the steep, easy ridge formed by
the junction of the reef and the main cliff-face.

I was quietly astonished again by the way they accepted everything now without question, not even as a conscious challenge, but simply the next thing to be done. They accepted the progression of 'adventures' as if it was the natural course of events — they'd jump from a plane tomorrow or climb steep ice if those options were ordained and to hand. Is this how armies get trained? At the heart of elation I felt unease: where does choice stop and programming begin?

They wouldn't dress though, insisting on climbing in togs, in case they fell in — though a parachute would have been a better precaution in that event. By now they were relaxed about ropes and belays, able to protect each other while I soloed along beside them and supervised. Soloing — unroped climbing, normal for an instructor — shocked them, and they had more difficulty with the apparent folly of this than with their own climbing. 'Sir, sir, if you farted you'd be dead, sir!' But now they'd accumulated confident experience and I found it amusing to see how smoothly they swung into gear, accepting things they had thought outrageous at first. Climbing the ridge safely, competently, I saw that — without even knowing it — they were thoroughly enjoying themselves. The warm rock bristled with good holds, but it was steep enough to require technique and attention too, for the sea fell away below us and the rock seemed excitingly undercut and exposed, as if it overhung the water, an optical illusion not uncommon on sea-crags. People, the mainland, the law, seemed to belong to another life — a drab, unappealing existence, the wrong side of parole.

I saw the tunnel-mouth, a pale outline under the sunken reef — but I knew better now than to point it out. Wait till they saw it themselves. Likewise, if I pointed out they were enjoying themselves, or even asked, their faces might still close and the innocence evaporate. So I said nothing, and sure enough they spotted the tunnel and were very smug indeed that I couldn't see it. Tommo went a step further and recognised a lobster in it from a hundred feet up, and when Joe reckoned the tunnel wasn't wide enough for the car and the lobster had to come in on foot like the entry to a particular block of flats, I thought they were back on the old footing again—Jacks among the Rednecks —and I felt a blaze of relief for Tommo. Weeks of sun, wind and hard going had taken the pinched look off their bodies—even if some of the faces could never be rescued from deprivation — they were fit and tanned, red anyway, as they swarmed up the cliff, clad only in swimming togs, climbing belts and shoes. We must have looked extraordinary — if he saw us at all; often the unexpected is invisible — to the small fishing-boat that chugged past the cove picking up lobster-pots. The group turned around on the rock waving fists, yelling obscenities, in case he took 'our' lobster. Fortunately the boat was out of earshot. I was afraid he might misinterpret the gestures and call out a rescue. I was about to point out the new line to be climbed tomorrow, a system of steep cracks wrinkling the centre of the face, but I remembered what I'd learned, waited till we stood on top where it appeared the most attractive choice, and casually suggested they pick something themselves. Sharp eyes narrowing on the options, Joe Curran picked the cracks immediately. He nominated himself and Brian for the first ascent. He made no mention of a third. The rebuff needled through the sunny afternoon. Tommo caught my eye as the others jostled, uncertain of priority.

'Me!' His face was raw, like a creature stripped of feathers.

'Every climb has a name. . . .'

'What'll we call it?' Joe raised the matter next morning. He had a strong sense of ritual.

'*The Jacks are back*!' Tommo whooped irrepressibly. Joe cut his sausages in silent sections.

'Call it *Penal Colony*,' Tuohy gibed; he was reading Kafka, 'Apt in every sense. . . .'

'Why not *Metamorphosis* so?' I was stung to foolishness, 'There's a change going on, you know!'

He grinned at me pityingly, 'You don't know the story, do you? . . .

'They're dung-beetles already.'

No sun that day. A relief; sunburn and salty backs made painful paddling. We were half-camped, half-resident in a deserted cottage, split into two groups of three, one to kayak around the island with Tuohy, in and out of sea-caves, land on inaccessible beaches, trail lines for mackerel, observe birds and seals, throw stones at them — no, we'd eliminated that. And my group, bound for the new route. On the way to the crag Tommo stayed close to me relating rough snatches of his life while Joe and Brian hurried ahead.

'Sir —' he interrupted himself abruptly — 'will it be hard?'

I stopped, examined him in detail, close up. Yesterday's glimpse had given me an insight far behind the bony nose, thin, anxious mouth, crooked eyes. His skull vibrated slightly as he focused on me. I stared harder, the way you examine someone sleeping, and know without doubt what you really think. He returned the scrutiny, attempting some painful exchange, his chin raised, the sad teeth jutting, and the slight vibration continuing all the time . . . was it the reason, I wondered, for that sense of jittering motion — his body chasing round to keep up with those eyes?

Climbing was not his strength, he didn't have precision-skills either — couldn't hit a dartboard or a cue-ball. An optical problem?

What to say? . . . I understood the power of the simple, universal fantasy, how he hoped to shine, to triumph, to reinstate himself.

I couldn't help him with it. The exchange faltered.

'No harder than what you've done, Tommo. But doing something new is always special. For yourself! . . . For yourself, Tommo! Do you understand?'

He broke away. All he'd heard was the special promise.

He withered on the rock. Turned his head and shot me a look of anger and despair. We both knew I shouldn't have let him try.

'Steady up, Tommo! Get a grip on yourself!' Joe mimed my advice with a vulgar snigger. Dung-beetle is right.

All Tommo had to do was reach up, grasp a pointed flake above his head, pull hard, and swing his left foot up to a large, flat hold. After that the crack leaned back again. The position was intimidating, not technical. He would have lunged awkwardly up without a second thought if the rope was above him, me anchored on a ledge taking it in as fast as he came. Now, with the rope below — leading — he couldn't climb. He knew immediately he couldn't do it, so the time he spent there had no forward motion at all. The day thickened around him, waiting. The sea rested against the foot of the cliff, the tide ceased to go in or out. Even the sun wasn't going anywhere until Tommo made his decision.

Standing on similar holds, five feet away, I saw how simple the moves were — easy for me, impossible for him — I felt a stab of impatience, angry that his big moment could collapse so simply, become such a trite catastrophe.

'Come on, Tommo . . . Do it!'

He found it difficult even to remain straddled where he was, his limbs wilting towards the belay-ledge. He shot me another stark glance, not angry, not imploring either; in his need he measured me for help — I failed him again.

On the ledge below, silence. They would not sneer at climbing-failure. Too close to the common bone. But he had thrust himself to the fore to lead the crux, 'the glory-bit' he called it, brushing aside their furious objections with my support — given against my better judgement, suspecting as I did that he'd been cultivating it on the way across under the guise of intimacy.

Joe and Brian stood braced against the belay, feet planted firmly on the rock. Joe held Tommo's rope in a belay-plate, there was no danger, even if he fell — and yet, in their cold silence, the refusal to console, something awful was occurring, a deliberate accident. I guided Tommo's heels back down an awkward move to the ledge. Through the suede I felt sharp bones tremble. I smelled failure on his clothes, a stale, distasteful whiff — cigarette smoke and nervous sweat. Hard not to avert my face. I chatted with hollow levity, patted shoulders, clipped and unclipped ropes. No response.

Brian was next. Too late to call it off, the inevitable was launched. He was animated, anticipation on his flushed cheeks. He had a fit, springy look today. Clothes always fitted him well — which is a quality of the body, not the clothes — his hair seemed to belong neatly to his head too; the others were all lank or shock-headed as if a casual scalp had been grafted to the skull. Joe kept his sleek and sharp, which wasn't the same thing at all either. He held Brian's rope with the cold concentration of a boxing-manager; someone else takes the punches, he takes a profit. Tommo hunched against the rock, staring blindly at the sea. The rest of us can creep home afterwards with the pieces. . . .

Brian reached up for two handholds, launched from the ledge; like grasping the handlebars of a bike and coasting smoothly away — reflexive as that. The holds conformed fluidly to his needs, a smooth climber, skill and balance. He took the hard move first try, not lunging or swinging, a delicate step.

I leaned across discreetly, placed a chock in the crack above him. He disdained the interference, lifted out the nut, jammed it in another position more to his satisfaction and clipped the rope through the karabiner. Independence. If he fell the chock would hold the rope and Joe could take the force below. Above the crux he paused in mid-move, giggled down at the belay. I moved up the crack beside him, ready to place another runner to continue his protection, I realised I was watching something new, blatant, exposed. Behind us the day was quiet; the sigh of the sea and the crying of birds underlined a tense, cinematic silence. Slither of soles on rock, hiss of breath. Faces below. I barely existed for these three — they were in an elemental, adolescent world. I sensed its secret, ugly terms making a parallel ascent along lines of tension that must not overlap ours.

Brian was showing off. I handed him another runner. He snatched it without a glance, placed it properly, clipped in. His moves were exaggerated now, made for effect, expressing his ability, celebrating himself and his exposure. I glanced down at the ledge; Joe smirked, Tommo's face was knotted.

I knew there would be another ropelength of easier climbing up above. Tommo could lead that, I thought, be first to the top of the cliff — a hollow satisfaction, having failed on the glory-bit — but the hardest part of growing up is coming to terms with hollow satisfactions. . . .

Brian performed an intricate series of moves in his private, smiling dance — wide bridges and high steps, leaning out on handholds, posing instinctively. I warned him sharply.

Fifty feet above the belay, with three good runners below, he pulled up on a steep flake, leaned far out in silhouette. The surge of movement stalled. He tugged sharply, grunting with annoyance, fingers whitening on the rock. The rope strained; 'Slack!' I yelled at Joe, and then I saw the problem. The rope had slipped into a sharp crack above the belay and jammed solid. Joe — it was actually his fault — tried to flick it out from below without success. I was reluctant to climb down and leave Brian alone.

'Tommo! Reach up and pull it out! Tommo . . . !' I called confidently on the kinship of the rope. He stood still a moment, his face a white blotch, then he obeyed. Reached up high, gripped the rope below the pinch, and tugged it sharply outwards. A few jerks and it came free. I turned back to Brian. Time for another runner. He was swinging nonchalantly on the flake, showing off again. Below him the rope still flicked. Angry, hissing voices, a scuffle. I thought Tommo mistook the runners for constrictions on the rope. He whipped it savagely. The first nut lifted out.

'Stop it, Tommo! Stop. . . .'

The second runner lifted. Joe's knuckles lashed. He knew how to hurt, the pain far sharper than the blow.

Tommo shrieked. Like an electric shock the sound whipped

up along the rope, the last nut popped, the rope stretched tight as wire.

If Brian fell he'd hit the sea.

I clawed across to place a runner. Another blow . . . a shriek.

Brian's waist jerked suddenly, arms shockloaded, one foot torn free, hands hooked tight . . . I clung to the rock — as if the whole crag moved.

'Tommo! Tommo — !' Shuddering, jolting, he clenched the rope. Then Brian laughed, sharp and shocking as a blade. Tommo slumped below. I saw him outlined against the water, misshapen, adrift.

Brian swung smoothly up the flake, sauntered towards a ledge. I vaulted after him, threw in a nut and clamped him roughly to it.

Safe! Safe! I tried to shake him, to yell with nervous tension, but he looked right through me, indifference in his eye. I did not exist.

I couldn't bring Tommo up to the same ledge as Brian, neither could I leave him alone below; he might untie. He had the look of exhausted options.

'Brian, bring Joe up here — then wait!' I shook him with violent satisfaction, 'WAIT! Do you hear?'

I climbed down to Tommo while Joe came up. It was chilling to see them, Joe moving coldly past me, while above him Brian fished tranquilly with the rope as if there were no vicious shadows darting for hooks under the surface. But I knew Joe wasn't going that way for long — no longer than he needed the rope to get him off the alien angle of the cliff. I'd learned to recognise intuitive truths from that zone they inhabited where instinct moved events and nothing seemed normal at first.

Joe was through with Brian — afraid of his unpredictability. Like myself, Joe understood he couldn't hope to control the source of that laugh. And just as he'd dropped Tommo for being arbitrary, now he would drop Brian for an even deeper inconsistency, a private anarchy that could not be resolved. But in their totally different worlds neither Brian nor Joe would ever be lonely — each was sufficient to himself.

As soon as I reached him Tommo broke down. Not a response to me as a person — more as if a witness, any witness, confirmed what he felt.

Misery, betrayal convulsed him with pain. 'He — was — *my* — friend!' More than a friend; blood-brother, tribesman. . . .

There was violent anger in him still.

'The bastard!! I'll get him —' he swore. For a moment I thought he meant Brian, then I understood again. And I knew what Tommo must do to survive; turn his pain into hatred, and freeze the wound.

WHOM THE GODS LOVE

No one will die in this story. That is a promise (as if I controlled events, pen slicing and splicing ropes at will). Good health to the unhappy child, and long life. He deserves it for a multitude of reasons, not least the coal-black wing of hair across (I swear) a green-eyed glance, or that grin of rapturous collusion with his mother when one of his many skills delighted her.

I do not control anything here. It wasn't I who chose climbing for him. She got him into that. Until then Alan held the reins; afterwards he was just his mother's son. And yet, how often does one encounter that much grace, talent, imagination, heaped upon each other without conceit or reticence, all reflected openly in a generous gaze that searches for the best thing in you, however deeply hidden. When it happens the world had better keep its distance, and its balance.

I fell in love with Alan's mother, incurably, long ago before he was born. Before the story started. We all did. We walked and climbed with her like courtiers on weekends in the Wicklow hills. Her vividness intoxicated us until gusts of wordless feeling strained the dullness of our skulls and our voices barked with ecstasy running wild on windy summer days.

We were in love with fantasy, an image by Mills & Boon, daughter of the mountains, hair blowing in the breeze, one hand shading a faraway, eclectic gaze, the other fondling a long-tongued adoring dog. That is not how she ever was at all — although she had that face, the impossible cheekbones, the rich hair, green eyes, slender, striding figure lost in lyrical distance then moments later laughing, singing, shouting out energy while we yelped and bayed at her heels, feeling, not like dogs, but heroes — or fine horses at the least.

She betrayed us for a stranger. He came strolling in from someone else's story, assured and powerful with officerly manners and swept her away for a whole day to climb an unexplored cliff. It hangs hideously on the hillside opposite the real crag at Glendalough. Born on the wrong side of a granite rift it is illegitimate geology, sunless, uncouth and overgrown.

She left the hut again with him in withered moonlight and returned alone at dawn. Though we were all awake no one stirred or whispered, not even I who blazed with pain in the darkness. I raged against the sound of tears. What right had she to cry?

She lay between us sorrowing as if no one else existed. What window had he revealed onto a radiance that none of us would ever feel? She owed us nothing, but it was still betrayal. A soldier on holiday, who never came again; only his initials appeared on that route-description, unrepeated and long-forgotten, and yet she bore Alan not like a grudge but with all the radiance of a state of grace.

I had no influence then, I have none now. Description cannot catch her for me. In truth she controls me, refusing the slow redemption that ageing memory should allow. I will not change her story! There is a tempting notion (you know it if you have been hurt enough) that existence is a thing already written, beyond revision. Too late to leap up on the page in the shadow of the fatal word and wrench the inky keys aside in a skid of asterisks and fractions; already, in some other universe, monstrous and sentimental, something turns the pages, devouring us. . . .

I do not believe it. All of us, Alan too, create our own existences. Independent of our creators. Some die on absurd mountains having brought themselves to that. Most live bedside lives the surer to die that way. Some are dispatched like crows as warning to the rest. And a few hang themselves with the shadow of a rope.

She took Alan to the hills before he was six months old. Always alone except for him. It was she who kept her distance. Some tried friendship and were shunned as if their sympathy was suspect. Alan grew to be extraordinary, no one could deny that no matter how they wished to hurt. He had her kind of beauty, and more. And he had something else that was less definable, more dangerous — a sense of intensely temporary presence, that vulnerability of the foundling, as if he might disappear as shatteringly as he had arrived. But the ache of his presence was irresistible, signifying urgencies we could never have known, never have suffered without him.

And none of us could have fathered a magical child like that. Our creatures, those of us who tried, were dull, wooden things by comparison.

He had talent of course. He glowed with abundance. Often, as he grew older, I saw them outlined on some neglected ridge in Kerry, Connemara or Donegal, the tall mother and her skipping child singing crystal-sharp harmonies that ached against the sky and rang close, too close, to — disintegration? Bitterly I questioned the clear air around my solitude, hammering these knuckles on its empty mirror that reflected everything in my heart. I heard them on frozen Brandon once, overlooking the Atlantic ocean when the child was ten, and then it seemed to me that a shivering fracture ran out across the sea and cold as ice I trembled there and felt the mirror shatter in the thin, high air.

I protest my innocence again in all of this. No, I do not choose climbing for the child, the way one might place a cherished thing in danger in case the urge to kill struck suddenly at midnight when the pen is drained of all compassion and only revenge will ease the pain. And death so easily written. . . .

She could have chosen music, painting, dance — anything but this frightful leap and recoil, leap and recoil, and the dreadful lunging for the edge of the obvious, struggling to re-enter this flat, simple world — as if being born into it had not been hard enough to last a lifetime.

Of course she wished to follow him.

Alan took to it with delight at first. He thought it hilarious, it seemed so extraordinarily ordered. And yet how subtly it changed the physics of his world. As if he had found wings and discovered the buoyancy of air. In every element now he saw the hidden ways and secret corridors of fantasy manifest themselves. If he could walk up cliffs then surely he could pass through walls, thought-transfer to other planets.

His mother's slow, uncertain progress gave him his first exhilarating taste of scorn. She who always seemed so proud and purposeful grew ponderous on the rock, could not see into it at all. She fought it blindly for concessions. Alan was gifted— rock seemed to flex to his hands and feet.

He played to his audience, she above or below, and I—I was always near, ornithologist with beard, tweed hat, binoculars and camera. And the third . . . The soldier still appeared in all my nightmares, bright and fleet as Mercury, mocking me. My only consolation was that he could not see the dazzling iridescence he had wrought. And yet with every year he came closer to reincarnation in his child. No one could forget.

She knew it, wanted it. She pushed him fiercely towards the source. Maternal love became a hard excitement, it was her will now that drove him towards achievement. He lost his own determination. He was leading hard, skidding through the grades and often now the holds were tilted upside down and all the cracks were blind. Surface had begun to close against him.

And yet he retained enchantment, though under pressure it became a fugitive charm, wide eyes too wide, the skin transparent, hair limp with sweat, limbs trembling towards escape as he reached the final holds on an adult route.

At thirteen he stands below his first Extreme. She fusses round him, plucking, fitting, fixing, crooning. In another moment she may attempt to comb his hair and he will wrench away. But that's not it at all; he doesn't want to leave. He lingers, clinging, until she straightens, shoves him firmly towards the rock.

At the base of a granite slab that steepens at twenty feet into a wall and then at forty feet becomes an overhang so that the whole climb points to the ground like a harshly polished chute, she stops to tie him on. Drapes the new rope on the ground and kneels to the level of his harness. Above her shoulder, released from observation, his face is a mask of fear. The camera whirrs.

The sun glares into her eyes from the mica-sprinkled slab with the dazzle of another day. Blind behind its prism she binds him to the shadow of his father's rope and pays it out into the past. He is gone, stepping gravely, grievously onto the slab without a kiss or any murmur of farewell. The old rope tears at her heart, she pushes it out to spare the pain, up the slab on tiptoe, onto the wall — it overhangs a little and he swings from hold to unprotected hold towards the looming roof.

Scrabbling at the lip his feet swing free, he starts the dreadful mantelshelf, she hears the breath rattle in his throat and her heart stammers in terrifying unison. The only sound in all the world. He drops to arms-length, feet kicking for support and then begins to haul again.

In her hands the rope is loose and useless as memory. It cannot draw him back. Panic-stricken she tugs and the coils twitch unattached towards her. Slowly the child unsticks from the rim of the story and tumbles backwards into space. The camera whirrs and whirrs.

Falling on her knees against the slab she throws out archetypal, anguished arms.

He will not die, for there was a promise made, but he has reached his highest point and failed. And now, throughout their lives, he'll be forever falling towards her.

THE WHITE GRAPH

It's been snowing now for three days, snow to 2,000 metres last night. I'm getting nervous; it's just like the first time twelve years ago. That summer, too, I came from chaos . . . drink, debt, divorce — I didn't care, I was in Chamonix where the sun shone and nothing mattered but sky-high rock, ice, and dreams. Rousie, Tut, Minksy — warlords of the Alps — were on Snell's Field pulling off First British Ascents every day of the week. Seemed you only had to stroll off the campsite to bag a first ascent if you were one of their gang. They hadn't heard of me yet — but I was determined they'd never forget. I came to the mountains of my mind like a thunderbolt, mad with pain and a rage to do great things.

The Blaitière was a buzz-route then, the West Face of the 'Blat', famous for the Fissure Brown. The good weather hadn't ended and we marched uphill the day we arrived. I'd a mate from Salford in tow, so morose he hardly ever spoke. We humped our new Joe Browns all the way to the Plan des Aiguilles full of paraffin, tins of stew, and no stove, broad feet tormented in narrow French boots. We bivvied badly by the Lac Bleu and ate the stew cold, grease and all. The Blat was the biggest crag I'd ever seen, but it looked easy. I couldn't make a figure 4 of that rock-scar though — more like South America, after an earthquake.

We left the bivouac before dawn and got to the Fissure Brown at nine. Started in the wrong place and climbed dribbling, gravelly pitches before we found the famous crack. From far below it looked like a secure hand-and-fist job, which meant it must be stinking offwidth. Close up, in the morning mist, it was a broad black cleft in cold granite. A short pillar at the foot, and after that nothing at all but the Fissure itself. The face leaned back a bit but the crack bulged to contradict it. No wedges either. I'd been promised wedges; sometimes, they said, you could climb it like the rungs of a ladder and get on with the real climbing then. It had been stripped by some thieving purist.

I attacked at the run in rucksack and boots, that mad flourish meant to bulldoze an obstacle with a frenzy of confidence. Like a bad fighter. Foreign leather thudded on foreign rock, and rebounded.

Fists, arms, shoulders rattled within the crack. I squirmed up a few feet and stuck solid, arm-wrestling the mountain. The right edge of the crack leaned out past my shoulder and the rucksack jammed. That crack had a feel for Joe Brown. The harder I wriggled the more firmly the sack jammed and dragged my hands out of the crack. I had no sense of discretion then, no idea how to retreat gracefully and sneak back streamlined so that the Fissure wouldn't notice me any more than it had to.

Instead I pulled brutally. Trying to pass through a narrowly-opened door with a rucksack on. Something had to give. And it wasn't even a French crack: I didn't have the excuse that it was some kind of Frog-stuff that a Brit wouldn't know how to stoop to. Brown did it first, Joe-bloody-Brown whose routes I was flashing in Wales with the arrogance always typical of the next generation but one.

Something gave. It sounded like muscle or bone, it should have been, but it was only the metal stiffener in the toughest sack ever made. Bending to my fury.

The left edge of the crack is composed of little overlaps, snub shapes as tightly moulded to the rock as paint-runs to a doorframe. Nothing to get the fingers behind, the rock gloss-cold and hostile. Higher up, a peg. Someone had nursed a blade into a fault. I hung on it, swung on it nearly an hour before I got the next moves figured — a hex wedged between crystals, slings to step in, slings to haul on and a sling to lasso, and the huge squashed rucksack still on my back.

My mate said nothing, but the pile of butts grew around his

solid feet. He accepted that this was how it was meant to be, because I said so, and there was no reason to doubt it. Above our heads a thousand feet of grooves and cracks burrowed into the low, grey clouds towards the summit — where we bivouacked exhausted and storm-tossed in the dark after twelve hours' climbing, never thinking not to finish what we'd begun, since life was hard anyway so why would climbing be any different?

So where does this wisdom — this sanity — come from at last? Is it a victory over myself, or just the peace of exhaustion? Hardly. Exhaustion brings dullness, not peace; and there are no victories, just compromise — between reality and desire. Wisdom, I know now, is a kind of dignified cunning. The same goes for sanity. Quote me on that.

What happened in those bitter years? I could describe the breakdown maybe — or the climbing, its occasional success — the lifestyle, relationships like feverish collisions, rebuttal and rebuff . . . but what really happened overall was — hardship. Emotional hardship — as if time was a long journey in bad weather and I could seldom see clearly enough to know if I was getting anywhere at all. But sometimes the clouds parted and there was flash of intense perspective. Lucid moments when the heart was seen to have failed again. The shape of my life linked those moments together.

A black graph. The white graph is only its shadow. An illusion.

In a cold dawn, less than a week ago, I left the Plan cable-car at a run. My partner this time was young and ambitious, a good rock-climber, if hints were facts. We met in the Bar-Nash. First route of the season for both of us.

He was keen enough to do the Blaitière though I got the feeling he was lowering his sights. He knew a lot about the trendier lines on the face but I was set on the old British route and there was no argument. He knew I'd been on it before — when he was a boy. I think he viewed the idea with as close an approach to indulgence as he could manage.

I tried rapport for a while — 'What d'you do for a crust, Andy?'

'I don't. . . .'

Shivering in the dark in Cham while the guides filled the first 'férique — 'You married yet, Andy?'

He jerked his head at the boring idea. They don't scramble to marry in their teens like we did. Not he smart ones anyway.

'You?' He had no interest. . . .

'Yeah. Four kids.' He was totally shocked; obviously I'd sold out. No commitment to climbing. He shuddered at the prospect of dribbling snapshots, or worse still—when courage was wanted on the route would I plead fatherhood?

So I didn't tell him I hadn't seen my kids for two years. While I'd been locked away. Or about their various mothers. . . .

I set a scorching pace across the moraine, breakneck boulder-hopping to rattle him. I know there's no way to beat these younger lads technically — all you can do is concede their strengths, and maybe gain a little on the rough ground. Andy tried to keep pace with me, once or twice he found quicker detours, until we left the moraine and headed up the glacier below the Brégeault Ridge.

The remote smoothness of the Blaitière had broken into features; the Red Pillar, the slabs, the grey scar, the sceptical wrinkles of the Brown Route — all showed the versatility of a face that used to be known for one route only.

Irritated by Andy's grimness I didn't pause for crampons. I counted on the gravel embedded in the ice to get me up the glacier, guessing from his comments that he might be less cocky on ice. Last year his first season finished in a crevasse in the Argentière Basin. Could happen to anyone, sure; those holes are so crowded it can be hard to get in.

'Ice is basically boring,' he'd lectured me, 'same move over and over. Now, Rock makes you Think. . . .'

A dead giveaway; never done any mixed!

No, I wasn't putting him down competitively—just storing up space for myself in what I feared could be an unbalanced day at my expense. It worked so well I was almost ashamed when he crawled onto the rock white-faced after resorting to crampons on the lip of a crevasse for the last snowbank. A fall there would have corpsed him. He admitted to feeling shaky but he put it down to a bad stomach, 'Dodgy bottle of wine last night. . . .'

Pathetic! Obviously it was altitude, acclimatization, arrogance — but he had to learn all that himself. He was in the right company. Efficiently sorting rock-gear and ropes I offered — without actually pausing — to sit around for a while till he recovered.

'Nah, I'm alright.' Curt, as if to say, Rock? I won't have any problems. It's you I'm worried about, mate!

The grey stubble and the belly can have that effect. But it never fails to disappoint me how fucking military the young alpinists are now, as if — under a veneer of anarchy — survival is a strict Commando-code forbidding any weakness or self-doubt.

Well, if he fancied discipline . . . 'You start,' I gave him his orders. 'There's the Fissure Brown. It's offwidth and it overhangs, but it's not too bad otherwise.'

He looked as shattered as his stiff lip allowed: 'Don't think I feel up to it yet. . . .' Nausea churned audibly in his stomach like an undigested fry. He looked around for a hole to crawl into. Not broken enough yet to drop his salopettes on the windswept terrace.

'Okay, I'll start,' I offered. Kindly, exultantly, I was prepared for this: one of those victorious moments brought about by willpower and pure need. It was going to be my day after all.

'I'll do the variation-start. No sense repeating myself. . . .'

To the left of the Fissure Brown — and climbing to the same belay — there is an alternative pitch, a hand-crack! Visually stunning. The first section is littered with easy flakes, and then the clean crack rises, sinuous and soaring, as if it had sloughed all its features without quite extricating its tail from the clutter. And up at the top there is a thin, sharp snake-bite.

Beside this elegant pitch the Fissure Brown is a boa constrictor. How had I missed it a dozen years ago when I needed it most?

And Brown? Had they ploughed their muscular furrow by choice, or had the hand-crack been cleaned into view since?

I'd been briefed and I came prepared; two big hexes and two large Friends, not the kind of gear you drag up alpine routes without advice.

I like jamming-cracks. Don't ever go by grade: there are cracks designed to encourage you up a wall, and cracks that try to throw you off — no matter how hard or easy. The two starts to this route are perfect examples of that.

After the flakes the pitch came clean, and then it was perfect handwidth, no holds, and so deep it must go right to the core of the Mont Blanc range. I swear a distant breath of lava warmed my fingertips as I reached inside. I might fail here for want of strength or will, but I could not fall off. The grey rock clamped me to it, clenched me hand and foot, owned me. . . .

I was gripped like a fossil, a lichen, a micro-insect whose wildest scuttlings down a hundred generations could not take it off the mountain. This crack absorbed everything. It was no random fault like the Fissure Brown but one of those points where the perfect geometry of rock forces the imperfect nature of the climber to submit, no — not to its difficulty, but to its relentless form and meaning. I'd been thinking a lot about climbing while I was ill, and it was as if I'd created this pitch for my return. But already, on the first move, I was afraid. Afraid of myself. Afraid I would be climbing this ruthless crack forever, jamming on past the belay, past the Fontaine ledges, past the summit, climbing on into personal space, permanently locked away in its cold, burning grip.

I climbed it to preserve my identity, my freedom — flailing forward the way a swimmer among sharks lifts himself whole out of the water; I climbed without a pause for protection, lifting myself whole from the rock with every stroke. . . .

Yeah, I know that's complex — schizoid maybe, but I take

climbing seriously. I'd a lot of time to work it out. Sometimes, at bare and powerful moments it stood for all the things I've never done or felt.

5a for ninety feet, at the top it squeezed, demanded more, a 5b finger-jam with the toes twisted and chewed, exposed ankles trembling a rope-length from the terrace, too fast and late for protection now. A huge handhold . . . Like too much dope too soon, heart and brain ejaculating through the skull. I doubled over on the belay to control the dizziness, the fear of pitching head-first down the crack — and found I was staring down the cold slot of the Fissure Brown, listening as I groaned and cursed towards the light in that tunnel of years.

Andy came up greyfaced, technically perfect, mentally stunned. No aesthetic spark. Looking at the thin mouth and inward eyes I knew he never recognised — never trusted — anything outside himself. And that he was ideal for me; I could do him no harm.

'You mad bastard!' he grunted, and then in case any admiration had shown through, 'Didn't have gear in your day, did they?'

'You still sick?' I didn't wait for an answer, 'I'll go ahead for a while.'

I felt great, perilously liberated from myself and yet complete, as if a thin gap — the width of that crack and no more — had opened up between me and the past. I'd have to cross over again on the way down, but things might be different, or I might have changed by then.

You can't change reality, I know, but you can see it differently.

For a while.

A groove hung above us, steep, tight, V-shaped, heading into overhangs. I had worked it grimly before, a miner in a sullen seam. Now I could bridge, chimney, shimmy, lean out or in, use the groove or refuse it. Clip a peg and skip the next three. I whooped past belays to run out a full rope every time, forcing Andy to climb with me till I reached the stance I fancied.

The overhang on good holds. Strenuous, not hard. Belayed above I scanned the routes I knew; the North Face of the Plan had lost its simple trick, the séracs a shambles, the ice-corridor gone and no safe way through. Over on the Peigne the North Ridge was deserted too, a grovelling grooveline totally out of vogue. But the routes on the slabs would be alive with dancers dressed for the crag, a cluster of bolts the only summit they sought. I could hear them yodelling on the Blaitière too.

'Wheeeeeeeee-Hah!' I responded. Good luck to them!

Andy was on the overhang. He'd solo it at home if he stooped to the standard, barely 5a, but he grappled with gritted teeth, body trembling with the effort of altitude. Yet he unclipped a sling from a peg and looped it neatly around his neck while clinging to the rock with failing fingers; just because I was watching him. Pride!

'Pull on 'em, Andy,' I goaded, 'That's what they're for!'

A ferocious glare, and I tried to think how to say I hadn't pulled on them either — because I hadn't *needed* to. . . .

The route unravelled at a manic pace, grooves, cracks, a delicate slab, all free and sound. Heart and breath raced like rock and roll towards a climax, yet I consumed every move with the greed of the half-starved, the long locked-away. What else is there, apart from good sex, to equal it? Big game hunting? Bull-fighting? War? Hemingway missed out on the best.

Andy was losing his grip. I had to be impressed with his staying-power, though, he'd a hell of a last gasp in him. He'd suit me alright. Badly dehydrated too, and I'd left the water-bottle at the foot of the route. Yeah, sorry. . . .

We were on target for a three-hour ascent; not bad for a first route. He was too burnt-out to argue, too proud to plead, but his whole manner was a violent complaint against the route.

He wanted to go down — I could feel it in the drag of the rope, hear it in his strangled curses. He couldn't handle the climbing on the day, so he didn't care about the mountain. It was not a thing in itself apart from his capacity for it.

I may come across as a hard bastard here, but I do have standards. I have respect. Even at my worst a dozen years ago I only wanted to match up to the magnificence of the Alps, to find some reflection of them in me. Andy wanted to use them to exhibit his own talent, and when it didn't work out he blamed everything but himself. Especially the mountain.

The last pitches to the Fontaine Ledges were sustained cracks, sweet and cunning as anything on a Yosemite wall. People abseil off there, the best climbing over, the summit irrelevant. I'd been to the top so I felt no need to go again—but I owed Andy a little further education. No, I didn't want to make a better man of him—I wouldn't presume—I was just trying to stop him getting worse.

'We're going to the top, Andy. . . .' He was slumped on the last belay, destination and descent on his face. '. . . It'll take another couple of hours.'

He had breath to spare for a snarl; 'I'm not going to any bloody top! There's just rubbish left. . . .'

'Is that so? You'd better traverse off the Brégeault Ridge then, because I'm going up. I'll nip down the Spencer Couloir on the other side, so I won't be back this way.' That was a bluff; I wouldn't touch the Spencer at dawn, never mind midday.

He almost came. The soldier in him struggled to submit to discipline. Then the human being, the failed mountaineer, conquered him for the best. 'I don't want to go any further,' he whimpered, 'I want to go down . . . now!'

'Want to?' I echoed with interest, 'Want to! Why?'

He scraped together the shreds of his ego, and threw them away: 'I'm not able to go on. I'm done for . . . burned out. . . .' If there had been enough liquid in him he would have cried.

'Why didn't you tell me, Andy?' Full of shocked sympathy and surprise I fixed an abseil.

Maybe I did rub his nose in it; but believe me he needed it—just as I need the elation, the power, the control that I know —I *know* — are only an illusion. The fact I can race up a small mountain won't make me any better at the other things I do and don't do.

Still, it will calm me if I make it endure; it will dissolve the poison in my blood, the anger that builds up and up till it threatens the heart and must be purged.

If there is any such thing as wisdom for me it means knowing when to cut loose. And choosing a victim, to spare the ones I love.

If I do half a dozen routes with Andy now, get the Walker and the Frêney done, maybe shoot over to Zermatt, I just might . . . pull things into shape this winter. If she's crazy enough to let me try.

DARK MOURNE

Steve was disappointed already. Green hedges and fields, green leafy trees, green sky . . . he had expected the Republic to start thinning out by now. Where was the red and blue of Northern Ireland? Standing up on his pedals, he scanned the wide, green landscape.

The three boys had left the train at Dundalk and cycled north towards the Border. Jim rode in front, as he had all the way. Fair haired, serious, stocky, he set the pace with muscular monotony. The trip had been his idea — a week in the Mournes, cycling and hillwalking, a little rock-climbing too — an exercise in self-reliance and observation. But he had failed to enlist ideal companions, friends who shared his own solid outlook and physique. The North was off-limits to most parents.

'Hurry up!' he shouted back importantly. 'We're near the *Border*!'

'What's the matter?' Steve grinned, 'does it shut, or what?'

Paddy, the youngest, had persuaded his family that the trip would broaden his horizons. He half-suspected his mother would let him go to a brothel if he could prove it was educational — and easy on his asthma! He was proud of her tolerance. To Paddy, everything in his life so far was an opportunity for the intellect.

His glasses were steamed up with the effort. The saddle was too high for his small body and he lunged at the pedals.

Formal education — he thought excitedly, sweat flying from his face — distorts reality. It does! It was obvious outside the classroom cage. Take geography . . . take history! Look how this landscape had absorbed its past like fertilizer and become ordinary, neutral farmland. He had been led to expect the topography of violent division. School history gave an impression of endless ancient conspiracy tearing the country. But this modern Ireland was not an extension of the past at all. It was an extension of the EEC! Bland as butter. And there's another thing — he thought severely — television! That doesn't do much for reality, either. . . .

'Why don't you shorten the pedals?' Steve interrupted cheerfully.

Paddy's brain seldom stooped to mechanics. 'I couldn't!' he flustered. 'It's my brother's bike. . . .'

'Oh well in that case — we'll drop the saddle instead.'

Jim cycled back impatiently, 'What's wrong now for God's sake. . . .'

'Looking for a spanner. . . .' Paddy explained,

'To drop the saddle. . . .' Steve added. 'The nut is rusty.' He eyed his friend thoughtfully. 'Maybe we could build up your feet. . . .'

The small intellectual poked a lurid packet hastily back into his saddle-bag. 'What's that?' Jim demanded, 'let me see. . . .' Paddy coloured miserably.

'*Snake-Bite Kit*!' Jim read in strangled tones.'*Antidote to all poisonous snake-bites including Rattlers, Cobras, and Black . . . Black Mambas . . .* Black Mambas? In the Mournes?' He goggled at Paddy.

'It was a mistake,' Paddy mumbled.

'That's right,' Steve defended breezily. 'Could happen to anyone. He meant to get spider-stuff instead. Tarantulas, Black Widows. . . .'

Paddy lifted a look of hurt betrayal but Steve was launched. 'You missed it, Jim. We were in the Mountain Shop last week. You know your woman there?'

'Martina?' The story threatened to dissolve into enjoyment already.

'Poor Paddy didn't know Martina's form at all. He had her on the gallop for half an hour, trying things on, changing his mind, asking questions — all in the interests of science, of course, and free exchange of information, nothing commercial involved. And she waiting to go to her lunch! In the end. . . .'

He giggled affectionately at Paddy's downcast face. '. . . In the end he bought a pair of bootlaces and when she slapped them up in front of him only asked if she had them in a different colour!'

Jim hooted incredulously, 'Martina?!'

'Well they were bright yellow!' Paddy muttered.

'. . . Just as she was about to break him in two, Paddy spotted all this junk on a shelf. *Commando* packets! There was a bit of sharp wire in one, a *Survival Saw* — that's for firewood, amputations, useful stuff like that . . . never know when you might want to whip off a leg — but Paddy zoomed in on the *Snake-Bite Kit*. You should have heard his voice! Pure rapture: "How much are *they*?" . . .

'Martina ripped one off the shelf—nearly took the wall with it and into the bag it went along with the yellow laces . . . "Snake-Bite Kit," she said, "Two Pound Fifty."' Steve choked on her husky snarl.

'*Two Pound Fifty*?'

'Well he couldn't turn it down. He'd have been bitten sooner than he expected if he had!'

'And you know what the worst thing was . . . ?' Paddy let out a snort of reluctant laughter. When she yelled the magic words "Snake-Bite", everybody in the whole shop turned round to gawp. They thought I was off to the Amazon, or somewhere! I couldn't let them down!'

He grinned and replaced the packet. 'Anyway it might come in handy some day.'

'If we meet Ian Paisley!' Steve giggled.

'Oh no!' Jim shook his head emphatically. 'That fellow doesn't bite you. He swallows you whole!'

The Border was an anti-climax: an ugly building by the roadside, shrouded trailers in a lay-by, Ireland stretching meagrely ahead. They obeyed the battered STOP-sign. Two cars flashed past, one in each direction, without a pause. Jim held his breath for the high-speed pursuit, the sound of sirens. Nothing stirred — officially. A crow settled on a verge and began unofficially picking seed.

A hand waved behind a window. Jim waved back—almost a salute. He was conscious of cultural identity clothing him like a uniform. Steve and Paddy were already careering into the North. Jim was forced to follow, unrecorded. His passport rankled in his pocket. He was fond of correct procedure.

'My God!' he exploded when they were clear. 'We could be smugglers or terrorists, or. . . .' He glared at his two companions, their pink legs protruding from wrinkled football shorts, innocent surprise in their eyes, ' — or schoolboys,' he finished sheepishly.

Round the first bend Jim pulled in. 'Map time!'

Next to his passport Jim loved his map. Paddy took his glasses off. An impressive spray of sweat sprinkled the dust. 'Don't bother,' he chirped. 'It's the A1 to Newry four miles, turn right B8 to Hilltown nine miles, B27 towards Kilkeel. Four miles to the Spelga Dam, four more — turn left towards Newcastle, mile and a half to the Silent Valley . . .'

He gasped for breath. 'Uphill all the way!'

Steve took Paddy's brain for granted, 'How far's all that?'

'Nearly twenty-five miles.'

'Are you sure you didn't add in the road-numbers?' The two friends rattled together with enjoyment. Thwarted, Jim fondled his map. 'I thought you said you were never here before. . . .'

'I wasn't! I checked the map on the train . . .' Paddy beamed, '. . . measured it with a thread. While you were chatting up schoolgirls. Or trying to!'

Before they moved away, Steve nudged Jim. Gleefully he indicated their small companion wobbling at the roadside. The bike was absentmindedly stuck in top gear and the loaded panniers clamped the back wheel to the tarmac. Paddy's pert features were concentrated with effort and his baggy shorts gave the impression of creeping up towards his armpits. Affectionately Steve tapped a hollow-sounding forehead. 'He's got it up here, though,' he said. 'Where it counts. . . .'

'This *must* be it!'

Twenty-five miles later a dark laneway, overhung with hawthorns, tunnelled into the night.

'Bloody dynamos!' Jim cursed wretchedly. 'Why did no-one bring a torch?' He felt their disapproval glow in the dark. Wasn't he supposed to be the expert?

'Shine a light!' he snapped. Sighing, Steve heaved his rear wheel in the air and kicked the pedal. The dynamo lit up wanly. Wheel ruts, a tufted ridge of grass . . . Jim slapped the map in front to the light and ducked towards it. Paddy ducked too. Their skulls met with a dull crack. The panniers dragged the wheel back to earth and the light went out.

A hopeless silence settled. Abruptly Jim shunted into the lane. 'This'll do me for tonight . . .' Darkness swallowed him instantly. The alien night tightened around Steve and Paddy. They were in the black heart of a Unionist landscape, clad only in shorts and sweat-soaked football shirts. Their scalps prickled with apprehension.

'This is the third lane in a mile,' Paddy breathed. 'We've only a one-in-three chance of being right!'

'Yeah, but there's three of us!' Steve strode forward his dynamo brightening with confidence.

'I found it. I Found it!' Jim's squawk rent the darkness. Lunging towards the sound, Paddy caught his bare shin on the steel pedal.

A large farmhouse loomed at the end of the lane. White-washed, two-storeyed, deserted. Jim cavorted in front of it, arms raised in the air as if he had just conjured it from the ground. Skeletal conifers leaned like dead sentries around the walls. On the gatepost a faint blotch of paint. Jim translated confidently, M-M-C, Mourne Mountaineering Club. I found it! I found it!

'Are ... are you sure we're allowed to stay?' Paddy quavered. 'There's no one here ...'

'Great!' Steve was in no doubt. 'Let's break in. I'm freezing.'

'I'm told they hide the key over the outhouse door,' Jim deliberated importantly. 'But which outhouse?'

He and Paddy darted off in opposite directions to search. Steve pushed open the front door and entered the house, where the others joined him a minute later, painfully rubbing bare legs.

'You might have told us, idiot! I barged into nettles looking for the bloody key!'

'Me too,' wailed Paddy, 'I got stung right where I scraped my shin!'

'That'll take your mind off the scrape,' Steve offered reasonably. His thin shoulders rose towards his ears bewildered by accusation. 'I thought you were gone exploring!'

'Put on the light! Idiot!' Jim snapped. 'Why are you standing in the dark?'

'There isn't any ...'

'What the hell do you mean, there isn't any?'

Steve made himself absolutely clear. 'I mean there isn't any ...'

Jim raked the wall for a switch.

'There's no poles ... no poles in the laneway,' Steve said.

'And no wires on the chimney,' Paddy added.

Jim's fingers faltered among the cobwebs. Something fat and squidgy jumped onto his wrist and galloped up his sleeve. 'There must be some kind of light,' he spluttered, scraping himself in disgust. 'They swore there was electricity ...'

'Here's a candle!' Steve offered brightly.

'Well light it, man, for God's sake ...'

'Give us a match, then.'

Jim cleared his throat and turned to Paddy in polite despair. 'Have you got a match? Please?'

'Sorry Jim. 'Fraid I don't smoke.'

Silence fell again. The house smelled of damp decay. A rustle came from upstairs, a hollow rattle,

'Mice . . .'

'Rats . . .'

'Loose plaster behind the wallpaper, that's all!' Jim scoffed nervously. 'Old houses make a lot of noise. They rattle like packing-crates . . . Everyone knows that.'

A stealthy creak from behind a door seemed to reinforce his words — it was as if a listener had shifted its weight. Jim snatched the door open. A stairway mounted into pitch blackness. He slammed it shut and lay against it.

'I don't want to scare anyone . . .' his voice quavered to a higher pitch, 'but I heard this place is haunted . . . Course I don't believe it . . .' The hidden stairs creaked again as if the listener had taken a sudden interest. 'Some of our club stayed here last year. They heard all sorts of stories . . . a lot of nonsense.'

'Like what?' Paddy demanded faintly. Steve slung a reassuring arm around his shoulders and cleared his throat at Jim. Too late.

'Oh noises and . . . things. Footsteps, screams . . . you know, the usual stuff. Someone got the chop here ages ago . . .'

'*Murdered*, you mean. Who?'

'We-ell', a family actually,' Jim said with uneasy relish. 'Butchered in their beds. Some of the fellows from our club said they heard it was . . . you know . . . people who didn't leave when they were ordered out. But it was a long time ago . . .' He pulled himself together. 'Of course the lads were only making up the story to frighten us when they got home . . . They didn't actually see anything themselves.'

'You mean *they* didn't have a torch either?'

'Lay off, Steve! They said there was electricity here. I thought of everything else. There must be matches somewhere. Where's the kitchen for a start? We'll poke around till we find something!'

In the yard the wind sighed. They heard a hasty brushing overhead, as if someone were sweeping a bedroom for their stay.

Paddy fluttered under Steve's arm, his voice high as a bat-squeak, 'We . . . we can't stay here!'

'Only a branch against the slates,' Jim growled uncertainly. 'Everyone stays here. It's a club hut for God's sake! Anyway . . . where else can we go?, He felt for the kitchen door, hands paddling cautiously in the dark. A loud ticking came from behind him, and every hair on his head tingled.

'Just bringing the bike in!' Steve barged his handlebars through the front door, then shrugged off the panniers and stepped on a pedal. The room trembled into cavernous existence, a stage-set in a lightning storm.

Paddy cheered, his glasses gleaming gratitude. Giddy with relief, Jim dangled his arms like a broken scarecrow and howled ghoulishly. Steve responded with the wail of a skittish banshee. As the brief light faded Jim was almost certain that Paddy had wet himself. 'Light up again!' he ordered inquisitively. The wheel whirred. No, just a wrinkle of shadow in the baggy shorts.

A doorway . . . As the light died Jim darted forward.

'Follow me — oooohhh!!' A low lintel! Steve rushed to the rescue. The bike stalled against the sofa. He tumbled across it and Paddy pitched headfirst into a tangle of arms, wheels, pedals, legs and handlebars. Jim drew a shuddering breath, postponed his headache and assumed control.

'On your feet Steve! You too, Paddy. Pull yourselves together now!'

The last command renewed the convulsion. Jim dragged them upright and straightened out the bike. 'You steer Paddy! I'll lift the back wheel. You're on pedals, Steve. Now when I count three, start!'

He lifted the back wheel by the carrier, 'One, two . . .' Steve leapt into the air.

'. . . .Owww! Get off, Eejit! Turn it with your hand . . .!' The room sprang to quivering life again, monstrous shadows swinging around the walls. 'And God said, "Let there be Light!"' Steve chanted, lurching towards the kitchen, '"and Jasus you could see for miles!"'

He was shorn off by the doorframe. The bike slewed and Paddy lost his grip. Jim's fingers entered the spokes. Steve thought the howl was aimed at him — for letting go. He grabbed the pedal again and churned mightily. The howl rose in pitch as if powered by the dynamo . . .

The kitchen was cold and stark; stone-floored, with a heavy wooden table. A shelf bore a litter of broken Primus stoves, cracked cups and a Cow & Gate tin. There was a stone sink, chipped and stained, two broken chairs, an empty dresser. The one small window was curtained with cobwebs, the back door secured by rusted bolts. No-one had ever been happy here.

Jim felt tentatively along the shelves.

'Mind the rat-traps,' Steve grinned. The hand retracted instantly.

'Doesn't s-seem to get much use . . .' Paddy whispered nervously, shrinking from a mound of bullet-shaped droppings on a shelf.

'Sure it does!' Jim was dismissing his own fear too. 'Most people bring their own gear. Like us. I've got a gas-stove, right!'

'I suppose it's got a pilot-light,' Paddy complained aggressively.

Jim glared at him. Bad enough taking that kind of guff from Steve without Paddy getting cheeky too.

'You know, I've been thinking,' Steve interrupted at knee-level. 'We've got three bikes here, right? And three rooms we want to use, right?' He beamed up at Jim. 'Why don't we hang a bike in each room, from the centre of the ceiling . . . We can take turns to pedal, and we'll save all this humping around . . .'

Overwhelmed by his own brilliance he paused. Darkness closed on the idea but Paddy saw potential: 'Good thinking Stevie!' He brightened, 'I bet there's a stream outside. We can rig up a hydroelectric scheme! All we'll need is a little waterfall, a paddle-wheel, and a belt-system to the back wheels . . .'

He was jigging with excitement. Jim gave the bike

an impatient jerk, 'Get moving, Einstein!' he growled. 'Upstairs. . . .'

The long, narrow stairway was panelled off from the living-room. Jim and Paddy gnashed the bike up the bare steps. Steve squirmed to reach the pedals. He halted them hilariously in mid-ascent: 'Did you hear about the fella that was sick in bed at the top of the house. . . .?'

Baffled, they glared at him. 'The doctor came up to see him. Your man was expecting a cure. The ould doc was puffin' and pantin' — "Begod Mick," he says, "they'll have a quare job gettin' the coffin down them stairs. . . . "'

The light revealed extensive desolation. A gaunt room had been adapted roughly as a dormitory. No bunks, but half the floor consisted of a raised platform scattered with mildewed mattresses. Another platform overhead was similarly equipped.

'A *Matratzenlager*!' Jim was proud of the technical informa-tion. 'This is what they use in alpine huts.' Paddy saw what he meant; the mattresses looked as if they had come down in a glacier. 'I don't want to complain but this won't do my asthma any good,' he warned dismally. Jim ordered him in to search for matches. As he scrambled reluctantly on to the top platform a sudden icy breeze whirled through the room. The door slammed.

'Draughty dump!' Jim shivered uneasily. He caught a look of frozen terror on Paddy's face and flung the light around.

'A man. . . .' Paddy gasped. 'There was a man. . . .' His trembling arm pointed.

'*Where?*'

'There! In the door. On the landing. . . .'

'Paddy, the door's Closed!'

'I know . . . but I *saw* him . . . he passed through it. . . .'

'Through the . . . the *timber*?!'

'Oh Paddy . . . for God's sake. . . .'

Paddy's terror was real. His teeth rattled, and his eyes — magnified already behind his lenses — were huge with evidence. The wheel slowed to an appalled whisper of light.

Paddy's arm still pointed. Its dancing shadow faded across the wall.

'A shadow! A bloody shadow!' Jim exploded with relief and disgust. 'That's all you saw, you EEjit. A bloody shadow!'

Steve released his breath in a long, whistling puncture. There were tears in Paddy's voice. '. . . Not a shadow,' he insisted weakly. 'It was a m-man . . . in a tartan shirt with sort of . . . yellowish hair and. . . .' He coughed defensively before adding in a small voice, '. . . and short trousers!'

Jim and Steve exploded in high-pitched laughter, 'Short trousers!' they echoed in hysterical relief, 'Ha-Ha' HAAAH!' Jim sobered abruptly, 'Clean your glasses or you'll frighten yourself to death. Short bloody trousers indeed! Look what I'm wearing!' He plucked at his shorts. 'You saw *my* shadow, you gobdaw!'

'Not . . . shorts,' Paddy whispered, ashen with fear and abuse, 'breeches. . . .'

Jim ignored him. 'Wind up that light!' he ordered.

Steve bent obediently to the pedal, and paused. 'D'you think. . . .' he wondered quietly, '. . . are we in the wrong place or something?'

The hall door crashed open. A scraping rumble resounded through the house. The noise increased until it came to a halt against a wall below. There was choked silence for a moment, the house catching its breath, then the intrusion rattled dreadfully. Steve pumped the pedal till the wheel hissed: 'Imagination. . . .' he droned hoarsely, 'Imagination. . . .' The radiant spotlight jerked across the walls and settled on the frail wooden door. Sharp blows below were echoed in grunts of effort. The bedroom door unlatched and silently swung ajar.

Paddy shrieked. Jim's fingers lost their nerveless grip and the bicycle crashed to the floor.

'What's goin' on up there? Is that you, Billy?'

Steve stumbled out to the landing. 'No,' he shouted in a ragged voice. 'It's us! What's happening?'

'That's what I was wonderin' meself!' A cone of torchlight

exposed Steve's gaunt form. 'Well, well! A footballer! That explains the noise. Ye're playin' a match up there!'

'Noise?!' Steve gasped in outrage, 'What about the racket downstairs? Was that you?'

'Oh that?' the voice chuckled pleasantly, 'Did I frighten ye? I'm sorry. I didn't know there was anybody up there.'

Steve scrambled downstairs followed cautiously by Jim. Paddy lowered himself weakly from step to step; clinging to the banister. The torchlight flashed across the floor to the fireplace.

'I was just bringin' in some firewood. See? Found it in the lane.' The voice was a chatty drawl. It went up and down the northern scale. 'Hey, welcome to the Hut! Ye should have lit the fire. It's cold. . . .' He rubbed his hands briskly. 'Did ye not find the candles either?'

Paddy's teeth chattered audibly. The stranger bent towards him in concern and Paddy shrank away, 'Hey, this wee fella's perished. . . .' He hurried into the kitchen and pulled out a drawer in the table. A lighter flared with an old-fashioned whiff of petrol and a candle flickered alight. He handed it to Jim. A heavy scent trailed the flame. 'Now,' he urged, 'there's whiskey-bottles out there for candlesticks. Set them round the room, one in each window, two on the mantelpiece, and mind you put a couple by the door. Hurry up now and we'll get this place ready yet.'

Steve examined him in the light of the second candle. He wore a heavy greatcoat with the collar turned up, and the peaked cap of a country farmer. His features were fleshy, a soft face with pale skin and uneven stubble. A good bit older than themselves, Steve thought. Impossible to tell though — the difference between age and experience. Loose, mobile eyes unnerved him as the man handed him his candle with a ceremonial nod. Large and liquid they squirmed uneasily in red-rimmed sockets. They belonged in a finer face. But the friendly concern was reassuring. They marched one by one through the draughts sheltering their candles with transparent hands. Paddy looked just like an altar-boy, Steve thought affectionately. Exorcism flickered through his mind, but the domestic ritual eased his imagination.

The stranger followed them into the room and fell on his knees before the fireplace. He began to chop kindling with the spike-end of a peculiar hammer. Steve peered at the implement, puzzled.

'It's a piton-hammer,' Jim opened his mouth for the first time.

'That's right,' the stranger displayed it, the head narrow and heavy, the spike viciously stubby. 'A climber's hammer. That spike is for pullin' out pitons. Pegs we call 'em. That was my job! Billy knocked 'em in and I pulled 'em out!' He smacked his lips in satisfaction.

'I thought pegs were out of fashion now,' Jim commented loftily, 'modern climbers don't use them any more.' Steve suffered a twinge of embarrassment for the friendly stranger.

'Aye, maybe so, maybe so,' the man smiled at Jim's presumption, 'but we're very traditional here. . . .' He laughed benevolently. 'You lads must be rock-climbers, then?'

'I've done a fair bit,' Jim boasted outrageously, 'They haven't.'

'Great! We'll have some fun on the rocks tomorrow so. If we can get round Billy, that is. Used to be a damn good climber, Billy. More of a walker meself. Hadn't the guts for the rock.' He whacked away with the spike, 'Billy was the boy for the climbin'. . . .

'Oh. . . .' he interrupted himself. 'Nearly forgot me manners. . . .' He threw the hammer into a meaty left fist and thrust out the right in a clammy handshake. 'I'm Robert Grey . . . I use this old place a lot. Me and Billy. There's not many comes nowadays. They go to the new hut up the road. But me and Billy, we're too old-fashioned to change.' He winked at Jim. Steve completed the introductions.

'First time up from Dublin, eh?' Robert grinned with pleasure.

'We'll give ye a good introduction tomorrow, so. Three wee

Fenians from the Free State, eh?' His eyes danced at them. 'Don't mind my big mouth. Nothin' to me where a man comes from. Long as he buys his round, eh? Only jokin' boys, only jokin'.'

A shadow crossed his face, 'Ye'll maybe find Billy a bit rough at first, understan',' he warned, 'but he's a good lad behind it. Used to be an army man. He misses it y'know. Excitement an' all. Damn good climber too . . . till the hand seized up. War-wound . . . made him bitter y'know . . . We might get him goin' again.' He sat back on his heels and the fire lit his flickering features. 'Let me think now. . . .' He scratched his head with the piton-hammer. 'We'll maybe start on Lower Cove and work up to Slieve Beg . . . or round to Annalong an' maybe Hare's Castle, how's that sound?' He beamed at their puzzled faces. 'Aye, I'll take care of Billy, don't worry about that. That's my job!'

Snatching up an iron kettle he headed for the door. 'Just goin' down for water. Only be a wee minute. . . .'

'Quick!' Jim hissed as soon as he was gone, 'get that bike downstairs or we'll look like right eejits!' Steve stuck his head outside. A shadow moved among the dead trees.

'— An illusion I tell you Paddy, that's all you saw. A trick of the light. Imagination!' Jim was arguing.

'But I *saw* it! I saw it . . . through the door. . . .'

Jim turned to Steve as if to an unimpeachable witness. 'Did you see anything upstairs, Steve?' he asked in a weary, long-suffering tone.

Steve hesitated, grappling with temptation, then grinned apology at his exhausted friend. 'Not a thing I'm afraid.' He shook his head in sympathy. 'Eyestrain, Paddy old son. Eyestrain and over work. Soon as you get home take a holiday. . . .' He launched up the stairs. Mechanical struggle erupted on the landing. The front door flew open and Robert hurried in with a slopping kettle.

'Soon have a brew,' he promised. 'Where's your mate?' He cocked an interested ear at the stairs, 'Kickin' football again?'

The stalemate in the stairwell broke and came crashing

towards them. A tangle of metal and flesh burst through the door and sprawled at Robert's feet. He peered up into the dark in case of further traffic, then he helped Steve gently to his feet.

'Son, don't take it personal,' and he shook his head sadly, 'but you look like you could use a big mug of hot tea!'

Robert produced a bottle wrapped in brown paper and laced his own cup. He tried to treat theirs too but Jim refused severely.

'Why not? Warm ye up, help ye sleep. No harm in it. ...'

Steve waggled his eyebrows in favour but Jim's refusal held. Lolling drowsily on the sofa it was obvious they'd have no trouble sleeping anyway. Robert occupied a bursting armchair. He pushed his cap back on his head and it left a thin red line across his glistening forehead. Irrationally Steve found himself looking for stitch-marks.

Robert regaled them with mock-heroic tales of cowardice and cunning on the local crags. Frequent sips from the bottle underlined the satisfaction of events ... 'I could see he was in trouble for all his big talk — not used to soloin' y'know — so I dropped him the end of a rope. Right in front of his big policeman's nose but he couldn't take a hand off to scratch himself, never mind tie on, he was that frightened, so he grabbed it in his teeth! An' hung on like a wee tarrier right to the top. I had to wring the spit out of it after. Only time he ever stopped braggin' — when his jaws were clamped around that rope. ...'

He interrupted himself at last when they yawned in unison.

'Ye'd best be off to bed,' he allowed reluctantly. 'I'll wait up a wee while for Billy. I'm afraid he's fell by the wayside again!' He clucked his tongue and the sad, dry ticking went on and on till he took another sip. Steve caught a look in the rolling eyes for which he had no words, but it startled him with an unexpected sense of pain.

Jim took a candle and they wobbled unsteadily upstairs, sleeping-bags bundled in their arms. The damp air in the bedroom roused them again. The candle stood on the window-sill. The reflection revealed wooden storm-shutters outside the glass.

'We're locked in!' Paddy shivered. 'I didn't notice that before. . . .'

'How could you?' Jim rebuked him sharply. 'Wasn't it dark when we came? That's only to protect the glass from vandals. All the huts use them. Still I'm glad Robert is here . . . even if he is a bit thick!' He smiled sheepishly and yawned, 'Old-fashioned is right. That's an army coat he's wearing. Did you see the state of the buttons? They haven't been polished in years. He should try that stuff he's drinking on them!'

Steve could not sleep. Urgency shrilled in his head. He couldn't reach its source. His brain rang and rang like a distant telephone. Sparks of perception flared and faded, left a sense of dread at the failure to understand. No idea what he was meant to know . . . he felt tiny voices scratching at the dark side of language. The candle shivered on the windowsill. Jim snored and Paddy's breath wheezed and rasped in his airways. Steve dozed at last. . . .

He jerked awake to the sound of footsteps. Creaking heavily up the stairs. The long, steep stairs to a child's ear. The nearer they came, the more his terror sharpened. He wanted to scream, to waken someone strong beside him, but already he was conscious of an extra presence in the room. And still the footsteps mounted the endless stairs. Steve peered through trembling eyelashes.

A heavy figure leaned towards the candle. The flame had dwindled to a midnight flicker . . . Thin straw-coloured hair, plaid shirt, knee-breeches . . . The man cocked his head suddenly and looked straight at the sleeping boys as if he detected an error in their breathing. Blood ran jagged and fiery in Steve's veins. Ugly shadows blackened the mouth, the eye-sockets, the nose. But the candle flared again and he was smiling over them, a strange tenderness dissolving the bloated face from within. . . .

. . . The light died. For a moment the sad, smiling stare lingered in the burnt darkness. Then Steve heard shuffling feet fade into the constant footsteps on the stairs.

He lay absolutely rigid in his sleeping-bag, every nerve stretched tight. Afraid to turn. Movement might snap his spine. His whisper clawed at Jim's sleep. 'Wake up! Ssh! For God's sake, Sssh!' Paddy sat up instantly. Jim shook his head, groaning.

'We've got to get out of here,' Steve hissed, 'There's something terrible . . . Listen to the footsteps. . . .'

Jim listened, his head lolling in the dark. Not a sound, except Steve's heart stammering in his chest and Paddy's wheezing breath.

'For God's sake Steve —'

'No. No! It's true! I saw the same as Paddy — It was Robert. . . .'

'So what? Go back to sleep —'

'No! I tell you — We've got to get away. . . .' his voice was a whispered wail. 'We're in the wrong place. . . .'

'OPEN UP!' Fists battered the front door. 'OPEN UP!' A raucous roar. They froze together. 'OPEN UP!!'

Steve felt his senses dissolve with shock. Sick, slow thoughts drifted into his skull like the shadows of stunned fish. It was starting again, and again, over and over. 'OPEN UP!' so frail Paddy's wrist in his frantic grip 'OPEN UP!' Frail and forever the bones of a ten-year old. . . .

Robert's feet running across the floor. His anxious voice as he struggled with the door, 'Oh my God, are you full again Billy? Keep quiet for God's sake you'll wake everyone. . . .'

'There's on'y us,' Billy laughed loud and coarse, 'out in the middle of nowhere. I'll shout as loud as I like! And you won't stop me —'

'Aye that's right Billy, that's right, there's no one'll interfere with ye,' Robert soothed nervously. 'Come over here to the fire. I was sittin' up for ye. . . .'

'Who owns all the fancy stuff?' Billy snarled suddenly.

'Ach, a couple o' youngsters Billy, that's all. Couple o' youngsters!' His voice rushed to reassure, 'But they're gone! Up the road Billy. They're gone! They'll be back tomorrow maybe . . . Sit down here now,' he wheedled, 'like a decent man, an' I'll make us a sup o' tea. . . .'

'Tea! Tea is it? Are you mockin' me with tea? Is that all ye have?' His voice cracked into curses.

'Och Billy! Billy! What's come over ye? It's a while since ye were this bad. I thought ye were gettin' better. What happened at all?'

A brief, charged silence. The boys strained towards the floor.

'Jesus Christ, Billy, don't take it all in one go! It'll kill ye. Give it here. . . .' An enraged, spluttering roar, a sharp blow. A bottle smashed to the floor. Everything stopped dead. Stunned by the explosion.

Paddy shuddered. His skull jolted against Steve's shoulder. The room filled with a choking rasp — an asthma attack. Steve threw an arm around him fiercely. 'Not now Paddy! Not now! Not now. . . .' he pleaded over and over again. 'Where's your inhaler? Where is it Paddy? Where is it?' He was shaking his friend desperately as if he could stifle the attack. In the relentless circle of his arm Paddy writhed and choked, his response a voiceless gasp but Steve heard him clear as a shout. Frail wet fingers clawed at his wrist as he broke away.

The voice began again below, snarling fury. 'You broke it on purpose, you — I'll KILL Ye. . . .' The darkness seethed with struggle. . . .

No impact. The disembodied violence of nightmare. Like the roar of a radio — sound without substance. Steve swam towards it. The shell of the house hung lifeless, deserted, around him. An old house should rattle like a packing-crate . . . He felt his nerves strain in a wave of unreason till he was barely holding on, wading through dark water.

He pulled the door open onto the landing. Paddy's crisis pitched him through. Struggle raged beyond the panelled stairs, bone on bone, snarl of vicious breath, boots kicking and skidding. But an icy stillness enclosed the turmoil; furniture skidded without vibration, bodies rebounded from mute walls. . . .

Steve shivered from step to step, wading deeper into the dark. He realised he was almost naked. Vulnerability froze his will.

No farther. The door at the bottom was closed. He could never open that . . . that . . . lid. He tangled his arms across his chest, crouched on his heels paralysed. Struggle reeled through the room inches from his head. He resisted the bloodless vacancy of a swoon.

There was no one in there . . . he knew it by the dead drift of the air, the stillness in the flimsy walls. The house echoed emptiness. Echoes and shadows. Reflections. Brutal memories trapped in place. . . Images not his own burned in his brain, things he had never seen; bleak faces staring into the ground; the corner of a soft mouth bleeding; hysterical shreds of battle; black trains thundering; blood trickling from the mouth, her body naked and vague; cold-eyed men with marching banners; and then — shockingly clear as a portrait — a child's face at the window and through the boy's eyes he saw a soldier running, running and screaming. . . .

. . . The trees! Those trees, leaning at the house like dead sentries! . . . Blood from the soldier's sleeve, running and screaming, the wrist slashed. Behind the eyes the woman lay, Steve could not turn his head, could not . . . blood from the soldier's sleeve, wrist slashed to the bone . . . could not turn his head.

It was old, old and still burning somewhere. His brain tightened fiercely against the invading flames. Threads of candlelight pierced the panel beside him, knitting and breaking in the dark. Slowly, with infinite abhorrence he leaned towards the crack. His cheekbone trembled on cold paint, eyelashes bending against the light. Thin neck, and brittle bones in his bare back. . . .

. . . Flailing shadows resolved to one transparent shape, Robert dancing through the room. His face swollen, sweating, hair in tangled locks. In one hand, the glittering neck of a bottle. In the other, the spiked hammer. No one else in the whole room. Thick lips strained across his teeth, a tormented whisper broke from his throat,

'Billy . . . Billy . . . don't! They're only children. . . . No!'

He shook his head hopelessly. A jagged wound in his cheek and the hammer bled softly.

Nausea closed Steve's eyes. He slumped against the stairs. Billy's voice grated through the panel, strangled with rage. 'I'll —KILL. . . .' Steve lifted his head to look for Billy. It took a long, long time. He saw Robert's bloated face again, eyes blazing through the flimsy panel, long teeth grinding curses, 'I'll KILL. . . .'

Fingers gripped Steve's shoulder. Ice round his heart. 'Come quick! Paddy's choking. . . .' Jim was shaking him.

He seized Jim's hair, dragged his head towards the crack. Overhead a terrible, tearing rasp. Tissues screaming terminal distress. Steve sweated terror. Knew what he must do — No. No! Impossible. That door —

In the dark pit of the stairwell the brown door pulsed. Paddy's inhaler the other side. He panicked, crawled upstairs. Jim caught him on the landing, 'Murder . . .' he mouthed frantically in Steve's ear, 'He'll kill Robert. . . .'

'Who — ?'

'Billy! He'll kill him . . . and then us. . . .'

'Billy? Did you see . . . Billy?'

'Yes, yes! With that hammer . . . We've got to escape. Now!'

'No! — Paddy . . . We can't leave Paddy!'

A strangled shriek rose from downstairs and dwindled to a bubbling moan.

'Oh God. He's done it. . . .'

Steve faltered into the bedroom. Paddy's efforts came at

long intervals. He was drowning under the air, his lungs sealed, brain starved. The fire in his chest lit the darkness for Steve. He crouched beside where Paddy lay sprawled on the platform, his head hanging over the edge. Steve saw him utterly clearly: the veins in his forehead, glazed eyes, blue lips, and the rigid arch of the throat. His inhaler downstairs. Too late. Minutes without oxygen and the brain decayed. He reached for Paddy's hand, found a cold, contorted claw. Tried a kiss of life — breathing into unresponsive bone. He turned from the platform, brushed Jim aside and stumbled to the stairs.

On the first step he pounded the panel with his fist. The whole house drummed. As he descended he began to scream, still drumming. It started as a wail of fear and grief trembling in his throat and rose to a wiry howl of outrage. In his bursting lungs he held all the air Paddy was denied. A scream to scar the ear. And the relentless rattle of the drum. He hurled the door open, entered an icy stillness. Candles guttered in their bottles. A circle of light sucked towards the centre of the room. The air shivered, swirling with invisible shape.

Steve crouched by the panniers. Cold force flogged his body and his skin crawled. The scream moaned in his mouth. His senses narrowed to a single point as he ripped through the pockets.

The inhaler ... Where? Dragged out clothes and shoes. *Where*? Pulled out a lurid packet. Forked tongues squirming ... 'How much are *They*. ...?' Hurled it away in anguish. Skidded under the sofa. No inhaler. Yellow laces ... Steve wept savagely. Grief and guilt. He found it in the last pocket. Intimate. Essential. Plastic. Useless. How could everything depend ... Too late. He saw Paddy's face again, glasses shattered, cold eyes staring through the rims. In the room candlelight swarmed among the shadows. Steve felt the skin flayed from his back when he rose, took a candle, dragged towards the door.

The house strained against a terrifying suction. Footsteps

raged behind him on the stairs. Steve entered the bedroom, locked the door. He pressed the inhaler to Paddy's cold lips and nostrils. The head rolled limply aside, all strain gone. Jim huddled on the platform, his eyes fixed on the door. A string of spittle hung unheeded from his chin. Heavy steps on the long, slow stairs. Steve faced the door. Robert was in the room again — and the steps still rising. A pulse! He felt a pulse in Paddy's wrist. It beat with every . . . No . . . Every step on the stairs shook the floor and echoed in Paddy's bones. That was all. He dropped the lifeless arm. The door rattled and shook. Vibration shuddered through the room.

'No, Billy . . . No. . . .'

A rending crash. The spiked hammer pierced the door above the lock, withdrew and smashed again. Wood burst inwards, splinters stabbing the air. A fist punched through the hole and groped towards the key.

Steve rose, remembering. He drew the candle from the bottle and broke away the neck. As he approached the hand it turned and offered him its urgent veins and tendons.

THE CLIMBER WHO COURTED DEATH

He left sheaves of scribbled description strewn in friends' houses where he stayed between trips. And wrote bundles of letters — everybody had them. No detail of his wandering was undescribed. In an effort to clear up his effects I collected all the known material, though I am sure there are folders and barely legible journals exiled in England and elsewhere that may never surface. The season in Africa, for example, which began with the Shipton-Tilman traverse of Mount Kenya in honour of two of his heroes, is missing, though undoubtedly recorded.

But, finally what was to be done with all these wads of words when I had them stacked in order, notebooks, foolscap, writing pads, and five — no, six! — piles of airmail? He was a very ordinary climber by modern standards, so a book of exploits would be unjustified. Neither was he literary in a creative sense — he favoured quantity of description rather than quality of evocation — so no original gem of mountain literature is about to surface. I read and re-read responsively in the hope that a significant form might arrange itself, an obituary or an epitaph emerge of its own accord. He used to be incensed by the media when they made a sensation of climbing accidents. And yet, when he died, there was not a single word in any paper. He would have resented that, too, in his contradictory way.

That was my fault—I could have informed them, I suppose. But I didn't, and this is perhaps an attempt to give him the obituary he would have wanted.

The earliest writing is a diary kept when he was twenty-three, before any of us knew him and before climbing became the motive force of his existence. The Alps appear marginally in these obsessed notes; he passed them by, a tumult on the horizon. Love had let him down, literature had failed him, mountains were not yet a distraction. The most recent record is a letter I received two weeks before his death at the age of thirty-four. He was killed in the Alps, below the Flammes de Pierre at the foot of the Dru. Killed by stonefall.

After this letter like a full stop comes Henri's telegram from Chamonix: 'Accident. Jack mort. Quoi faire?'

The first and last writings are the most affecting of all. They reflect the contrasts of the life between with a stark clarity. The final letter bubbles with self-assured opinions and exploits from Yosemite and the climbing-resorts of the American West.

> Yosemite is a dream of El Dorado and Disneyland, valley of invincible legend and tasteless tourism. Escape via paradisal rock from the trash of expensive leisure. . . . Camp 4 is a Who's Who of international competition. Every exchange of greetings is a discreet clash of swords. I'm relieved by my own mediocrity. . . . Went up to do the C.H. [Chouinard-Herbert] on Sentinel with a bowery bum but he chickened out on the walk-in. Raged on alone and did the Steck-Salathé instead. Took me the whole damn day. Not quite your respectable free 5.9. either. More like 5a, A1. Got my skull stuck in the Narrows. The scene is burnt into my brain like a colour-slide, 1000 feet up, 15 feet inside the face, headjammed in a rock bottleneck, staring out between granite blinkers through a chink in the cliff at a vertical slice of sky, a strip of Sunnyside Wall, a green stripe of Valley. Picturesque, but I had to push on. . . .

Of course he was rubbing in (with his light allusion) the two days I spent on the same route last year. He never missed a chance to compare and excel.

When Jack said he soloed a route it could mean a lot of things. The only definite interpretation was that he climbed it without a partner. But he seldom ventured above VS without a backrope and the possibility of protection. He picked routes which should be well within his capacity and so a good deal of his soloing was authentic with the backrope trailing in case he needed to throw in a nut and rope off. For longer, less predictable routes he developed self-belay techniques to a high degree of speed, and claimed he could abseil a pitch to clean it and jumar back to his high point faster than the average second could have climbed it. Or so he liked to think.

Not that he was particularly concerned with ethics anyway. He climbed to get up the route, and enjoyed it best on his own. Lack of technique was never allowed to interfere if a sling could pull him over a problem. He didn't give a damn about great climbers either. Except for Walter Bonatti. Bonatti was his hero. 'It would take ten of your average great climbers to do what Bonatti did alone. And they'd all die young,' he wrote back to me in a kind of postal yell when I expressed reservations about one of Bonatti's books. But that was another time, another needle. That last American letter continued:

> Those slab routes on Glacier Apron and the Tuolumne domes are the most enjoyable climbing I've ever done. Getting used to friction is like being a novice again, you have to learn techniques, tricks, tolerances. We get jaded by habit and experience, and lose the fun of novelty; but I think I've rediscovered enjoyment — especially this sunny honey-coloured stuff, if you can imagine that in the drenched deprivation of an Irish summer!

I could imagine him alright, front-pointing up golden acres of slabs, invisible crampons on his rock boots, and the rope tied off to a skimpy bolt. (It was the sourness of my envy that turned the sun to ice.)

There isn't a trace of shadow in that last summer; it's all sun and jubilation. He enclosed a slide, unroped on a slabby arête, his wiry figure bunched in concentration, black hair tied back in a pony-tail, and his dark skin smeared with chalk in elaborate patterns of war-paint. That was meant to provoke, some of us didn't agree with chalk at that time. But the overall effect was electric — I looked for the tomahawk.

But that was the summer chapter. The previous winter had been a different story: the winter of his thirty-fourth year. He came into the States deviously from Canada. He had been to

Alaska, to climb McKinley of course, and to work, to do whatever occurred, but some kind of muscle injury in his leg began to gnaw at his nerves, and he moved south instead. Not far enough though. He spent an appalling winter working in Connecticut, an even worse fate than spending it in Scotland he reckoned. The leg kept him out of good jobs, the heavy work, and he had to double-shift to earn enough, working in a hotel kitchen and then bartending at night. He felt he aged unbearably that winter, while all his claims were on youth and being young.

> Hartford is a fatal city, a precast mausoleum. The Insurance capital of the world reeks of security and death. I'm staying in the YMCA for the sake of the gym. I play endless games of handball in streamlined alleys with elderly fitness-freaks who accept me as one of their own. We're a sorry crew, Budweiser and small cigars, our knees strapped up in pink elastic, stinking of wintergreen . . . .

Whenever people asked me for news of Jack in the ironic tone of voice that expresses the envy of the bound for the free I heard myself reciting landmarks on an exotic itinerary; Peru, Nepal, Africa, Norway . . . All the places I wanted to go myself. Sometimes it was hard to resist using him as an *alter ego* and pretending it was me out there gallivanting around the mountain-ranges of the world, impervious to paternity, impecunity, mortgages, the various conditions that shackled the rest. Not to mention motivation. Jack maintained we married and bred to excuse our lack of motivation.

But, on the other hand, it wasn't really difficult to understand how much his freedom cost. After a while it became obvious that Jack's mobility was not by choice. He always grew irritable and irritating after a long lay-off, pettily argumentative — and then just on the margin of dislike he disappeared. He abandoned people and places not because he wanted to — in fact he never stopped talking about involvement — but because he grew bored with himself and his own restrictions. He couldn't bear that sense of futility that most of us have to put up with and learn to ignore.

'The claustrophobia of the quotidian,' he growled in an English diary with that tedious taste of his for genitive phrase-making. 'This must be how a battery-hen would feel if it could think.'

It seems a bit melodramatic because he liked a lot of people genuinely, and kept in close touch with them. In fact those letters are usually cheerful, extrovert celebrations of some exotic environment, and there is little if any pressure or resentment apparent.

But the diaries are the shadow-side of the story. It seems as if the private writing is a kind of one-man dialogue to talk away isolation. It is ironic that, in spite of all his efforts at communication, his best writing occurs in passages that were never meant to be read. He unleashes real feelings there, even if it is a kind of despair.

1st of May, feastday of the sun, national day of distress, Mayday! Mayday! Outside the window it is snowing vehemently, all the apple-blossom in every suburb of the world stripped violently from the boughs and whirled before the wind. A naked shrub in the garden disposes snowflakes among its branches like bleak petals, but lower, on the slushy grass, daffodils thrash in panic. How bitter that yellow. There is nothing redeeming in it.

Staring through the window into the ironic snow on Mayday, rubbing the fogged-up glass of April and March, peering through the February pane, breathing on the January ice, I am struck by the sense of winter as a taste, a taste remembered like a clot of glass in the miserable mouth, and I cannot spit it out, and I cannot swallow it, it is there until . . . until it dissolves.

Something grievous that happened long ago is settling into a groove of years. Something else is jagged as ever — like an accident hidden beneath the skin. We are wrapped around our secret accidents. Continuity freezes in the blood; it scrapes against the bone.

When I was twenty I regarded myself as about sixteen — it wasn't a matter of numbers, just a feeling. And the decade that wound up to the thirty mark passed as if I was just slowly, thoroughly, turning seventeen. Then suddenly Time couldn't take the strain any more; like stretched and stretched elastic it shot back into shape this winter and I was catapulted viciously into the fact of my consolidated years. For a fraction of time things continued out of focus like the final, brief vibrations of rubber in its regained shape, but the images quickly overlapped, and now I am what I am, and there is a slackness where elasticity has been lost.

Loneliness is a tangible aspect of things, the sour rind of existence.

It seems after his break-up with Margaret there were none of those alliances of the heart, or even of the head, that contain assurances of a future. In fact I think the failure of all his attachments — to romance, creativity, or work — must have wiped out *any* future. He was dedicated to climbing; a terminal devotion in more ways than one, for when the body and the nerves began to go downhill at an unreasonably early age, what is there left for the mountaineer? Is there any future in gradually climbing down the grades at lower and lower altitudes, watching unrequited aspirations vanish behind impossible clouds?

So he was desperately impatient to get things done. Especially when he began to suffer what he described variously as rheumatism, lumbago, arthritis, sciatica, and fibrositis, sometimes all at once. He wrote to me with a savage snap when I turned down an expedition he was trying to organise. He never understood the mundane problems and responsibilities of normal people. When I told him something would turn up to salvage his arrangements he wrote back, 'What's the use of saying "something will turn up."? Half the world is waiting for something to turn up. They die of waiting, and that's the only thing that ever *does* happen to them.'

He had been climbing, it seems, on and off for a while before he really discovered it as a lifestyle; that is to say, he might struggle up three or four VS's a year if he happened to find them in his vicinity, but it wasn't a passion. Water was his element then. He lived in Kerry, Clare, Galway, Donegal, along the Atlantic as much as he could, working on trawlers, diving for illegal lobsters, selling black sea-urchins to the exporters.

Margaret lived with him through most of that time — about five years, she says. We wrote to her after the accident to tell her what happened. It seemed the right thing to do, although I have only met her once. She teaches in Mayo and never comes to Dublin. She confirmed a few hints he dropped about that period, his urge to write, copious drinking, irritating restlessness. But she refused to let me see any letters. They were private, she said. Of course I shouldn't have asked; it's just that I was collecting them from others, and forgot that hers would be different.

I knew his original ambitions had been literary. Margaret says he slaved over it hopelessly. When he gave up there was nothing left, not even a manuscript. He told me once on our way through Germany how he left his entire *opus* in a luggage-locker in Frankfurt. When he returned to empty the locker he didn't have the money to pay the extra charges, so he abandoned the lot. It was a gesture. He accepted there was no loss to posterity. And I accepted the story as a metaphor.

And that brings me to the notebook, the first one. It is a brief diary of that brief trip to the continent during which he lost touch with everything, including Margaret and his epic novel. ('Epic novel' is a guess, but it feels right.) He was a shattered twenty-three year old, a depressed romantic, wandering around in a bad winter with a cheap sleeping-bag and a Gibson guitar. The disjointed entries show him busking in freezing subways, sleeping under bridges, drinking malevolently in bars where he refused to tip the waiters. He gets beaten up twice in two months. The writing shows lingering traces of the literary urge in its tone of the studied throwaway.

Slept in a tennis-court in Liège last night. It froze viciously but it's another luminous day. At daybreak I *heard* a leaf fall from a tree at a distance of at least thirty yards, a staccato measure of the sharp frost. The leaf snapped decisively from its twig and rattled down a lattice of bare branches hitting the concrete below with a final crackling report.

He moved across to Paris in a shower of unquotable references to Joyce, Beckett, and Ezra Pound. 'The sturdy, unkillable infants of the poor.' he called them mysteriously, without any justification that I can think of.

Awoke shattered this morning, in ribbons, in a doorway near the Gare de Lyon. Cambodian Airways, I think. The usual fragmented memories of an excessive evening. Luckily I had the instinct to encase myself in cardboard, because it froze poisonously last night.

Hounded by a sequence of hangover and venomous frosts he explored the city, 'I walk, and walk, and somehow waste the city. I walk until my legs ache from hip to ankle. Scenes impinge upon my retina, slide off, are lost, without awe, indifferently. My mind will not connect. I cannot experience enthusiasm.'

Arrested by the police for persistently busking in the subway under the Etoile — it was the warmest one — he spent a miserable week in jail, the rhymed entry reading:

> All dreams are sad dreams;
> sad in their failure to come true,
> Sad in their consequences if they do.'

But that week in the cells seems to have given him the necessary perspective on his drinking, because he moved to Germany, distractedly noting the Alps *en route*, intent on saving some money and establishing a 'sense of purpose'. Weeks later, after a harrowing excursion northwards involving a blizzard and tattered tennis-shoes, he is on the ferry out of Ostend where he landed a few months earlier. The last stilted note reads:

The circle curves into its final arc.

As we leave Ostend the continental coast is visible only as a carious ridge of apartment blocks trailing their disjointed geometry along the shore. The sky is in virtuoso mood, a full range of variations from inviolate blue to hammersnouted thunder clouds down the edge of which the sun streams in yellow strains onto a turbulent sea, sullen with shadow and the hue of churned sand.

It must have been soon after that morbid interlude that he arrived in Dublin, and I met him for the first time. I was looking for a climbing partner and he was enthusiastic. We met in Dalkey Quarry in the evenings and went to Wicklow or Clare on occasional weekends. He let me lead a lot at first, though I suspected he was a better climber than I. Afterwards I understood that this was because his interest had not yet focused into the passion it later became.

Fascinated even then by the idea of soloing he was certainly not an ideal partner. The classic route on a crag which anyone else would have wanted to lead he aspired to solo on sight — so he was constantly avoiding those plum routes that I particularly craved. If there was no one else to do the necessary, he would reluctantly concede and second me on a classic, although he did refuse point-blank to follow Pis Fliuch one weekend when we were alone. He held my rope of course, with a suitable blend of regret and determination and I only had to abseil to retrieve my gear, but I missed the fellowship of shared climbing while he shakily soloed the pitch afterwards, and I could not make up my mind whether I should wait below to scrape him off the rocks, or above in case he needed a top-rope.

It was the same in Wales — he had to solo Cemetery Gates, though he followed my lead on it then. I tried not to feel upstaged, but sometimes I felt it was becoming a bit of an act with him. Afterwards he seconded Cenotaph Corner — he expressed no desire to solo that one — and pulled heartily on the upper peg. When I ridiculed him for this breach of ethics he showed no particular interest in the issue.

When leading, he climbed rapidly, using strength as much as technique, placing competent protection if it was available. Soloing was a different matter; he rested a good deal, and moved in short, sharp bursts between stances. He was not averse to pulling up on a sling for prior inspection of a move, though afterwards he might climb it free.

He lashed across Dream of White Horses one sunny afternoon as if it were the cliff-path walk — which I suppose it is — and I got the best sequence of pictures I've ever taken. Perhaps that's not a bad image for our lopsided partnership — the leader way out in front on a top quality route, unfortunately without a rope, while the second consoles himself with a camera. But that doesn't mean he took advantage of me either! I was no more a *natural* second than he was. Climbing, to me, means leading. I had no hesitation about finding another partner whenever a route rankled between us.

Vector, for example, was a glint in his eye and a taste in my mouth at the same time. I argued that it would be a clear suicide verdict if he attempted a free-solo of that poisonously polished route, and that anything less than an ethical ascent would be cheap. The glint remained however and I did the route with a Yorkshire climber who found the whole episode a great Irish joke. I've searched his notes for any later mention of Vector but it doesn't feature, and I somehow doubt that he ever ventured onto it.

Still, despite its imbalance, the partnership had its rewards. He was intense company and would go anywhere, anytime with or without money. We spent several seasons in the Alps, shivering in wet tents, while the routes snuggled deeper into the eternal snow. But we met everyone through his celebrated Gibson. We became acquainted with a whole generation of musical mountaineers over Bob Dylan, Woody Guthrie, the Dubliners, and the bit of Bach that was obligatory then in the late sixties and early seventies.

To pay our boat-fares home we busked in Geneva and Paris, and here his infuriating obstinacy revealed itself again. Though an exceptional guitarist — he was only an average singer. His voice was pleasant enough, but it didn't have the power for cinemas and subways. But he always insisted on singing when he busked, though he could have made a fortune as an instrumentalist, playing blues, ragtime, classical. When he sang — usually Dylan — he let the guitar lapse into simple background rhythms, and it was only between verses that he impressed passers-by. But he insisted that singing was what *he* preferred. It took a week to raise the money we could have made in a day.

After two or three of these sodden seasons he began to travel further, managing trips that were off limits to me with a career to look after. But I upstaged him on America by combining a seminar in Los Angeles with a month in Yosemite. I'm still paying for it in credibility to the job, but I'll get over that.

Jack resented me getting there first. It took him completely by surprise; like a mutiny. I was supposed to be his shadow, his photographer, following behind. He was building up for a long time to Yosemite — he wanted to be good enough to solo the Nose! — but when I broke away and asserted my independence and *my* values he had to get there quick and set the record straight. People tell me I'm being paranoid about things like that, but I can't see why else he would have soloed all my routes, and made such a point of telling me about it. There is no further mention of the Nose either. The nearest he got to that was the East Buttess of El Capitan.

I certainly have happier memories of the Alps. Competition doesn't seem to have soured our climbing there, but maybe that's only because we never got a great deal done anyway. Despite endless misfortune with the weather Jack never relented in his alpine ambitions, and he headed back there this summer as soon as California overheated. That last letter from Yosemite ends

Henri has invited me to stay with them in their chalet, but I rather think not.

I suspect I don't get on too well with Julie; she thinks I'm a bad influence on her cher Henri. Personally I think *she's* a bad influence on cher Henri, but anyway I shall probably be on Snell's Field if you make it.

There was no chance of me making it. I was due to become a parent in August, and still placating the firm over that embezzled month. But I enviously anticipated the next letter. Was I wishing him success, or hoping he would fail without me? His prime ambition in the Alps was to solo one of the routes on the Dru. Not the famed Bonatti Pillar, nor the excessive American Direct, but the beautiful and original North Face route, the Allain-Leininger. Of course it is the most visually arresting aspect of that improbable monolith, with its snowy niche like an eye of paradise blind to the inferior world. He felt that a man alone, frontpointing across that olympian névé would have transcended the flat laws of destiny. And though he had climbed harder and more technical lines, that one was always 'the great route in the sky' since the first day we stood in Les Praz and stared up in mystical awe like savages confronted with the Statue of Liberty.

People will want to know what he was doing in the couloir under the Flammes de Pierre if it was the North Face of the Dru he was interested in. That couloir leads to the Bonatti Pillar. The North Face is around the other side. *I* would say it was just typical Jack. He was gratifying a fantasy, taking a look at the Pillar—that sheer monument to his deathless hero Bonatti who soloed the first ascent over six days of total immersion in self. Jack would have looked, and then gone round to the North Face. The weather would turn bad as it always did, and he would go down. If that sounds sour it is only because it's sad. With people like Jack all truths, like dreams, are sad truths.

So, I suppose, here too at thirty-four, a fuller circle curved into its final arc. But I owe one particular, last debt.

It is a memory of a sombre June morning a year or so after our partnership began. We were attending the funeral of a friend. Jack and I had found the broken body at the foot of a crag and gone through the grim recovery process without flinching. But in the church he suffered an attack of nausea. Pale candles guttered beside the polished coffin, the brown benches creaked with mourners, he saw the old priests genuflecting, gliding, dipping, like birds of prey he thought, and he turned visibly green before stumbling out into the world of sky and air. Afterwards, in the gloomy fellowship of grief, he said defiantly:

'If it happens to me I don't want any of those mealy-mouthed bastards near me. Chuck me out to sea or something instead.'

I saw what he meant alright — though I tried to make a joke of it.

'I won't have it either. Over my dead body,' I said.

And that is the final reason for this valedictory memoir; that no one was there to see the dealers in death didn't get him first. My daughter was born in early August, two days before Henri's message arrived. We were expecting congratulatory telegrams and it took some time for the truth to penetrate. Under the circumstances I could only reply: 'Enterrez.'

THE OLD STORY

As soon as the three men climbed above the shelter of the lower slopes the wind hardened against them. It ripped through the falling snow, flung a bitter flurry in their faces, then swept the hillside clear.

Another mountain was revealed.

We saw their tiny figures, high above us, as we escaped down the valley out of the smothered hills. We said nothing, unwilling to trip the rhythm of descent.

Farmers, we uneasily supposed. Going up for stranded sheep. But there were no dogs. And it was too late.

Where the snowbound bogs began a rough, upward curve we saw them halt in a straggling line. Three black dots printed on the white slope. They were a poignant Morse S $\cdots$ an abbreviated stammer of distress. Above them the mountain grew and grew into the sour murk of the evening, the snow-shower lifting steadily up the slopes, yet never clearing the horizon. It seemed there was no top to this mountain.

We shuffled downhill towards the distant car, casting anxious glances back.

There was a morbid sense of dislocation in the scene, like a landmark exposed in the wrong context; a row of familiar rocks shrouded in snow. But our boots were cold and wet; we had defied the taboo of Christmas Day and struggled high into the snowy hills. Condensation soaked our clothes inside the windproof anoraks. Delay was impossible. We might have tried a warning, if we'd been near enough to shout to them, three black dots dwindling towards obscure conclusion across the grey page of the evening. All around, the language of outrage was snowed under, leaving only that last $\cdots$ apotheosis of silence.

There was nothing we could do. The remorseless snow

began again, cold ash of time drifting down between us. They disappeared slowly behind the weather. Into the past, one by one.

Darkness thickened across the mountains.

Hugh stared up into the appalling gloom. Rory, the guide, had abandoned them finally. Vanished without a shout or a backward glance. His surging footprints grimly rejected the funeral pace.

Hugh staggered forward another step. A swirl of wind whipped up snow and scoured his face. His legs were numb from the hips to the toes. He dragged a foot out of the flat powder and lurched forward, hit rising ground, no momentum. He was going uphill again.

His feet clubbed through the steepening surface and sank between tufts of buried heather. Loose snow piled into the clogs and wadded around his ankles. Tilting forward he saw his shinbone scrape against the frozen crust of the footprint. A cold, bloodless wound, ivory-white, bracketed each shin.

He concentrated on placing his feet in the deep holes Rory had kicked in the snow, but the gaps were too great for a boy. Air rasping in his throat he fought for the energy to match that rhythm, the powerful stride of survival, but he stumbled at every step and was forced to plunge his cringing foot again in a fresh trail.

Higher up there were heavy drifts of snow banked in rolling waves with miniature cornices, blue-shadowed and blade-sharp. Feathered patterns of snow-ice, bitterly frozen, encrusted the humps of hidden heather.

A steep, sliding step up a bank, his foot skidded, a fierce gust wrestled him back a place. The tips of his broken teeth sang bitterly in his skull in a mouthful of icy wind.

Slumped in shivering defeat memory assaulted him with a rage of loss. He remembered the speed of his thin bones flying; legs leaping and hurtling, racing over sandhills in sea-storms— eyes, teeth, every inch of skin flogged by sand and salt spray—

skimming the wind-lashed reeds that thatched the dunes, bare heels thudding and plunging in solid banks of sand, their scalloped edges blade-sharp and smoking wildly in Atlantic gales. . . .

Battered beaches in Donegal, Hugh racing the hounds of Castle Doe through the endless dunes, his wild red hair streaming on the sea-wind. . . .

Fierce disciplines of his beleaguered culture and its medieval wars. Elizabethan intrigue squeezing the North-west kingdom. At fourteen he was ripped from fosterage, kidnapped from impending kingship, four years held to hostage in the imperial stronghold of Dublin Castle. . . .

Now he was out; on the run.

In a stupor of exhaustion Hugh swayed in his footsteps facing the barrier of snow. Thin garments were stiffening ominously against his skin. He trembled convulsively, the blue of his hands shading to bone-white towards the fingertips.

Old scars lividly ringed his wrists, the marks of manacles that bound him to the Castle walls since his last escape. A jagged cut to the bone on the right wrist where the rough file slipped in haste last night.

Down at the car, darkness drifting in like a lapse of memory, we dropped our rucksacks. We had Cicatrin in First Aid boxes and enough bandages to cover a body whole. But we dared not linger, looking back. We must escape before the roads were buried.

The car skidded precariously out of the hills, and back to the city. We could not be responsible for the consequences of the past. We are only guilty of the repetition of events, the endless failure to correct.

History comes round and around like winter.

The soldiers get there first. The stretcher-bearers are always last.

And the vice-regal soldiers, bounty-hunters on horseback with sword and halberd, they are out there too, combing the frozen hills for the fugitives.

If they dragged Hugh back from the jaws of winter he would hang for his liberty by the starved neck; red head and white face preserved in a skull-cap of black pitch, a weathered lump on a flagstaff above the battlements.

And if he eluded them too he would survive to suffer heaped up tragedy in a brief future, traditions erased, a whole history unhinged at Kinsale. And death handed down for centuries.

Hugh dared not look back down the slope, refused even to turn his head.

If Art O Neill had fallen behind he was beyond help now in this fatal half-light. That was why Rory had finally forged ahead. He was leaving Art to fate. If they dragged him any further they would all die.

Images of his friend and fellow-hostage tormented Hugh's imagination. Art O Neill had been larger than life. In prison he loomed over Hugh's wretched spirit, sustaining him, subtly tempering his passion for escape.

But while Hugh paced the cage of the jail Art rotted, as if all the strength of this will was being absorbed by the younger boy. Hugh could not clear his mind of the round face that had swollen slowly in front of his eyes twenty four hours a day during four bitter years of hostage.

He saw Art again and again slump belly down in deep snow, a bloated carcass bulging in a thin silk shirt. He saw the heavy head strain hopelessly, imploring uphill after Hugh's disappearing back. Brutally he blinked away the image, clubbed the snow from his face with frozen fingers, and stumbled on. He must catch Rory. The guide was strong and knew the way. Nothing else mattered. Art would drag himself along behind, crawl out of the Pale on his belly if need be. Art O Neill would not yield to a blind mountain in Wicklow. This was his second flight too. There would not be another. Again Hugh imagined him sprawled on the white slope below, arms outflung in desolation, embracing a curve of snow, lacerated feet helpless in his small, tight clogs.

An open wound tore Art's forehead above one staring eye.

Thin blood trickled from the wound into the eye and down the creased cheek.

The watery blood arrested Hugh. Stopped him in stumbling flight. He knew if he turned back he would tumble downhill, down the steep slope of his own will. He stopped in despairing resignation and shuffled slowly around.

Art was staggering grotesquely towards him, huge body swaying on buckling legs.

Soft flesh quivered on his great bones, fattened on the flour and grease of prison. Heavy thighs shuddered in his sagging hose. No exercise in years but the daily shamble to a closet-squat, and still he had covered twenty-five miles of wintry Wicklow in a night and day, clad in sodden indoor clothes. He had hung between their shoulders until Hugh and Rory could no longer support him, and he was left reeling forward alone.

It was too cold for blood to flow, but a rusty stain caked his forehead, matted with wisps of hair and masonry grit.

Hugh shuddered in the sickening grip of the accident — descending the rope. Art's gross body squeezing down the shaft from the high prison-closet.

Art was violently opposed to that escape-route, but at the end of all the arguments he had no choice. If he remained behind he would be hanged for his friend's escape. His power had wasted away, he had lost control of Hugh.

It was a tight fit, even for the boy's wiry form, sliding down the knotted tapestries, a hundred feet down the loose shaft cringing at every touch of the slimy walls.

Hugh had plugged his nostrils and filled his mouth with wine-soaked wool before he gripped the twisted cloth, but by the time he lowered into the main sewer that ran into the moat he was retching violently.

Art couldn't possibly squirm down that filthy constriction. In a guilty panic Hugh thought of swarming back up again, but that was impossible.

He crouched shivering and sweating in the dark sewer, the

anal canal of Elizabethan imperialism. Upstairs the raucous soldiers celebrated Christmas.

The tiny circle of light at the top of the shaft was suddenly obscured. A shower of debris rained down, then bigger stones and broken bricks came ricocheting fiercely down the tunnel.

Art was struggling and wrestling inside the wall of the tower. His kicking feet and hoarse breath were audible below through the rattle of rotten masonry. Inch by inch he squirmed downwards, and every rumbling, stinking second Hugh awaited the clamour of pursuit. The knots in the cloth rope had been tied in a frantic hurry, with the minimum overlap to increase the length. If a knot slipped under Art's enormous weight. . . .

Hugh understood that this was Hell he had chosen; not escape any more, but descent into Hell.

At last Art's legs kicked out of the shaft through the roof of the horizontal culvert. The forked shadow of a monstrous delivery fought across the roof in the light of the taper Hugh held aloft to burn the vapours.

Hugh turned his face away in revolted pity.

The emerging body was beyond recognition. Art had become the shape and substance of his own decay.

His feet touched down and he crouched to enter the culvert. A spray of dirt and splinters rained down on his shoulders as he released his grip on the cloth rope.

Then a vicious, whining rattle, thud of stone on bone, and Art toppled limply forward into Hugh's arms.

The taper fell from nerveless fingers but in the last second of sizzling light Hugh saw the dirty, dizzy blood spurt from Art's open forehead.

Across the whipping snow Art came toppling towards Hugh. His glazed eyes were fixed on the stalk of support outlined in the shifting wilderness, a streak of lank, red hair glowing against the sky. Art's body was finished. He felt neither cold, nor tired, nor hungry. A vast numbness stirred fitfully by sparks of reason; Rory running to Glenmalure. Hugh . . . Hugh waiting.

His knees folded without resistance, tumbled him forward against an unbearable bank of snow. Hugh waiting.

He whispered, sinking 'Ní thig liom ... dhul ... níos faid. ...' Confession of defeat.

As he fell he saw Hugh move.

But no touch on the shoulder. No tugging hand. When he opened his eyes and raised his head Hugh was gone.

Two rows of overlapping footprints marched away into the dark. Art levered himself to his hands and knees, and crawled towards the steep bank. Origin and destination meant nothing now. Continuity ...

The mountain levelled out. Hugh was traversing a dark plateau. Less snow here. The fierce wind scoured it off, the air stinging with icy powder. Rory's tracks half-obscured already.

Round clumps of mountain-grass grew clear of the hard crust. As coarse as sedge the rusty tufts resembled wild scalps of warrior-hair.

Head after head marched in mourning ranks beside Hugh's stumbling feet, an army of Gallowglasses buried on a hopeless mission, the rough, red hair blown down in fringes over the frozen faces beneath.

Hugh realised the entire mountain was the treacherous crust of a burial ground. He was lost, sinking deeper in the grip of the cold; ankle-deep, knee-deep, wading into the deadly snow, down among the ranks of buried soldiers.

He dragged himself out of delirium, hallucinations dissolved behind his eyes, reverted to shapes in the blowing snow. Night already, and he was nowhere. A wasteland of ice and pain and hunger. Christmas Day darkening and he knew he was treading a deadly frontier; light and dark, hope and despair. Life and death.

Through the early hours of the escape Hugh had fiercely sustained the fantasy of a last gentle ridge somewhere on the rim of the Wicklow sky. ...

Mid-day, the sun high and healing, pouring benediction into a deep, green valley. Bowing sentries step silently aside, a tumult of cheering faces, reaching hands, powerful arms bearing him aloft into the unsubdued sanctuary of the Gael.

He peopled his illusion with aching felicities. His own mother, queen of the north, standing shoulder to shoulder with Fiach O Broin, warrior of Wicklow, at the heart of the valley stronghold to welcome him home to freedom.

A banquet, a bed, fast horses, north to kingship; and then years and years of vengeful victory, reversing the tide of empire. Replacing it with his own?

As the day wore on, and the agony increased, and Art began to die slowly, Hugh's paradise dimmed hour by hour, until finally he would have traded freedom for a hint of food and rest. He was gone too far and too far gone, and there was not the faintest dream flickering in the savage arena of the night.

Hugh stood rooted in the vacant tracks. The footprints were old and obscure already. He trembled at the ultimate isolation.

His body knotted suddenly with shock, then doubled over on itself in rigid, empty shudders. He was pitched abruptly to his knees weeping in convulsive terror.

Tears flooded from his eyes, slid without sensation down his numb cheeks, over the frozen knuckles clenched against his mouth.

And with the clarity of despair Hugh understood that his face and fingers felt no trace of the hot tears, felt nothing at all. And his feet too were lost, victims of a frost creeping steadily towards the core, feeling for the frantic heart.

A movement behind him. He jerked round, at bay. Saw the huge silhouette swaying again in the dark.

Art's features were sunken holes in the flesh of his face. His feet ploughed through the snow, every movement a last refusal to lie down and die. Grey all over, bleached bloodless.

Arms folded across his chest; lifting himself bodily across the snow.

Hugh crouched, open-mouthed, transfixed by the apparition, tears congealing on his cheeks. He saw Art stumble, the arms slid loosely apart, limp hands tumbled down by his side.

There was no hint of life in the gesture. The collapse of motion itself.

Hugh was close enough to see the blind glazing of the eyes, and the loosening skin, as the will finally released its grip.

Hugh's arms lifted in desolate supplication. He grappled the toppling body to him, and shook it savagely.

Not to be alone . . . the only one. . . .

He begged Art's folding flesh to go on enduring, to survive. A mute, massive weight leaned upon him.

Feverishly pleading, Hugh dragged an inert arm over his own shoulders, around his thin neck, and staggered forward in the frozen embrace. Rory's prints had vanished. Art's feet were anchored in the snow. On the windswept side of the mountain Red Hugh O Donnell wrestled with death.

We knew them of course . . . Just as you did. They moved vividly against the background of their history, so vividly we sometimes reached to touch, fingers faltering in confusion against the tracked white of the page.

There was nothing there. Twinges of memory and premonition.

But they were part of us, because the story refused to end in a hole on a hillside, a shallow grave.

Rory brought help from Glenmalure the following day.

And Red Hugh rose from the dead. He transcended time.

They dug him, barely alive, from under the snow, gave him back to history with the irresistible force of resurrection.

He tore the country asunder for the last ten years of his short life.

Envenomed with frostbite and fury he drove us violently towards the penal centuries.

But Art was dead.

His death underlines the miracle of Hugh's survival. he is the victim history and faith teach us to need.

We could never arrive soon enough to save him. Not from Glenmalure or any other point in terrain or time.

We are cursed with a need for human sacrifice.

THE GIFT OF TONGUES

'Brake!' Jacko yelled. 'Now!'

The silver car dug into the road. Invisible impact. Rubber howling, the back end skated.

'Handbrake. NOW!' Light and noise streaked the dark. Was it a roll? Jem's skull shrank. Long, shuddering skid, hurled round the handle in his fist. Still upright. Police lights scorched his eyes, veered at him.

'Now! Ram! Now!' Powerful blast in first, lift-off in second. The blue flash jerked aside. Space-invader. White-hot glimpse of faces, gaping mouths, bonnet vaulting the grass.

'Chicken! You shoulda creamed him —'

'Too fast Jacko! Too fast! We woulda been wiped —'

The car was loose in Jem's hands. Sweat and streetlights blinded him. The needle at eighty and creeping up. It controlled the car: Jem only clung to the wheel. Too much road all of a sudden, a whole runway. Headlights flashed panic at him.

'You're on the wrong side!' Jacko whooped. Wrong side of the carriageway. Weaving through a chaos of traffic-lights, pinball reds and greens.

'Where are we, Jacko? Where —'

'Cabinteely bypass. Headin' into town. You're gettin' the feel of her, Jem. The handbrake turn was ace.'

Rush of pride along strained nerves. Cars scattering, horns blaring. The dashboard winked and glowed below eye-level. Jem saw the bony fingers fiddle through the static on the radio. 'Want to hear what they're saying?' Jacko's left arm was folded in a sling inside his jacket. Smashed in a head-on a month before. Then, he drove twenty miles in a wrecked Orion, two cars on his tail and shook them off. Jem envied the cool nerve. Nerve pulled Jacko's face tight as an axehead, sharp forehead, beaked nose, pointed chin, the cheekbones flattened back to wiry hair.

. . . BMW. Silver. British reg. Foxrock 9.50 towards city-centre. Aggressive. Stand clear. . . .

Jacko bared his teeth in pleasure. Jem felt the net closing.

He slipped out of it, into the TV thrill. Waiting for the silver car to punch across the screen, chrome flaring, hunched stuntman, squad-cars closing like jackals. He'd turn up the sound, light a smoke, drink tea, scratch an armpit, sit back — but he was into a bend, wrestling the wheel, real walls rushing. The car went down on one knee and wailed around, tyres shrill as sirens.

'Can't take it Jacko. Too much —' Too much for Jem, the real thing.

'Get a grip, man!' Contempt. 'Get off the main drag. They're waitin' in Donnybrook. Get a grip —'

A trail of shock, Foster's Avenue to Dundrum, outraged lights and horns. Denim stuck to Jem's short legs. Sweat slid into his shoes. The seat held his plump body like a catapult, skull aimed through the windscreen. He peered out onto the flying bonnet, jet-wing touching down, taking off. Another mistake and Jacko would take her one-armed. Pull over! You short-arsed spa!

Swooping from the Bottle Tower down to Terenure. The fancy arch. Trees on the pavements. Houses hiding. Toy cars behind tin gates. A park by a river. No caravans, no horses.

Red lights. Jem put the boot down. To show Jacko. Through the junction, blind. Jolt of terminal fear — like the electric chair.

Jacko didn't blink. Colour-blind and speed-crazy. The best.

'Coppers!' Jacko pointed. In the park, running figures. 'Stop!'

Jem went through it again. Brakes, handbrake, car writhing all over the road. He saw them coming. Two cops, one shadow. Jacko threw the rear door open.

'In!' he yelled. 'Take her away, Buttsy!'

'Taxi —' the passenger gasped, 'Taxi, I —' Foreign. A fit of coughing. Jem spun around. A featureless silhouette.

'Jacko!' he hissed, 'he's fuckin' Black!'

Jacko was clicking fingers, impatiently. 'Got smack, man?'

'Taxi, I —'

'Don't come the tourist, Sambo! Them coppers weren't runnin' for a bus. What is it, H? Coke?' Full of harsh threat.

'Friend. Friend, I have nothing —' The voice had leaned forward, spoke behind Jem's ear. Never heard anything like it before. Like water feeling its way in dry ground. Words poured between pebbles, polishing edges. . . .

Jem pursued the voice. It seemed to come from somewhere remote, over distance and effort. There was an echo in it too, a strange sense of chorus. It was more than accent. His ear had to work to recognise language trickling in the complex sound.

A siren slashed. Close. Jem panicked. 'They're coming. In front! What'll I do?'

'Put the boot down, and Keep it down. Don't stop for Nothin'!'

The squad-car swung off the road. Word of the ramming had got through. Jem saw the strength of Jacko's tactic. Lash out loud and early. Violence had right of way. Confrontation wasn't Jem's style.

Cunning. But he was learning. The lesson continued; 'Don't bullshit me, blackie! You're dealin'. Cut us in or you'll have to be scraped off that road.'

'I have nothing to give but gratitude —' Deep resignation saddened the voice. Jacko lunged one-handed. Jem stalled him. Honesty stuck out a mile here.

'What were they after?' His voice sounded like broken glass in his mouth. 'The police. Why were they chasin' you?'

'They were not police. Not *your* police —'

'Drug Squad,' Jacko snorted, 'I smelled them a mile off.'

'No I am alien —' Jacko spun again. ' — Refugee. Illegal immigrant in Ireland.'

'Where you from, George?'

'I come from B——' Consonants buzzed in Jem's ear, 'near to Ethiopa and Sudan.'

'Africa?'

'Af-ri-kah —' The syllables sighed, breath of the burnt continent, land of safari and starvation.

'What brought you here?' Jem was interested.

'Dope, man! Dealin' dope,' Jacko was still certain.

The voice cut him off with passionate insistence, 'I did not come to buy or sell. I have nothing that you need. My people are lost and broken. I come for help . . .to Mister Geldof.'

Dun Laoghaire 2, Jem read, dislocated. Picture of a car-ferry.

'Kick him out!' Jacko raged. 'He's takin' the piss. Geldof!'

'*Sir* Geldof!' Jem sniggered. 'How'd you get into the country?' He was always interested in the angles. A planner.

'On a ship to your city.' A shudder of disgust. 'An oil-ship. Many days and nights from Suez. I was sick, hidden in a sm-a-a-al place.'

'What do you want Geldof for anyway?'

The silhouette in the mirror trembled. 'Our mountains have turned to dust. Soon they will blow away. Four years without crops —'

Jacko exploded: 'Are yez bleedin' hungry *again*?! Turn around,' he ordered Jem, 'He's not gettin' a lift home!'

The African resumed, his words booming gravely and for a moment Jem imagined the single voice came from many mouths. 'Our people were proud. We lived among high mountains. In dry seasons we held the soil with the weight of our existence. Now we are scattered below and our blood sickens. There is nothing for us there. I am sent to seek help.'

'All the way to Ireland!' Jacko yelped. 'We can't even help ourselves!'

'We know your country is an enemy of hunger. A priest was with us many years. He spoke often of your own famine. We could not accept his teaching. We do not change our ways. But he taught us anyway.'

The interior of the car was drenched in familiar, ghastly amber. Jem recognised the bypass once again. Perhaps it was another one. Round in circles. The law was gone to ground and the car seemed to float above the road drifting in and out of light traffic, the occasional air-pocket rippling the wheels. Jem dreamed of a jet-wing swooping across continents and oceans.

Day and night, dark and light around the spinning globe. Palm trees, blue seas, brown bodies on golden beaches ... Broken bodies in ditches ... Hunger and health, rags and wealth, life and death, day and night, dark and light, hour after hour after hour, boats, trains, cars, bikes crawling below him. He saw a tall, black figure race across a blazing desert, slipping over the surface like the shadow of another plane. Disturbing images. Not the way he was accustomed to dream. He pulled backwards on the steering-wheel with a sudden longing.

The car lifted smoothly and soared away from the earth. A hostess brought tea to the flight-deck. Nice take-off, Captain. Barrels and a bumpy junction and he broke blind lights at the church for Jacko.

'What do they call you, George?' he enquired over his shoulder.

For the duration of the impossible syllables the confusion surrounding the voice was resolved. Then it returned, a weave of echoes.

'Will you take me to Mister Geldof, please?'

Jem felt a frightened chill at the back of his neck. It shivered down his spine and he accepted it. The power in the voice! Not asking a favour. Just stating a right, politely. His leg flexed in a decision and the brake bit slowly. Halted on the crown of the road he switched on the interior light and turned around. Silence — except for Jacko hissing *Don't like Mondays* through his teeth, rapping the rhythm on the dash.

Jem stared at the man behind him. His own body was squat

with a short thick neck and to look around he almost had to flop on to his belly.

In contrast, the African almost touched the roof of the car with his astonishing head. He did not look hungry; indeed, like sculpture he seemed self-sufficient as if capable of maintaining the same polished shape forever. The skin was absolutely black, so black that streetlights, reflections, the pearly radiance of the interior lamp, drowned in it without a glimmer. With its delicate features exquisitely drawn the face at first looked small and childlike and it was only when he realised again the height of the man and the size of his extraordinary head that Jem understood the nature of the person gazing quietly down at him. A child grown old without the loss of innocence.

Pain had spared the dignified, dark eyes under arched eyebrows and there was no bitterness around the mouth. But as he gaped in fascination Jem slowly penetrated the illusion. Something had worn away the flesh beneath the skin and brought the bones agonizingly close to the smooth surface, and soon the skull would be exposed without any camouflage at all.

The cropped hair shaped to the head was dusted with silver and Jem's sacrilegious fingers itched to feel where the texture lay between black lamb and steel-wool.

He sat in the back of the huge car with his knees heaped in front of him and his arms draped around them as if those were his only belongings, although a small, incongruous suitcase rested on the seat beside him. He wore a loose boiler-suit, probably — Jem reckoned — the property of the distressful oil-tanker.

He seemed relaxed now, as if he had placed himself with total confidence in the hands in which he found himself. Jem and Jacko and their silver taxi.

Jem broke the hard news.

'Geldof's not here,' he said. 'He lives in England. Sorry.'

'He is here.' The answer was not contradiction. A guttural sigh of assurance.

'He's not bleedin' *here*!!' Jacko exploded. 'Wrong country.

Tough shit!' Yet he stopped short of eviction. Was he afraid, Jem wondered? Jacko was afraid of nothing. It was the compulsion in the voice, the madness of belief.

'It was a long, hard way. For a long time I ran. Without food or water. Then the sea. I was guided on my journey. We know many secrets.' And again he said it, infinitely confident, 'He is here.'

He sat behind Jem solid as a hump on his back. Jacko scratched his narrow jaw and scowled. 'Leave him. We'll find another jammer —'

He prepared to walk away. Fast lights in the distance raced towards them. He leapt in again. 'Go!'

Newpark Avenue down to Blackrock, out the seafront to the Punch Bowl the shore of the world black beside them. They lost the tail in Booterstown. Jem handled the car as if he was born to it. All the time the impassive face stared over his shoulder hardly rocking with the motion of the chase. The great dark eyes were open, but they glanced neither right nor left, nor did they blink at the strobe-lights of frantic cars. They simply stared straight ahead to a final destination.

'Any ideas?'

'Try the Pink,' Jacko growled.

Jem stared at him, amazed at the concession, then he covered it smoothly. 'Time we had a pint in anyway. And a change of wheels.'

He turned to his passenger with the self-importance of a guide, 'We'll ask in The Pink Elephant. They'll know if he's around.

'Don't count on it, but. Far as I know he hasn't got the boat-fare home. He gave it all away an' now he's skint. The Rats haven't had a hit in years.'

'Like hell he's skint!' Jacko jeered —

'Yes,' the voice interrupted, 'we must find him soon —'

It sounded faint and faraway and when Jem glanced in the mirror the statuesque head was no longer directly behind him but slumped sideways against the seat. He recognised the symptoms, screeched to a halt outside a chip shop and threw Jacko a fiver.

'Burger and chips. Quick!'

'Bloody hell, do they never feed themselves —'

'Smoked cod for me and whatever you're havin' yourself.'

Jem waited nervously, engine racing. A thought struck him,

'D'you eat meat?' The head shook weakly, but the eyes remained closed. He hopped out and roared after Jacko, 'Get fish! He's a bleedin' vegetarian.'

Jacko streaked through the door, loaded with food and pursued by a fat man in an apron. The car sped away and Jacko stuffed the fiver in his own pocket. He dumped a steaming package in the African's lap. 'Meals on bleedin' wheels!' he grumbled.

'Get that down ya,' Jem advised generously. 'You can't go drinkin' on an empty stomach.'

Jem spilled his own chips into the space behind the gear-stick, apparently designed for that purpose, and angled the greasy mirror to watch the performance behind.

The passenger sat up weakly and held the food in his two hands. His eyes were open again in a visionary gaze, and his lips moved in clear, poignant silence.

'He's Prayin'!' Jem was staggered. The chips in his own gullet turned to wet ash and he gobbled fiercely at the smoked cod to overcome an extraordinary distress.

The African was still praying. Or else he'd forgotten where his mouth was. Jem could stand it no longer.

'When did you eat last?'

The man bowed his head and thought. He selected a chip between long slender fingers. 'I cannot say. A long time. Before the ship—I do not know.' he admitted simply. And ate. A little. Some chips. The shrivelled fish he ignored.

Jem was suddenly terrified. He felt himself on the verge of the unthinkable. Alien. Far worse than foreign. Foreigners ate

four or five meals a day like himself. They were human. Now
the idea of starvation as a way of life struck him with the force of
blind terror. Again he saw the shape racing across the broad,
burnt earth. It was thin and tall, hard as a needle. A bone
needle.

The city centre was quiet. Jem drove decently now. No coat-
trailing.

'Dump it!' Jacko ordered impatiently as he sought a
parking-space,

'We'll get something else after. Turbo maybe'

Jem stopped in a loading-bay. No Parking Day or Night.

'Right George,' he invited the African, 'let's go find
Geldof.'

He was amazed at the gentleness of his own voice. Never
sounded like that before. He spat on the pavement to
compensate.

The stranger grew suddenly agitated at the conclusion of his
mission. There were tears in his eyes and his hands fluttered up
and down his person. He seized the small case and drew out a
long, coloured garment, fold after fold of radiant material.
Handling it reverently he slipped it over his head. As it
unfolded down his body he shed the boiler-suit, rolling it neatly
with fastidious care and placing it in the suitcase. Jem and Jacko
prowled uneasily trying to seem a thousand miles from the
stolen car.

He lifted each bare foot in turn, dusted it carefully and
inserted it into a sandal of soft leather laced with thongs. Then
he handed the suitcase to Jem who received it without
question.

Stepping out onto the pavement the African stood up
slowly to his full, uninterrupted height. Even Jacko stared,
helpless.

The man was ridiculously impressive, a head and neck taller
than Jacko but slender as a sapling and somehow leaning gently
backwards all the way from his waist to the tapered crown of his
head as if he possessed, instead of normal balance, some

defiant sense of grace designed for looking upwards rather than down.

Jem was totally convinced, and knew this was his weakest moment.

He could go along with a joke or a whim or any mad dash in the night, but this dark truth was too demanding.

He was about to point the way and disappear, but Jacko was already striding towards The Pink, and Tzammeniya Maseratu Harathanazu followed in his wake.

'Who?'

'Geldof! I said Geldof!' Jacko rapped. 'Is he here?'

'You mean *Bob* Geldof?

'You mean *Mick* Jagger!' Jacko mimicked the barman.

Typical, Jem reflected. Hadn't the brains to get the pints in before he started a row.

He nudged the African who stood aloof from the crowd, arms folded within his sleeves. The serene face and huge, unfocused eyes burned with a clean, ebony flame through the clamour, the colour and the smoke. In the long, loose robe, standing perfectly detached, he looked like a supreme magician who had just materialised on the spot and was about to do something simultaneously simple and stunning. Every voice hushed in expectation.

Jem was overawed but manners prevailed. 'What'll you have, George?'

No answer. A cup of water I suppose, he thought obscurely and called three pints.

He saw a rock-star on a velvet bar-stool between two blonde companions. The girls stared at his African. The rock-singer stared at his drink.

Jem thrust his low, fat grin into the group. 'Hey,' he enquired, leaning on one of the velvet girls, 'Is Geldof around? My friend wants to know,' he indicated the African for support. 'Matter of life or death.'

The rock-star shrugged. The pupils of his eyes were saturated.

His companions giggled. Jem felt he was not being taken seriously.

None of his guest's charisma had rubbed off on him.

'Who is he, your friend?' the rock-star mumbled.

'You mean you don't know who he _is_?' Jem's lip curled in contempt.

'Well he's not Joan Armatrading! So who the fuck is he?'

'Nelson Mandela.' The first name in Jem's head.

'Yeah. Heard of him. You his roadie? Tell him Geldof's not here.'

He turned away, and one of his attendants cradled his petulant face in her thin hands.

Farther down the bar Jacko was engaged in a row of his own. In a revised mental aside Jem wondered was it a reflection on the upper classes that he and Jacko could never enter their pubs without trouble.

The impassive stance of the African was unnerving Jem. If he was left there much longer this crowd would hang coats on him.

Time was running out. Voices raised — chiefly Jacko's.

'Hey Roadie!' Jem was tapped on the shoulder. A tough, handsome young man with the muscle-vest, worn jeans, battered boots, and the cynical face of a roadshow driver.

Geldof's in Wicklow,' he drawled. 'At a party. They flew him over. Don't mind your man.' He nodded at his disgruntled boss, the rock-star, 'He wasn't invited.'

'They flew him over? For a party?'

'Yeah, man. This evening. In a private jet. Just to be there—'

'Where's the party?'

'Near Ashford. The Viscount's place. They won't let _you_ in though.' He should be alright. Some kinda witch-doctor is he?'

'Yeah.' Jem whistled between two fingers. 'Let's go Jacko!' One on each elbow they hustled the African like a hijacked statue out of The Pink.

While Jacko slipped back to hurl bricks Jem stole another car. Something dignified. He had a stylish sense of mission now. A limousine with tinted windows? CD plates?

He found a silver Mercedes, beautifully sleek, so sleek it was hardly a Merc at all. He had to check the badge. He stumbled heavily against the car. No alarm.

Smiling apologetically at his black friend — again the feeling was new — he reached inside his jacket and drew out his personal persuader. It was a metal bar shaped like a small starting-handle. The resemblance was oddly appropriate for there was a slender key-shape made of hardened steel mounted on the end of the bar.

It was obviously harder than an ordinary key because Jem stabbed it into the keyhole and with a sudden wrench of the starting-handle he burst the door lock.

'Belongs to a friend. He won't mind,' he assured the African.

As the long, black legs disappeared into the cream interior Jem saw that the bones were entirely without flesh or muscle. He reckoned they must work on will-power.

The steering-lock went the same way as the door. Jem hoped it belonged to the rock-star. He stared at the knot of wires behind the steering-column. Might as well be looking into a bush.

Jacko arrived at a run, hostilities concluded. In one second he had ignition, two seconds, power.

'*Nice* car!' He exhaled rare approval.

'Hope it doesn't rain.' Jem pointed at the naked windscreen. No wipers. Like an eye without eye lashes. 'Some hoor musta broke them off. Jasus you can't leave anythin'.'

Jacko stabbed a button and from below the lip of the bonnet long arms silently climbed the windscreen. 'Retractable. Helps the air-flow. No rifle-sight on the bonnet either. Aerodynamics. *Nice* car!'

Jem wondered about retractable wings and wheels.

'Over the mountains or down by the sea?' He offered the choice to his passengers.

'Take the high road. Sally's Gap. Your man'll feel more at home.'

Jacko was on the crusade, too. 'No law up there,' he explained defensively.

Out of the decayed city through the redbrick suburbs the silver car slid smooth as water on the broken streets. Dublin looked and felt like a film before the action starts. Not a whisper on the surface but the tension rasping like a chainsaw underneath. 'While the city sleeps Danger stalks the streets.'

Guided by Jacko, who knew it like a taxi-driver, he struck the road to the Hellfire Club and the noble bonnet of the car lifted to the angle of the Dublin mountains.

The hostile darkness that surrounds a city closed in on the winding road, until they broke out suddenly above the trees at Killakee and saw below them a broken branch of stars blazing in the bay.

'Jasus,' Jem breathed reverently. 'Great place to bring a bird!'

Behind him the African sat silently seeing something different. He stared down upon a jungle, and Jem following his eyes caught a glimpse of the black holes between the lights and the sinister blocks of darkness that had almost swallowed the stranger. For a second Jem felt the rotten undergrowth stir within the phosphorescence of the city. Heartbeats raced in the distance like naked feet chased by the whip of a siren. For reassurance he looked to the home-lights of Ballymun, brave rampart against the northern night, and pride restored itself.

On a whim he joined the row of parked cars and lay back luxuriously in his seat. Flying must be like this; swooping at night out of the Milky Way, across the burning city the velvet streets and the neon river, houses streaming like candleflames, the sci-fi airport lifting up to meet him, concrete tilting to the wheels.

He couldn't admit his fantasy to Jacko. 'Nick a plane. What's stoppin' you?' It used to be horses—now it was all one to Jacko as long as there was an engine in it. A race, a chase, wreckage, a fire. . . .

But flight was Jem's private dream, too pure for crime. He saw himself — not on the run flapping in panic — but seated coolly in a cockpit, the uniform sharp as only respect could make it, a model of authority and skill, adored by tall, blonde stewardesses.

He was a street-pigeon with the dreams of a hawk. A patriot too. He'd fly for Aer Lingus only, he was adamant on that. He imagined a laser-gun in the cockpit for sorting out the foreign airlines.

Ah well—he sighed for the moment—great place to bring a bird!

A savage poke in the ribs —

Beyond Jacko's warning hiss and the hand that hid his face, beyond the electric window and not two feet from the side of the silver Mercedes—both vehicles facing the city like seats in a cinema — a huge, black car was parked, bonnet bulging with a V8 engine and bristling with aerials. Two big, red faces on top of jackets, shirts and ties snarled at Jacko, Jem, and the thin African as if they had found the ultimate subversion.

'Branchmen. *Hit it!*'

The Merc lunged for the road, stalled, shook itself in a spray of gravel. Deep in his throat the African growled. The first hairpin doubled back above the car park and Jem saw the city lights reel below as if something monstrous had smashed into the night.

Real driving now. Not brute power. Control was everything. Jacko rapped commands. Skill and nerve. No streetlights. No guiding kerbs. No walls to throw him back on tarmac. As if he had driven over the edge of order the white line stopped. The road humped, tilted, swerved. Bog sprawled on both sides. A blur of black trenches, steel flash of water. Nightmare beyond the wheels. Rip the skin off the country and this flesh was bared. Only concrete kept it down. Jem prayed for concrete —

for the erased city. If he lost the road the silver bubble would submerge in cold, black slime. He searched in panic for pursuit. Craters and ridges threw the flying car into the air. The road behind never appeared in the mirror. He was either too far above it or travelling broadside. Above the bog the sky was soft with summer night and the higher hills ran smoothly along-side, devoid of detail, dark curves closing the horizon. Silent space sucked his blood. The dam burst; the African was speaking. Speaking. . . .

The sound filled the car, drowned the engine. No ordinary speech. Hardly speech at all in the way that chant and exhortation are not speech. There were no words that he could seize. Solid, sibilant sound pitched high and strong against the rumble of the road. It issued like the roar of falling water and its meaning should have plunged down the valleys below the ridge but the car contained it, threw it back upon itself in waves of resonant repetition.

Jem felt potent emotion washing through him, dissolving his greasy skin, surging in his blood. He glanced in elated terror at Jacko and he too was in the grip of fervour, eyes bulging, mouth wide open, passion corrugating his forehead. Then Jem went careering through the bends above Glencree, swatting ditches, walls clubbing at him, frenzied sheep leaping into holes in the dark. Jacko's face was in his hands, head down, as Jem pulled miraculously out of the turmoil and began the long burn up beyond Lough Bray.

The voice in the back still poured forth. Jem slowed. No tail could have held that pace; there was no light in the sky behind, and he had recognised something else. On the underside of the voice there was a flash, a quicksilver gleam of language.

Cruising uphill, his ear strained; he seized a loose thread of English. Overlapping it there was a guttural tongue — German, was it, or Russian, African? — while the English also shaded away into a gabble of French, Italian, Spanish . . . Jem could not identify anything but it was like listening to random radio after midnight. Except that this was not electronics. This was one man, beyond himself, speaking passionately in tongues. To anyone, anywhere, who might hear.

Not about his own people, or the hunger they inhabited, or Af-ri-kah, but everyman—as if he had experienced everything possible on his journey and now he spilled its meaning over Jem and Jacko, the only witnesses to a doomed truth.

> *. . . like blown leaves and feathers loose in air enter the earth only to begin again and again . . .*
>
> *. . . do not drift in corners and multiply. Sand that settles chokes the soil . . .*
>
> *. . . in the high branches of the world the air is sweet and sudden. Hide in the uplands above the poisoned world . . .*
>
> *. . . travel only on escaping wings, alighting to hide, not to plunder or to build . . .*
>
> *. . . put away machines. Until the spirit learns to float, go on foot. In silence . . .*
>
> *. . . slip like shadows over the surface under the sun but let your substance be elsewhere — in memory and dream . . .*
>
> *. . .do not take root. Earth is the one root and it is poisoned . . .*
>
> *. . . now. That time is over . . .*
>
> *. . . I have seen the agents of the new world, who are everywhere. They are here. . . .*

From a childhood pulpit Jem caught the echo of persecution. Biblical. Feathers weren't his idea of flight. He latched on to one thing only. Put away machines . . . Get out and walk? Jem cringed like a slug. The car was a shell against the bog. The black breath of night swamped his eyes and headlights. He wouldn't last a minute out there. Clinging to the steering wheel for survival he wept for the livid tunnels of the city.

Why? Why? Hurtling through midnight mountains for a stranger.

Why?

The moment they picked him up power and direction had changed utterly. Now the prophet was commanding them to live like crows. He must deflect these harsh orders before they got a grip.

He yelled desperately into the flow; 'Hey! George! What's your place like, George? Home? Is it like this kip?'

Tzammeniya Maseratu Harathanazu fell completely silent. It was a vacant, eerie silence, a gap in the air, as if Jem had tuned to a source that was no longer even there.

When he spoke again his voice had ceased to boom. It thinned to a single strand, a dusty thread trying to spin delicate images in the air, to fix bright colours on the flying night. There was a faint rhythm of sun and rain, seasons and moons that meant nothing at all to Jem wrestling the car through tangled bends.

He heard of sand and snow, of mountains that were more than elevations of the lowlands, they were separate elements in themselves, homelands above the setting sun. Sometimes in the mid-afternoon the mountains barely existed, they were painted dimly on the sky and called for faith; at night they were their own shadow against the stars; in winter they cut the surface of the earth like broken bones. In the growing season green buds sprouted in secret hollows. Sometimes they came to leaf.

Near Ethiopia and Sudan, yes, but not of either, remains of an ancient, uneroded Af-ri-kah above the borders. On one side, now in Ethiopia, there were Russians, on the other, Americans in Sudan. The people on both sides starved. They could not eat ideas.

The crops withered, the animals died, then the children and the old. The high ground turned to dust, the dust blew away from the rock, blew away between their fingers. The sun had turned and burned them out of the mountains. The survivors were led down to the famished valleys and herded into destitution-camps, the strongest loaded in army lorries and taken a thousand miles to the south to be resettled.

In Jem's hands the car slowed to a crawl as the dusty voice whispered of travelling day and night for a week in wheel-ruts and dry river-beds through the famine lowlands, crushed together on the hot steel under a canvas sheet. The weakest died and were buried in passing. The mountains dissolved in shimmering air and the sky burned down to the ground on every side. There was nothing ahead but cracked, black earth and withered bush. Once they saw a line of people who envied the awful lorries and the unknown destination. Some held their children up to be taken.

When the journey ended the earth offered no welcome. They were released without resources in an alien place.

A few turned their faces at once and began the long march home. There were dead voices calling and they could not be deserted. They walked a thousand miles through the hot season to reach the mountains before the rains came. They trudged the borders for three months living on memory and when they reached home — two men of the score who started — the rains failed them again. . . .

A faint glow silhouetted the speaker in the mirror. It came from behind and was increasing every second. The Sally Gap. A crossroads caught the silver Mercedes in its net. Jem swung left. The car knew instinctively where to go.

. . . But a crop was impossible anyway, for there was a road now, a ragged new road cut into the mountain, and high up a fence surrounded the harvest-plateau, squat, grey buildings stood where the maize-fields used to be, and helicopters, jeeps, uniforms — Yanks or Reds, it didn't matter. There was a hole in the mountain near the ruined village, an enormous mine. . . .

'What were they after?' Jacko's voice had diamonds in it. The African had not heard him right, 'Hunger,' he said, 'they had found Hunger.'

And after he had left his mark in blood the second man turned to travel south again. But Tzammeniya Maseratu Harathanazu faced north this time — and started running.

The light behind was relentless now, burning like a laser. The tapered head caught in the mirror seemed transparent.

'Hit it!' Jacko roared. Jem thought he wanted a handbrake

turn and ramming-session, but he was doing eighty, downhill, the road no wider than the car. His eyes blurred. The road wriggled faster than the lights could find it. At the bottom a twisted bridge! He skidded bluntly, sickening slam against the side, stonework shearing past his shoulder. Through and into another bend. The engine note was higher, harsh with injury. The lights behind clawed the darkness. No ordinary chase. Jem expected bullets.

A second bridge. He slammed the other door. Screech of steel, silver sparks. Jacko clutched his wounded arm. He was ready for the third bridge, took it like a slalom-gate.

Uphill again, clean sweep along a slope, kick through a hairpin and then the steep road narrowed, pinned to the mountain by a fragile wall, vacant space below it. Sheep on the verges luminous with terror.

And then the long descent urgent as gravity through forest thick with spiky shadow, and out below into sleeping fields and farmland, Roundwood, reservoirs, and everywhere the random roads of Wicklow. The car found its own way, always trailing the lights behind, sometimes a glow above the trees, sometimes a ravenous glare until Jem stamped on the throttle and broke away.

Jacko was awed, disbelieving. 'They can't be this good. . . .'

'They are not what you think —' the African warned. He was ignored. They had their own skins to save.

Whether the car found it or he did Jem could not say, but the huge gates gaped open, black and gold, between ornate pillars in a high stone wall and he swung on burning wheels. Shouts from the gatehouse, running shadows. Up the avenue, lawns and woodland, torn fence trailing like ivy-strands. Between tall trees the floodlit castle stood. Fairytale towers and terraces, a forecourt packed with cars. Jacko jerked reflexively. Limousines, sportscars, huge saloons, two helicopters with rotors discreetly folded.

On a low terrace under blue and silver lamps guests danced in imitation moonlight.

Jem skidded against a C.D. Jaguar. The familiar cruelty of steel. Gravel strafed the granite steps. The music broke. A squad of burly men bore down. Jem struggled with the welded doors. Jacko stabbed a button and the sun-roof opened. He slithered out on the shadowside, disappeared in the bushes. Jem already knew which car was marked. He tried to follow as the tuxedos tightened, but the exit was too small.

'Please?' The African tugged him down and climbed out onto the roof where he rose thin and splendid in his radiant robe, hands folded, head high and tilted back.

Jem decided to see it through. He poked up head and shoulders and addressed the heavies in a well-bred croak. 'Is Geldof — Mister Geldof about?'

'No Reporters! Get Out!'

Jem gestured at the figure on the roof. 'Does he look like a newshound?! Geldof!' he bellowed, 'GELDOF!'

The terrace stirred. A shiny blue dress suit detached itself and slouched towards the steps.

Entirely unnoticed a black car with a bulging bonnet and dimmed headlights slid towards them along the drive. Without any lights at all another passed it, escaping sleek and low across the shadowed lawn towards the gates. Only Jem felt Jacko go.

The man in the blue dress suit scuffed onto the gravel. He wore sneakers. He came with the casual assurance of one used to spotlights. Some distance from the car he halted, shook lank hair from his forehead to examine the supplicant with shrewd eyes. Slowly, affirmatively, he lifted both hands in welcome. In the lazy gesture of those arms was the power of mass approval.

Jem felt the stranger tremble with conclusion. His eyes closed, he bowed from the waist. Tiny splashes hit the silver steel.

In the midst of his own panic Jem felt enormous pride and pity. The African moved down invisible stairs towards the outstretched hands. In slow motion, gliding through sea-level air, in the dim reflection of the spotlights. Brightening — savage engine-roar, full headlights. The bulging bonnet hurtled across the gravel, struck the stranger behind the knees, hurled him in the air. He crumpled back across the roof and drifted to the ground as light as a fall of leaves. The car vanished into the avenue.

On the terrace, hysteria, screaming chaos —

Jem and Geldof remained motionless, staring, leaning slightly away from each other, as if the tightrope had not yet broken and the figure was still in mid-air.

Voices announced police.

'That *was* the police,' Jem whispered, 'they followed us —'

He heard water shifting pebbles in his head, 'Not your police —' and Geldof nodded. Not your police.

Jem slipped through the sunroof to kneel by the dead stranger.

Skin and bone, no blood. The face was serene and final. He fumbled with the eyelids as if his fingertips could hurt. The garment drooped between the hipbones across the stomach as if the body had already melted in the ground.

Sirens screamed along the avenue. He jumped for the Mercedes.

Squeezed through the sunroof, headfirst. His hips jammed. Rough hands hauled on his ankles. Suspended in the car he clung to the inert steering wheel and rattled it in a fury of injustice. A gap opened in the uniforms and Geldof's head appeared. It seemed upside-down to Jem but the eyes were full of questions and unmistakeable importance.